Praise for the Lucy and

CW00499616

A curiously magical thriller wi
sparkle.

**Helen Lederer**, author of *Losing it*, comedian and founder of
the *Comedy Women in Print Prize*

This is a thriller, a chase, a buddy story, a mystery (certainly
for Dawson, who starts out off the back foot but manages to
survive several rugged encounters), all smoothly told with
hugely engaging characters, and rips along at a hectic pace. If
you like some smiles, even chuckles, with your reading, this is
great fun but doesn't dissolve into slapstick.

**Adrian Magson**, author of *Hostile State*

My goodness! What a hilarious, energetic and entertaining
roller-coaster of a read this is. The pace never lets up. Dawson
(for he is our hapless hero – and never was a man more lacking
in hap) starts off in the UK, hops over to Australia and there is
chased by a colourful collection of Germans and Russians, Brits
and Aussies. Some are goodies, some baddies, and some lurk in
the grey area in between. All are intent on solving the mystery
of the eponymous teapot, or preventing others from doing so.
It's as clever and witty as its title. I certainly enjoyed the ride!

**Sue Clark**, author of *Note to Boy*

A very entertaining read that kept me guessing all the way
through. I needed to have my wits about me as there is a large
cast of characters and the chapters switch rapidly back and
forth between them, but this only added to the book's fast
pace. Steve's skilful storytelling and sense of fun made this a
rollicking good read.

**Imogen Matthews,** award-winning author of *The Hidden
Village* and *Hidden in the Shadows*

# Poor Table Manners

STEVE
SHEPPARD

CLARET PRESS

ISBN paperback: 978-1-910461-76-1
ISBN ebook: 978-1-910461-77-8

A CIP catalogue record for this book is available from the British Library.

This paperback can be ordered from all bookstores as well as from Amazon, and the ebook is available on online platforms such as Amazon and iBooks.

Cover and Interior Design by Petya Tsankova

**www.claretpress.com**

To my brother Rob, for a lifetime's inspiration, in the hope that he'll forgive the fact that Rachel Whyte has not reappeared in either this book or *Bored to Death in the Baltics*

## Acknowledgements

Despite the gratifying, if relative success of *A Very Important Teapot* and *Bored to Death in the Baltics*, the unending battle with imposter syndrome means that I tend to plough a rather lonely furrow when writing. I am always astonished when I read pages and pages of thanks and acknowledgements in other books. Who can all these people be? Sometimes there are so many that the author's copyright to the book seems open to question.

Me? Not many. However, there are a few, a gloriously tiny few to whom I owe a deep debt of gratitude. Firstly my beta readers, the amazingly funny Sue Clark and the extraordinarily punctilious Justine Gilbert. Ladies, thank you both for your time and helpful comments given freely and willingly.

After that, well, it's pretty much just the wonderful Katie Isbester and her ever-evolving team at Claret Press; in particular, for *Poor Table Manners*, Alex Green as well of course the brilliant Petya Tsankova for another stunning cover.

I also need to thank a few friends of mine for allowing their good names to be besmirched in this tale, some more than others. I hope it doesn't spoil the friendships. I believe I've forewarned most of you, particularly those of you who don't necessarily survive until the end of the book.

If you've enjoyed *Poor Table Manners* (or indeed *A Very Important Teapot* and *Bored to Death in the Baltics*), please don't be afraid to spend a few minutes of your precious time and leave a review somewhere useful (Ama*on, Good*eads, for example). They are the beasts that we little-known authors, perhaps unfortunately, cannot do without and reviews do help to find new readers, they really do. Thanks.

Table Mountain had always been on Dawson's bucket list, but this was not how he had envisaged it.

He glanced across at Lucy and then back at the young couple pointing guns at them across the cable car. They were barely into their twenties and looked nervous. The guns were real enough though and the hands holding them steady enough. Dawson had originally taken the pair for tourists. He'd been surprised that there weren't more passengers but it was only eight in the morning.

With two automatic pistols pointing in their direction and the cable car travelling slowly upwards through a thick mist, it was starting to look as though Dawson and Lucy might have to send their apologies for missing tomorrow's meeting with Rebecca Erasmus of the South African State Security Agency. The thought gave Dawson an idea.

'Excuse me, guys,' he said cheerfully, holding up his phone. 'Just got to make a call. We've a meeting booked and I'm guessing you might have other plans for us.'

The man grabbed for the phone. 'Give me that,' he snarled, but Dawson, who was a few inches the taller of the two, simply held it higher as the man came closer, gun beginning to waver away from Dawson as he did so. His female companion's attention was momentarily distracted and it was a moment that Lucy barely needed. It had been months since she'd had the opportunity to practise any of the skills learnt in the MI6 dojo earlier in the year and she was more than ready for a bit of fisticuffs. Dawson had been counting on this.

The fight was over almost before it could be called a fight with their female assailant's gun transferred to Lucy and the woman catapulted into her male companion, whose attention was split between Dawson's mobile and Lucy's unexpected assault. Unfortunately for him, when his colleague cannoned into him, he was already on tiptoe attempting to reach the phone. Equally unfortunately he was standing by a window which Dawson had pulled down to aid some photography he'd been attempting. With one hand holding his gun and the other now wrestling for the phone, the man was unable to prevent himself toppling through the open window. To assist, Dawson let go of his phone at peak-topple.

The man grabbed, despairingly but with surprising success – especially with the cable car rotating slowly through 360° – for the window sill and, displaying admirable gymnastic finesse, managed to swing himself up on to the roof before either Dawson or Lucy could react.

'Watch her,' Lucy said, tossing the woman's gun to Dawson. Before he could stop her – which would have been an exercise doomed to failure in any case – Lucy had slithered out of the cable car window in pursuit. Dawson didn't care to speculate exactly how far above ground they now were.

'She's mad, your friend,' mumbled the woman. She was slumped on the floor of the cable car, attempting to stem a heavily-bleeding nose with the fingers of both hands.

Up on the slowly turning roof, Lucy suddenly realised that her opponent, now with one arm wrapped around the stanchion linking the car to the overhead cable, still had his gun in the hand not wrapped around the stanchion, while she'd passed her own newly-acquired pistol to Dawson. Possibly I should have considered that, she thought, but too late now. She crouched at the edge of the roof, not daring to look over the side. She didn't think she suffered from vertigo but glancing down might be pushing her luck. Luck: she could do with some now. Currently her options seemed to consist either of falling to her death with a bullet in her or falling to her death without a bullet in her.

When the shot came though, it didn't come from the man in front of her, who was trying to steady himself against the jerky swaying of the cable car to get a clear shot at the crouching Lucy. Instead it came from beneath, and the bullet caught the man right between his splayed legs. Lucy winced. She'd always supposed that when a man got shot in the balls he'd scream. After all, she'd been informed (by men) that getting a knee in the bollocks was akin to the pain of childbirth, so a certain amount of screaming was to be expected when a bullet, rather than a knee, was involved. But there was nothing. Just a look of complete surprise on the man's face as he let go of the stanchion and disappeared silently over the side of the cable car into the mist.

'Just skill,' Dawson said immodestly, when Lucy had scrambled back inside the car and asked him how he'd managed to get such an accurate bead on the man through the thin but opaque steel of the roof.

She let that go. He deserved his moment and had just saved her life after all. 'Thanks, lover,' she said, kissing him on the cheek and retrieving the gun from his grasp at the same time. 'I'd better take this. Now that you're a cold-blooded killer it'd be dangerous for you to keep it.' He didn't demur. The cable car continued its slow progress up the side of the mountain. 'Some bloody holiday.' But she was smiling as she said it. Dawson looked at her, not a blonde hair out of place after her expedition on to the roof.

'I've lost my phone,' he said.

'Never mind; it was a rubbish phone. You must have had it about six years. Modern ones take colour photos, you know.' She turned her attention to the bleeding woman on the floor, who looked stunned at the unexpected turn of events including the death of her colleague and the state of her nose. 'Now then, who exactly are you and what gives you the right to ruin our holiday?'

The woman remained silent, glowering at Lucy through the blood. Dawson said, 'You need to think about answering my partner's questions. You wouldn't like her when she's angry.'

At that moment the car's clanking signalled their arrival at the upper station of the cableway. 'At least I can say I've been up Table Mountain,' Dawson continued. 'Even if it's with a bloody-nosed gunwoman in tow and the death of a complete stranger on my conscience.' They drew to a grinding halt. 'What are we going to do with this one?'

Lucy was already pulling the woman to her feet. At least the bleeding was beginning to ease off. Lucy hadn't hit her very hard. Definitely out of practice, she thought.

The automatic door slid open and they stepped out into the covered station, where two middle-aged cableway employees in bright green fleeces were staring open-mouthed at the three of them, focusing particularly on the gun in Lucy's hand.

'Hi, chaps,' said Dawson, stepping forward and smiling at the two men. 'You don't by any chance have anywhere secure we could put this young lady for a couple of hours, do you?'

Lucy stared at him. 'What are you talking about? We're turning straight round and taking madam here to the police.'

'I'm going nowhere until I've seen a dassie,' said Dawson.

The brief exchange was all the distraction the woman needed. Previously diminished and well-beaten, she now turned and hared for the door, out on to the top of the mountain, pushing one of the cableway staff out of her way. Lucy spun round and raised her gun, but a staff member was between her and the door, and by the time she'd taken a step aside to get a clear shot, the woman had disappeared into the thick mist.

NINE DAYS EARLIER

___ In which Lucy Smith takes a phone call,
   and Dawson books a holiday

'Ms Smith?'

Despite owning the name for nearly a year, Lucy was nevertheless unsure how to answer this. 'Mmm,' she said into her phone neutrally. The number had been withheld and she almost hadn't answered the call. However, the slight chance that it might herald a work opportunity plus the fact that she'd been doing no more than staring listlessly out of the coffee shop's window at the rain and a few hardy-but-drenched passers-by had prompted her to tap the green icon.

'Ms Lucy Smith?' Actually, spammers never called her by that name. It wasn't the name on her passport. Well it was, but not her original passport, the one which was currently sitting in a locked box at the back of a wardrobe in her old bedroom down in Dorset.

The voice was female, Irish – southern Irish to Lucy's expert ears – and sounded unsure.

'Who wants to know?' Lucy waved and smiled at a waitress who scurried off to brew another latte. Lucy's smile did not extend down the phone. These days, the long days following Charles Gulliver's death, she rarely felt like being polite, especially not to cold callers.

Although Lucy and Dawson had known ex-Chief Superintendent Gulliver only a few months, he had soon become a close friend. Following their unjust dismissal from MI6, he had been quick to offer them jobs in the newly created investigations bureau that bore his name. And something about the road accident that had brought his life to a premature end seven days ago sat uneasily with Lucy. She considered it more than suspicious and, despite Dawson being much more inclined to accept that it had been a genuine accident, she'd found herself brooding about the whys and wherefores ever since.

'Oh, yes, sorry.' The woman on the other end of the phone now sounded flustered as well as unsure. 'My name is Waters.' She paused. Lucy said nothing. She knew nobody of that name. The waitress brought her another latte. 'I work for Mr Underwood.'

Now that was a name Lucy knew only too well.

'Bad luck.' She knew she was being needlessly rude but she'd worked for Jason Underwood herself until the summer. It had been he who sacked her. Her and Dawson. Given a list of a thousand people she didn't want to see or speak to, Underwood stood at about 999. She couldn't at that moment work out who the thousandth might be.

'Er, yes,' the woman on the phone said. 'Mr Underwood has asked me to pass on his condolences.' Condolences? He'd taken his time; Gulliver had been dead for a week. The Waters woman was on a roll now. 'He wonders if perhaps he could meet you and Mr Dawson after the funeral on Tuesday.'

Lucy's second latte needed drinking. She hung up.

The door to the coffee shop opened, bringing with it a blast of cold air, a spattering of rain and Dawson. 'All done,' he said cheerfully, kissing her damply and plonking himself down in the chair opposite.

Lucy said nothing.

'You could look happier about it. I'm the one who's been braving the rain and mildly incompetent travel agents while you've been relaxing in here drinking coffee.'

Lucy summoned up a vestige of a smile from somewhere deep inside. 'I haven't just been drinking coffee. I've been answering phone calls from strange Irish women and thinking dark thoughts.'

'You can put aside your dark thoughts. We's goin' on an

'oliday, missus.' The attempt at Cockney was worse than Dick van Dyke's.

'I remember holidays,' Lucy said. 'That's when you go to foreign places and don't get shot at by the locals. Go on then, surprise me. Where are we going?' She'd left that decision to Dawson. Somewhere warm had been her only stipulation. Somewhere it wasn't raining. Sleeting, she corrected herself, peering past Dawson through the window. Sleet which looked to be turning to snow very shortly.

'Cape Town.' Dawson announced this with the bravura of a game show host revealing a million-pound jackpot.

'Cape Town,' she repeated. 'Where 3,000 people a year get murdered. I think I specified that not getting shot would be ideal. I was hoping for something a little more Caribbean.'

'Well, Jamaica's not exactly safe. I mean, nowhere is these days.'

Lucy sighed. Having left the decision to Dawson she couldn't really complain about his choice of destination. 'Cape Town's fine. Lots of Brits go there and they don't always come home in coffins.'

'Exactly. It's where the sun goes for its holidays and also, and you may not know this, but it appears they have a big mountain with a flat top there. I mean, how weird's that? Mountains are supposed to be pointy.' He was grinning. Despite everything, Lucy grinned back. 'Anyway, you said something about a phone call. Some strange woman?'

Lucy thought for a moment. She shouldn't have mentioned the call but he had a right to know. 'Someone who works for Jason Underwood,' she said.

'Underwood? What does he want? Not offering us our jobs back, is he?' The prospect seemed to excite him. Lucy felt the exact opposite of excited.

In which a vicar's cassock fails
to keep out the cold, and Dawson
falls over a grave

Lucy had been correct about the prospect of snow. The weather really was absurdly foul for mid-November. A biting wind originating in the chillier parts of Siberia had brought flurries of thick white flakes to south-east England and some of the snow was enjoying itself so much it had decided to stay put. As the church clock of St Martin's, Stallford sonorously tolled twelve, the temperature dropped well below freezing and looked likely to dip even further before the next hour was struck.

The mood of the mourners matched the weather as they shuffled out of the mild chill of the church into the genuine cold outside, buttoning overcoats, tightening scarves and donning hats, many of which looked less likely to keep out the cold than bare heads would have. Who wears a baseball cap to a funeral? Some copper probably, thought Dawson. He scanned the congregation through the mists of their collective breath. There were more than a few coppers present. They weren't difficult to spot as there weren't that many mourners in total, fewer than forty, which included the vicar who was apparently intending to brave the freezing temperatures wearing just her cassock. Maybe she sported full-length thermals underneath or was happy to trust in the Lord to keep her warm. Or was that a hipflask raising a contour in the cassock?

Lucy tucked a gloved hand through his arm and snuggled closer. 'Bit brass monkeys,' Dawson observed cheerfully.

It wasn't a mood Lucy shared. Charles Gulliver's unexpected death, whether suspicious or not, dealt a mortal blow to the ongoing viability of Gulliver Track and Trace Ltd – or Charlie's Angels as Dawson insisted on calling it. The company's finances had been stretched even before Gulliver's sudden demise and without his contacts and leadership, the investigations bureau looked likely to founder before its first winter was out. They'd already laid off three members of staff, including Sam Bunter, who'd been with them from the start. At least Sam had smiled when Lucy gave him the news; it turned out he'd already decided to return to Surrey Constabulary. Something about being more comfortable in uniform.

Dawson pulled his new, navy-blue scarf tighter around his throat with the hand not currently being commandeered by Lucy. It was the first scarf he'd worn since the age of twelve and he was only wearing it now because it had been a birthday present from Lucy. He'd turned thirty-three yesterday. A third of a century, all but. Did that mean he was approaching middle age? Bearing in mind how close to death he'd come several times already this year, reaching middle age might be an achievement. As for the scarf, he found it itchy and restricting; it was clear that already, less than a year into their relationship, Lucy was trying to change him. He'd been warned that women did that. The scarf was the first sign. Time to dress like a grown-up, she'd suggested, and not volunteer for an unnecessary bout of pneumonia. He looked around. Scarves were *de rigueur* amongst the thin congregation, even the bloke wearing the inappropriate baseball cap, so perhaps she was right. She normally was.

'Unusually cold for a twenty-first century November, my darlings,' remarked the vicar, heaving to beside them. 'When I was a lass, I remember being all mittened-up on bonfire night, but these days I'm often in shorts this time of year.' Dawson found the idea of the vicar wearing shorts somehow disturbing. She was, to say the least, a substantial woman.

The vicar was, though, correct about the unseasonable temperatures. Global warming had presumably decided to take an extensive holiday, and the three-month heatwave of summer had been replaced by winter without first bothering to go through the colourful rigmarole of autumn. One day the trees were green and leafy and the next browny-grey sticks of despair.

'Cheer up, Luce,' said Dawson. 'Pub?' Most of the attendees were dispersing and Dawson and Lucy had already said their goodbyes to Gulliver's only surviving relative, a thin-mouthed spinster sister of few words who had organised the service tidily and efficiently. She quickly disappeared to wherever thin-mouthed spinster sisters disappear to as soon as the vicar had finished proceedings with a rousing rendition of *Abide With Me*, a rousingness shared only by Dawson amongst the congregation.

'Excellent idea,' said Jason Underwood, arriving at their side. He seemed to have apparated from nowhere, so much so that Dawson jumped and lost his footing on an errant piece of ice on the path, disappearing behind a headstone belonging to one Isaiah Turmot (1808-1871). The shadowy MI6 man, early fifties, tall, elegant and immaculately dressed, had sat in isolation at the back of the church. Dawson thought he'd seen him leave before the vicar had brought the show to a close, but apparently not.

'Not for me, I'm afraid, my dears,' said the vicar. 'I'm not really dressed for the pub. Actually, I'm not really dressed for standing out here either. I'm so cold, I think I've got icicles hanging off my nipples.' Dawson found another unwanted and disturbing vision creep into his brain. 'I'll bid you *adieu*.' And she bustled off back inside St Martin's slightly warmer embrace.

___ In which Dawson decides lamb is
off the menu, and Lucy locks
a child in a bathroom


'I was expecting Mr Bunter to be at the funeral,' said Underwood once the three of them were ensconced inside The Cricketers with drinks. His own was a double brandy. Dawson had bought the round. It seemed only right as the pub was his local but Underwood hadn't offered in any case.

'Sam was sorry to miss it,' said Lucy. 'As I'm sure your spies have told you, he's rejoining the police and they wanted him in today to work on some new piece of equipment or other. Knowing this government, water cannon or tear gas.'

'I don't employ spies, Lucy. I prefer to call them colleagues.'

'Any particular reason you wanted to see Sam?' said Dawson.

'Indeed. I wanted to ask him if there was anyone at the service he didn't recognise.'

'Why him?'

'Because I'm guessing that most of our fellow mourners were Surrey Police and I'm interested in those who might not be. Strangers.'

'What are you getting at?' said Lucy. 'Strangers? One of them was Charles's sister, and since he was a nice bloke I'm guessing he had friends. Friends we wouldn't necessarily know.'

'You didn't consider it your job to talk to them?'

'Not really. We're not family.'

'Did you notice anyone failing to pay their respects to Gulliver's sister?'

'Not me,' said Dawson. 'I wasn't really taking note.'

'You're MI6. You should be taking note of everything. Have neither of you wondered about Gulliver's death?'

Lucy kept silent but Dawson said, 'He was driving across

Exmoor in the dark, ran into a sheep and swerved into a stone wall at fifty miles an hour. That's what Devon police said. We've seen a pic of the sheep, or what's left of it. I'll be steering clear of lamb for a while, I can tell you. Shame Charlie didn't steer clear of it. Still, all in all, not much wondering to do really. Oh, and in case you'd forgotten, I'm not MI6. Neither of us is. You sacked us, remember?'

'Why did he hit a sheep and why was he going so fast?' asked Underwood, ignoring Dawson's remark. Dawson, used to life's regular unfairnesses, was quite phlegmatic about it after five months although Lucy remained bitter.

'He wasn't a very good driver,' Lucy said, keeping her suspicions under wraps. 'I don't want to speak ill of the dead but seriously, Charles was a man for whom chauffeurs might have been invented. He'd never have made it as a traffic cop.'

'Even so,' Underwood said. 'Exmoor, twisty road, dark, raining as I understand it. No one would be driving that fast.' He paused. 'Unless, perhaps, they were being chased.'

'Any evidence of that?' said Lucy. 'Much CCTV on Exmoor is there? He was a crap driver, I told you. I don't scare easily but I'd rather face a dozen armed Russian thugs again than be in Charles's passenger seat.'

'And it was late,' Dawson agreed. 'He was probably hurrying to get back to his hotel before the dining room shut. And those Exmoor sheep are buggers. They've no road sense at all.'

'You don't seem to be taking the violent death of a friend and colleague very seriously, Dawson.' Underwood looked at his nearly empty brandy glass but made no move towards his wallet.

'Violent in the sense that he hit a sheep and a wall,' said Lucy, 'but you're suggesting something more.'

'Why was Gulliver on Exmoor?' asked Underwood.

'He was on a case,' said Lucy.

'What case?'

'Without wishing to be rude,' and here Dawson could hear

the faint strain of sarcasm in her voice, 'that's none of your business. As Dawson's just mentioned, we're not part of Six any more. In fact, I'm not clear what you're doing here at all. What exactly is Charles Gulliver's death to you?'

Underwood leaned forward, hands clasped in front of him on the table and looked around the pub, whether to spot possible eavesdroppers or to collect a few stray thoughts, Dawson wasn't sure. He wasn't sure about a lot of things. Like Lucy, he couldn't really see much reason for Jason Underwood, MI6 Control, to be at the funeral at all. He'd hardly known ex-Chief Superintendent Charles Gulliver.

'Nice pub,' said Underwood eventually.

'Thanks,' said Lucy. 'We'll put your review on Trip Advisor.'

'How would you like your old jobs back?'

'No thanks,' said Lucy. Dawson had been about to say 'Yes, please,' but held his tongue. Lucy looked at him as if daring him to unhold it. 'We're perfectly all right as we are, thanks all the same.'

'Really?' Underwood leaned back and took a sip of his drink. 'Your little investigations bureau was losing money hand over fist even before Gulliver's departure from this life of toil. Your remaining resources are virtually non-existent.'

'Leaving all that to one side, you were just about to tell us why you think Charlie Gulliver's car crash wasn't an accident.' Dawson was as much curious as anything else.

Underwood drained his brandy. 'What if I were to tell you,' he said, 'that Charles Gulliver did not have a sister. But that he **did** have a brother, Andrew, who is a lawyer working with the South African State Security Agency. And Andrew went missing two days after Charles crashed on Exmoor.'

'South Africa?' said Dawson. 'We're going there on Friday. On holiday.'

'I know.'

'Of course you do,' said Lucy. 'I mean, we booked it all of two days ago. Why wouldn't you?'

'You would expect nothing less, I'm sure.'

'All of which is entirely irrelevant,' said Lucy, 'as neither Dawson nor I is coming back to Six.' Dawson wished she would at least give Underwood the chance to elaborate. Going back to the security service held a definite attraction as far as he was concerned. It was true that Gulliver Track and Trace had fallen on hard times. Not so much fallen as been born into them and with very little prospect of times becoming softer before the limited remaining capital they had ran out.

'I understand you've been working as some kind of bodyguard, Lucy,' said Underwood. 'Not entirely the sort of work that Gulliver's was set up to undertake.' That much was true. Close protection had never been part of the company's remit but even before Charles's collision with the sheep, dwindling resources had prompted her to accept a position in Hampstead as live-in bodyguard to the six-year-old son of Prince Arshad bin Salman, a distant member of the extended royal family of Saudi Arabia, albeit not so distant that he wasn't entitled to call himself Prince.

Dawson hadn't been happy as he considered it would be better if Lucy continued to be his own live-in bodyguard and it was soon apparent, regardless of the generous and much-needed salary, that her employment prospects *chez* bin Salman were unlikely to be long-lived. Little Laraib, despite his name translating as "Faultless", was anything but. He was in fact an uncompromising trainee bastard who seemed to think Lucy was his personal slave and demanded she refer to him as Your Excellency and curtsy every time she entered his exalted presence. Lucy, refusing to pay homage to a six-year-old brat, had done well to survive eighteen days, at which point she'd cracked and locked the tiny, wannabe dictator in his bathroom for two hours. At that point, Prince Arshad had unsurprisingly terminated her employment, although how Underwood had known about the job in the first place was, like his knowledge of their forthcoming holiday in Cape Town, a mystery.

Lucy took a pull of her lager. 'Yes, we're short of money. Yes, Gulliver dying hasn't helped. But no, at the risk of repeating myself, we do not want to come back to work for MI6.'

Dawson, however, was keen to keep the conversation going. 'Tell me if I'm wrong,' he said. 'You're asking us to have a look for Charlie's missing brother while we're on holiday.'

Underwood looked around the pub again but the cold weather had kept people at home and it was nearly empty. Despite the absence of potential eavesdroppers, he said, 'I'd prefer to continue this conversation back at Vauxhall Cross.'

'And I'd prefer it if you buggered off and had the conversation with somebody else,' said Lucy. 'I am **not** coming back to Six and I am **not** having my holiday turned into work.' She downed the rest of her pint, got up and stalked off to the ladies.

The two men watched her retreating back. 'Tell me about the fake sister,' Dawson said when the toilet door had shut behind her. 'Do you know who she is?'

'I have someone working on that.'

'Why didn't you arrest her at the funeral? Or get one of the many coppers there to do it?'

'Oh, I don't think this is anything for Surrey Constabulary to worry their pretty little heads about.'

'I imagine you're having her followed. Who by? I didn't see anyone.'

'Which is hardly surprising as you've just admitted you weren't taking note.' Underwood rose languidly to his feet and buttoned his expensive coat. 'One other thing. Why has neither of you mentioned that the car Charles Gulliver was driving across Exmoor is registered to a certain Joanna Leigh Delamere? In other words, Lucy. The crash wasn't an accident, Dawson. Despite the coincidence with his brother's subsequent disappearance, maybe, just maybe, Charles wasn't the intended victim. Mull that over and talk to Lucy. Then call me. There's a time for stubbornness and this really isn't it. You'll be in Cape Town in seventy-two hours and it would be helpful if you weren't there just to look at dassies, particularly if there's a target on your girlfriend's back.'

'What are dassies?' Dawson asked, but Underwood was already out of the door to the street, exiting as smoothly as he'd earlier arrived at the funeral.

I gave myself a full ten minutes in the loo before returning to the table to find Jason Underwood gone and Saul
consulting his phone, trying to decide if dassies were
the same as rock hyraxes. 'Yes, they are,' I said as I sat
down.

'He thinks they were after you,' said Saul quietly,
pocketing his phone. He told me what Underwood had
said while I'd been in the toilet counting the sheets on
a roll of loo paper. Then, seeing as both our glasses were
empty, he fetched refills. I was in sudden need of a second
drink. If Underwood was correct, if it was me who should
be dead and not Charles, then what had seemed like an
unlikely coincidence had just got personal. But that made
even less sense. Who wanted to kill me? I thought back.
Charles had gone to Minehead to chase up an anonymous
lead on a missing bloke, a case that had long since gone
cold. I'd suggested it was too far to chase wild geese but
he'd made the valid point that even a tenuous lead was
better than nothing. His car was in the workshop having
the most recent dent he'd inflicted on it straightened out
so I'd reluctantly loaned him mine.

Underwood seemed to be basing his supposition entirely on the fact that Charles was driving my car. No, I
decided, it was too thin. For once, nobody was out to get
me. And Charles had simply crashed. It had been an accident, nothing more. If you wanted to kill someone, there
were more reliable ways of doing it than depending on a
sheep to do the job for you.

But where did that leave the unidentified woman at
the funeral, the one who had introduced herself as Julia
Gulliver? I had no doubt that Underwood was correct
when he'd said Charles had no sister. There did seem to

*be a mystery unfolding, a mystery that was starting to intrigue me.*

—

*I still wasn't sure how I felt at ten o'clock the next morning when Saul, against my better judgement, called Underwood with me shouting something to the effect that my better judgement was better than his better judgement. I stopped shouting when Underwood answered. I didn't want to embarrass myself and I'd also realised that Saul taking charge of a situation – any situation – and making a decision of his own, particularly a decision I might disagree with, was actually Quite A Good Thing.*

*'OK, we're listening,' Saul said. Well, he was at any rate. I stomped off to have a shower. When I emerged from the bathroom, Saul was busy cleaning up the now-broken crockery I'd thrown in his general direction at about the time he'd dialled Underwood's number. It hadn't been an entirely serious throw. And while my throwing hand had hovered over the Australian teapot (which, despite being hideous and lidless, continued to hold pride of place on the shelf) I'd passed it by and chosen instead a collection of appalling Chinese-themed plates given as an engagement present by a maiden aunt of Saul who obviously loathed him. Or maybe she just hadn't approved of the sort of woman he'd got himself engaged to.*

*Engaged? Yes, indeedy. It had taken him long enough to ask. Too long, actually. In fact, it had been me who'd brought the subject up a few weeks after we'd got back from Estonia, Saul with a bullet hole in his shoulder. I had to wait until he'd recovered sufficiently to stop squealing during sex. I mean, there was still some squealing going on but I like to think that was more to do with the quality of the lovemaking than sheer pain.*

I'd posed the question of betrothal as a question, the question in question being: 'Are you ever actually going to get around to asking me to marry you?' He'd ummed and aahed for a while before it dawned on him that I wouldn't be mentioning it if I hadn't been planning to say yes if he did ask, so he rolled over, grinned, placed one hand on, shall we say, my right upper stomach and said (and I quote): 'Hey, sweetcheeks, will ya marry me?' in what could have been an attempt at a Brooklyn accent but which actually hailed (and I have a highly tuned ear for dialects) more from Cardiff.

So I punched him for the "sweetcheeks" and the appalling accent and then said 'Yes' in case the punch had hurt. It shouldn't have; I'd deliberately aimed for the shoulder which hadn't taken the bullet.

'Tomorrow, ten o'clock,' he said without looking round, which he usually did when I emerged from the shower to check I hadn't forgotten to wrap a towel round me. I hadn't forgotten, as it happened. 'You and me, Vauxhall Cross.'

Tomorrow: the day before we were due to leave for Cape Town for what was starting to feel less like a holiday with every passing minute. At least he hadn't got us rushing up to London this afternoon. Apart from anything else, I hadn't packed yet.

'You, maybe,' I said. 'I'm not coming.' That wasn't actually the decision I'd come to but I was interested to see how far Saul's new-found masterfulness would stretch. It turned out that it still had some elasticity to it.

'Yes, you are,' he said. 'Even if I have to pick you up and carry you.'

'I'd pay to see you try that,' I said, laughing. It was just as well he could make me laugh.

He laughed too, at the same time checking that I wasn't within touching distance of any more of Aunt

*Harriet's faux-Chinese porcelain. 'Anyway,' he said. 'If Charlie's Angels are going to show up at MI6, we don't want to pitch up two wings light.'*

— In which Sapphire Waters pours coffee,
  and Lucy stands up


'Discovered who wants to kill me yet?' Lucy asked as a tall, pretty secretary with curly red hair, bright green eyes and round, black spectacles showed her and Dawson into Jason Underwood's office in the MI6 HQ at Vauxhall Cross. 'What about the Julia Gulliver woman, or whatever her name is? Any joy finding her?'

'And good morning to you too, Lucy. You're looking radiant, I must say. Unless those are temper-spots on your cheeks. Take a seat. You too, Dawson.' Underwood gestured towards four deep armchairs surrounding a Persian rug that probably cost an arm, a leg and several other assorted limbs. He trekked across the acreage of carpet to join them. 'By the way, when's the wedding? I presume I'll receive an invitation.'

'How did you know about the...? began Dawson before being brought to a halt by a snort from his fiancée.

'Bugging our bedroom now, are you, Jase?' she said witheringly.

'Absolutely not. What do you take me for? I simply like to show an interest in the lives of my colleagues.'

'Ex-colleagues.'

'Can I offer you coffee?' The pretty secretary came in with a tray of coffee and Bourbon biscuits which she placed on a low table in front of them before perching herself on the edge of the fourth armchair and starting to pour, unasked.

'Ooh, Bourbons,' said Dawson. 'My favourite.'

'Of course,' said Underwood.

Lucy tilted her head towards the secretary and raised her eyebrows in Underwood's direction.

'Oh yes, of course, forgive me. Allow me to introduce Sapphire Waters. I have asked Sapphire to take temporary charge of putting together a little sub-department I have in mind and tasked her with identifying the particular parameters of its remit.'

Lucy, who remained undecided about how angry she was at being dragged up to London the day before leaving for South Africa, nonetheless began to think the situation demanded a certain amount of rudeness. 'Departmental Heads reduced to pouring the coffee now, are they? And... Sapphire Waters? Really?'

'I'm thinking you're hardly in a position to start questioning peoples' names, Lady Leigh Delamere. At least my parents didn't name me after a motorway service area.' Sapphire spoke in the gentle southern Irish lilt that Lucy had previously heard on the phone. It only emphasised the slightly mocking tone of the comment. 'How would you be liking it, Mr Dawson?' Sapphire continued, milk jug poised, green eyes wide and expressionless behind the glasses. A few Bourbon crumbs fell from Dawson's mouth; he hoped nobody had noticed.

'Black, please, Ms Waters,' said Dawson. 'No sugar, I'm...'

'Sweet enough? To be sure.'

'Moving forward,' said Underwood, 'I need a front for the new sub-department and this is it. You know, there are lots of valuable lost bits and pieces out in the great wide world: gold, paintings, diamonds you haven't yet managed to trouser, Dawson. For example, are you familiar with Gaddafi's lost millions? We're pretty certain that South Africa is home to some of his ill-gotten gains. But for now, let's concentrate on why Charles Gulliver has been murdered and Andrew Gulliver is likely to have suffered the same fate.'

'Unless you've found some proof in the past forty-eight hours, you can't be certain that Charles **was** murdered,' said Lucy, 'and if, as you hilariously suggest, I was the intended victim, then it has nothing whatsoever to do with his brother's disappearance.'

'In this building, we're never too concerned about the sort

of proof that a judge might accept,' said Underwood. 'You know that, Lucy.'

'The non-sister,' said Dawson, trying manfully to recover from the Bourbon-crumb incident. 'What's she doing arranging Charlie's funeral? Did she kill him? And if Lucy was the real target, what's "Julia Gulliver" got against her?'

'She didn't arrange the funeral,' said Sapphire. 'I've spoken to Charles Gulliver's solicitor. All the arrangements were made by them. It was stipulated in his will. A will which mentions his brother, Andrew, but no sister.'

'If she was responsible for Charles's death, she wouldn't be hanging around to shake hands with half of Surrey's police force, would she?' said Lucy.

'Agreed.'

'Which means she didn't kill him and was at the funeral for another reason entirely.'

'We don't know who killed him,' said Underwood. 'But let's assume for the moment Charles **was** the planned victim and that the same people were responsible for his brother's disappearance. If so, the answer lies in Cape Town. You have a meeting booked next Tuesday with a Rebecca Erasmus, a senior officer at the South African State Security Agency. She's leading the hunt for Andrew Gulliver who, you will recall me mentioning in that delightful public house on Tuesday, is – or, more likely, was – a colleague of hers.'

Lucy decided that enough was enough, that Underwood booking meetings for her and Dawson in South Africa before she'd even agreed to return to Six was the straw that broke her back. She got up abruptly. 'I told you Cape Town was the wrong place for a holiday,' she said to Dawson. 'Thanks for the offer,' she added to Underwood, 'but we're not interested. I think we'll stick with a job that doesn't include the likelihood of being shot at every five minutes.'

Even as she said the words, she realised that actually, being shot at was the part she missed most and, furthermore, there was still the possibility, however remote, that it should be her, lying in the freshly-dug plot in St Martin's graveyard currently occupied by Charles Gulliver. 'In any case,' she continued, while giving Dawson the sort of look that said if he didn't get his arse out of his armchair in the next millisecond she wouldn't be answerable for her actions, 'you couldn't afford us.'

*Saul grabbed me by the arm as soon as we were outside and pulled me across Vauxhall Bridge and on to a bench in the Riverside Walk Gardens opposite the SIS Building. The wind gusting off the Thames was considerably keener than I was, although the temperature was several degrees higher than at the funeral. It wasn't bench-sitting weather but neither was it as chilly as the look in Saul's normally warm brown eyes. I knew what was coming.*

*'What the fuck was all that about?' he said. 'You know as well as I do that there's no future in Charlie's Angels. The mortgage on the flat won't pay itself, nor will the rent on the office. If Charlie Gulliver's been murdered, why the hell would you not want to find out who by and why? Even more so, if it was you they were really after. And you loved working for Six and being all kickass. Our old jobs are being offered to us on a plate and you're turning them down. And for what? Pride? I've been on the dole and I don't want to go back on it.'*

*I took a deep breath. He was right but then again, he was wrong too. Typical Saul really. 'It's not our old jobs though, is it?' I said ungrammatically. 'Not with Miss High-and-Mighty in charge.' Saul slid away from me, which was a first and wouldn't do his chinos any good, judging by the pigeon droppings on the bench. He looked at me appraisingly and nodded.*

*'Is that why you spent the entire meeting being rude to Sapphire? She seemed fine to me.'*

*'I could see she'd won you over as soon as she dangled her Bourbons in your face. She's just a kid. I can't work for her. And what about this Erasmus woman in South Africa? Why does she need us swanning over there? Is South African Security so crap they can't investigate*

their own disappearances?' There was a thin drizzle starting up, sweeping under the bridge from the direction of Battersea, which wasn't exactly helping my mood.

'I doubt if Sapphire's much more a kid than you are. In case you've forgotten, you're younger than me and you didn't find me complaining when you insisted on taking charge.'

'That's only because you were desperate to get in my pants.'

'I'm not denying that.' He put a hand on my shoulder and turned me to face him. 'But it's also because you're clever, intuitive and much better at making decisions than me. In any case, at no point did Jason say you – we – would be working for Sapphire. He said, and I quote, "I have asked Sapphire to take temporary charge of putting together a little sub-department I have in mind". The salient word being "temporary".'

I was impressed both with his use of the word salient and the feat of memory. 'No mention of her continuing to run it once she's put it together. And even if she was nominally in charge, Underwood knows full well you don't take orders from anyone. You've certainly never taken them from him. So whoever's name's at the top of the headed paper, we all know who'll be running things. Bottom line: we both want to find out what this is all about and we're not going to do that cap in hand for cash to keep Charlie's Angels afloat.'

Maybe Saul was right. Just occasionally, he was. He was unquestionably right when he said there was no future in Gulliver Track and Trace. And if Gulliver was murdered, deliberately or through mistaken identity, Saul was also right that I wanted to find out what the hell was going on. Who for example was the woman posing as his non-existent sister? I'd stormed out of the meeting without getting a reply to that question.

I stood up, walked to the wall above the river and stared across the Thames through the drizzle to the SIS Building. Despite myself, I was struggling to resist its pull. It was five minutes before I returned to the bench. Saul had waited patiently. He smiled up at me. I scowled back.

'So, Lucy Smith,' he said. 'What do you say?'

'Not going to be Lucy Smith for long,' I said, resuming my place on the damp bench next to him, 'since you seem to have somehow tricked me into becoming Lucy Dawson.' I'd never actually been Lucy Smith in the first place of course. 'I suppose you think, being a sort of a man, that'll make you head of the household and I'll have to do everything you tell me. So all this taking charge stuff is you getting in the practice.'

He grinned. 'I don't think that, dearest heart. Mind you, it would be nice if you accept that I'm sometimes right. Once you've finished all the cooking and cleaning of course.'

I couldn't keep the scowl going any longer and grinned at him. At that point my phone rang. It was Underwood. I looked at it for a few seconds, then at Saul, who raised his eyebrows and nodded.

'So, Lucy, are you coming back upstairs again or are you going to carry on getting wet across the river? I think I can run to something a little stronger than Sapphire's coffee if it'll help you make your mind up.'

_____ In which Sapphire kicks some equipment,
and Dawson trips on a rug

When Lucy and Dawson returned to Underwood's office, he and Sapphire didn't appear to have moved from the deep armchairs where they'd been sitting thirty minutes earlier. But the coffee tray had been cleared away and in its place stood an unopened bottle of Cardhu single malt and four crystal tumblers. Also on the table lay several A4 black and white photographs.

Underwood leaned forward and shuffled through the photos as Lucy and Dawson resumed their seats. 'Sapphire took these at the funeral,' he said. Most of them showed various groups of mourners following the service but one was a blown-up shot of the woman who had introduced herself as Charles Gulliver's sister, Julia. She appeared to be staring straight into the camera lens. The image was of exceptional quality, helped by the clear, cold air. Underwood picked another photo from the pile and passed it to Lucy. It showed the same woman getting into the passenger seat of a car, an inconspicuous grey Vauxhall. A second figure, another woman, could be seen in the driving seat. It was possible she was Black but the angle of the shot and the darkness of the car's interior provided no certainty. Lucy took the photograph and stared at it with Dawson leaning across to look too.

'Are you going to ask us who that is?' he said.

'Why, do you know?' said Underwood.

'It's hard to see her face but no, I don't think so. I'm pretty sure she's not a resident of Stallford.'

'The facial recognition software here is the bee's knees,' said Sapphire, 'but I wasn't able to get a clear shot of the woman's face. However, we do now have a 62% probability on Julia Gulliver.'

'At last,' said Lucy. 'You could have mentioned it when I first asked.'

'It only came through while you were sitting out in the rain,' said Underwood, pouring four measures of the whisky. Dawson noticed that Underwood's own was significantly the largest measure.

'I took the opportunity to give the equipment a kick,' said Sapphire, smiling. 'And then made a couple of phone calls.'

'You're a busy woman, Ms Waters,' said Lucy. 'Setting up new departments, taking pictures of mourners, pouring coffee, kicking stuff, making phone calls. You should slow down a bit.'

Dawson glared at his fiancée. 'And?' he asked Sapphire.

'We have her down as CIA,' said Underwood. 'Name of Stella Fish. But Langley, somewhat reluctantly it must be said, told Sapphire that she left the agency a few months ago. And before you ask, no, they were not willing to say why.'

'I don't have that sort of clout,' said Sapphire, picking up her whisky and draining her glass in one. She made a face. 'Well, it's not exactly Jameson's, but it'll do.' Lucy, despite herself, found she was beginning to warm to the Irishwoman.

'She didn't sound American,' said Dawson. 'And if she swam away from the CIA, what's she doing at the funeral?'

'Accents mean nothing,' said Underwood. 'I'm waiting for a call back from a friend of mine in the CIA. Chap called Anthony Melhuish. However, and you'll find this interesting, he's currently in Cape Town.' He sat back and, aware that Dawson was long-since hooked, gave Lucy his full attention. 'You in or out?'

'Let's get this straight,' said Lucy, picking up her own glass and, like Sapphire, downing it in one; she couldn't help her competitive nature. 'An ex-CIA officer pretends to be Charles's sister and as she didn't organise the funeral, we still don't know what she was doing there until your American buddy calls you back.'

'And he might not call you back,' said Dawson. 'And if he

does, he may not know himself or, if he does know, might not be willing or able to tell you.'

'Oh, he'll know,' said Underwood. 'But I'm not counting on him telling me. The Yanks aren't always the biggest sharers and I have a sneaking feeling that this might be one of those occasions. Perhaps you could arrange a tête-à-tête with him while you're out there.' He paused. 'There's someone else you might be keen to track down, Lucy.'

'Oh?' She raised an eyebrow. 'Who would that be?'

'Your old friend, Songsung Rong, was spotted at Heath-row two days before Charles Gulliver died, getting off a flight from Johannesburg. She was using the name Gao Chang. The day after the so-called accident, she flew back to South Africa. Unfortunately, we don't know what she was up to when she was here but...'

Songsung Rong, the absurdly tall Chinese Intelligence Agent Lucy had shot twice in the the feet in Estonia. Even with two bullets in her, she'd been terrifying and terrifyingly lethal. Lucy really didn't want to see her hale and hearty and haring down country lanes. No wonder Charles drove into a wall.

'What you're inferring is that Rong popped over to kill me in some sort of revenge attack and got Charles by mistake.'

'Maybe. Or maybe she meant to kill Charles anyway. The Chinese are getting more and more involved in South African politics. They've been investing an awful lot into the rest of the continent – railways, ports and just good old-fashioned real estate – and South Africa's a natural progression. That level of financial investment tends to create a certain political interest on both parts. The Chinese want to make sure their investments are safe and the South African state wants to make sure that it remains independent. Rebecca Erasmus can doubtless fill you in with more detail. It's possible that killing Charles Gulliver was intended as a warning to his brother, Andrew, to stop poking his nose in.' Underwood shrugged. 'Go and find out.'

'If we say yes, are you going to refund the cost of our holiday?' said Dawson.

'Of course not, although there's nothing to stop you staying in Cape Town after you've found out what's going on. Anyway, your meeting with Rebecca Erasmus isn't until Tuesday. I don't like the delay but it can't be helped and by my reckoning, that gives you three full days to enjoy yourself first. Cape Town's not very big. Go up Table Mountain, visit a vineyard and frankly, you've done it.'

'What about this loot of Gaddafi's?' said Dawson. 'We could hang around and try to find it.'

'Gaddafi's missing money is merely an excuse for the new sub-department.' He thought for a minute, refilling his own glass but absent-mindedly failing to refill anyone else's. 'Mind you, it's an idea. Sapphire can draw up a list of possible targets.'

'Targets?' said Dawson. 'Does that mean we get given guns this time?'

'Absolutely not. It's proved quite dangerous giving you and Lucy guns; you tend to shoot people with them.'

'And it's just us two going?' said Lucy. 'Not Sapphire.'

'I'm sitting right here, Lucy,' said Sapphire, although she was smiling as she said it.

'I'm sorry,' said Lucy, 'but I need to know who's doing what and who's in charge.'

Dawson sighed. Underwood sighed. Sapphire was too busy to sigh. 'I'm in charge,' Underwood said. 'You'll all be reporting directly to me but I do have many more calls on my time so your first contact will be Sapphire, like it or not.'

'I'm backroom,' added Sapphire. 'I'm not a derring-doer like you two. I get scared getting on a bus by myself. I'm more than happy to leave all the exciting foreign travel and consorting with enemy spies to you guys.'

'Sounds good,' said Dawson, pleased that Sapphire considered him to be a derring-doer.

'Right, that's that,' said Underwood. 'Now, get to it.'

Lucy and Dawson rose but, as they did so, Dawson tripped on the Persian rug and crashed into Lucy, sending her sprawling on to Sapphire's lap in the next armchair. There was a slightly tense pause before Lucy, smiling at the red-headed woman from a distance of three inches, said, 'I thought it was time we got better acquainted.'

'You could at least have taken me out to dinner first,' said Sapphire. 'A girl has standards, you know.'

\_\_ In which Lucy wears a hat,
   and spots a non-shark


Now that Lucy was fully committed to the job, the delay in getting on with it was irritating her. But Rebecca Erasmus would not be available until Tuesday and she and Dawson could hardly go tromping around Cape Town waving their newly reissued MI6 IDs without getting clearance first from South African State Security. Like it or not, they had three days to kill. Wrong word, she thought.

Or Rong word. They'd heard nothing further from Underwood on the current whereabouts of the Chinese agent. If she **had** killed Charles Gulliver, the motive of putting pressure on his brother, seemed implausible, especially as Andrew himself had disappeared a couple of days later. But equally implausible was Rong flying to England and trekking all the way to Exmoor just to bump off Lucy in some sort of revenge attack. It was far-fetched to say the least. Lucy was hoping she'd have the opportunity to pose the question to her: spying wasn't supposed to be about personal vendettas.

She and Dawson had arrived late on Friday and had time to do no more than book into the decidedly budget hotel that Dawson had found. Having hired a car first thing, the hot sun had drawn them to Bloubergstrand, across the bay from Cape Town and affording a view of Robben Island in the middle distance. 'After a day at the seaside, minds refreshed and bodies bronzed and toned – well, mine bronzed and yours toned – we'll be able to set to on Gullivergate with verve and gusto,' Dawson had said as he'd driven the small Toyota out of the city.

So, here she was, sitting on the beach at Bloubergstrand. She wore a wide-brimmed hat and stared alternately at Dawson's head bobbing about twenty metres out in the surf and the cloud-shrouded flat top of Table Mountain across the bay.

She watched a small cabin cruiser chug towards them, the sun reflecting from its white paintwork, but soon lost interest and didn't notice it change tack a hundred metres out and head off towards Cape Town.

Lucy glanced again at Dawson, now a further ten metres out in the bay ploughing manfully through the choppy waters. He'd been disappointed when Lucy had declined to join him in the sea; the steeply inclining beach and heavy waves had put her off. They had the beach all to themselves. Apart from the occasional vehicle speeding along the road behind them, there was little sign of life anywhere except the restaurant which, judging from the number of cars outside, seemed to enjoy a certain popularity.

In half an hour or so, Lucy thought, she'd be more than ready for a tasty piece of snoek. The absence of people venturing outside the restaurant or their air-conditioned cars was probably down to the unseasonable heat as the clock moved sluggishly towards midday. Mid-November temperatures in Cape Town, Lucy had read, weren't supposed to go much beyond 25 but the Toyota's thermometer was indicating 30 when they'd arrived an hour ago. The phrase "mad dogs and Englishmen" hadn't actually been uttered in their direction when they'd left the hotel but you could see what the locals were thinking as the two of them sploshed on Factor 50 and drove off.

Lucy suddenly noticed that Dawson's head wasn't the only object she could see in front of her. Ten metres north of him was a larger smudge in the waves. She removed her sunglasses and squinted more closely. Whatever it was, it didn't seem to be making much headway through the water. Her first thought had been Shark and her second, Would I have to go and rescue my fiancé from being eaten?

If this was a shark, it was a very lazy one, doing little more than just lolloping about on the surface. Nevertheless, Lucy hauled herself to her feet and strolled down to the water's edge.

'Hey, Neptune!' she called. Dawson stopped his forward propulsion and waved at her.

'Changed your mind?' he shouted back. 'Come on in, it's fantastic. Stops you getting sunburnt too.' Lucy wasn't getting sunburnt. A lifetime with the inconvenient possession of pale skin and freckles had taught her to take great care in the sun: Factor 50, t-shirt and broad-brimmed hat were keeping her skin the colour she preferred it to remain. Dawson, being quite brown, was less bothered and therefore getting browner and yes, redder, even on day one of their working holiday.

'You're not getting me in there with that shark,' Lucy shouted and laughed.

'Shark? What the fuck?' Dawson looked around wildly and started splashing – not so much swimming now as an active avoidance of drowning – towards the beach. But then he stopped again, having finally spotted the non-shark Lucy had seen. He broke off from flailing entertainingly around, bobbed up and down a few times and then started swimming towards whatever it was. Lucy wasn't sure whether that was entirely wise. To be fair though, most things Dawson attempted weren't entirely wise, so she was used to that.

_ In which Captain Temba Yeboah
  notices something missing,
  and looks at an iPad

Captain Temba Yeboah had seen more bodies washed up by
the sea than he cared to remember and this one didn't look
to him as though it had been in the water very long. Lying on
the beach at Bloubergstrand in the noon heat, it was clearly identifiable as a white male. What age of white male, the
captain wasn't qualified to guess, although he could make a
fairly accurate guess about the cause of death. The absence of
anything resembling a head was the sort of clue that Yeboah,
with ten years as a police officer behind him, could not easily
overlook.

He signalled to two hefty constables to zip up the body
bag before it got too odorous and fly-infested, and turned to
the young English couple who'd called in the macabre find.
Yeboah had had a bad morning and the discovery of yet another murder victim was unlikely to improve things for the
rest of the day, especially given the lack of a head to aid identification. He'd already sent word to the local maritime safety authority to keep a lookout in case the head appeared. It
would be helpful if it did, but it would be more helpful if it
wasn't first discovered by a small child or a pensioner with a
heart condition.

Even so, things weren't all bad, he reflected as he looked
across at the two people standing a few metres away, the
woman especially. She was definitely worth looking at, small-
ish, blonde and very pretty in an English Rose kind of way.
Late twenties, maybe thirty, Yeboah estimated. Her male companion was rather more nondescript but then looks weren't
everything. He wasn't exactly Dwayne Johnson himself.

'Is this going to take much longer, Captain?' asked the
woman. 'We're starving.'

'A man is dead. It will take as long as it takes.'

'But we didn't kill him,' said the man.

'If you say so,' said Yeboah. He didn't believe for one second that these two were responsible, and he was quite hungry himself, but if he had to stand sweating on this baking beach for a few minutes, then he didn't see why they shouldn't too – even if they had been public-spirited in calling the police. In his experience most people would have climbed in their cars, driven to a different beach and forgotten all about it.

He looked at the two passports that the nondescript man had collected from their hire car up on the road but was interrupted by a third constable, who was carrying an iPad rather than a body bag. Yeboah glanced as the constable pointed at the screen and then, with an almost theatrical double take, grabbed the iPad and stared more closely.

Lucy noticed the double take and suspected that her snoek was going to be delayed a while longer. Yeboah handed the iPad back to the constable, motioned for him to stay close and, face hardening in so much as he could make it harden, approached the couple.

'Mr Saul Dawson and Ms Lucy Smith,' he said. 'What is the purpose of your visit to South Africa?'

'We're on holiday, Inspector,' said Dawson, smiling cheerfully. Finding himself in the same small piece of the Atlantic Ocean as a headless corpse had made him even more upbeat than usual.

'Captain,' said Yeboah. 'We do not have inspectors in South Africa.' He secretly quite liked the idea of being an inspector. It sounded a lot more police-y than captain.

'And we're trying to have lunch,' said the woman, butting in on his thoughts. If anything was going to butt in on his thoughts, he could think of worse things than Ms Lucy Smith, whose scowl, if anything, made her look even prettier.

'Do spies go on holiday?' he asked, trying to keep his voice neutral.

'Where did you read that?' asked Dawson, dumbfounded. Even now, after the action-filled year he'd just experienced, he found his dumb constantly rising to the surface.

'What we may or may not do for a living is entirely irrelevant, Captain,' said Lucy, the scowl deepening. 'As Mr Dawson says, we're presently on holiday.' For two more days anyway. 'Now if you don't mind, we'll be off. Hopefully, there's still a portion of fish with my name on it in that restaurant over there. If you want to talk further, and I don't see why you should, you have the name of our hotel.'

Yeboah wasn't giving up that easily. 'A man has been murdered,' he said. 'And here you are at the scene of the discovery, a woman responsible for the death of at least one Russian citizen in Estonia.' He pointed at the iPad. 'I have every right to arrest you.'

'Hmm,' said Dawson thoughtfully, looking at Lucy's face. 'You may find you need more than one constable.'

_ In which a woman leans on a car,
and Temba Yeboah's shirt sticks
to his back


Waiting by – or more correctly leaning on – Yeboah's police Volkswagen was a slim white woman with shoulder-length brown hair and a face largely obscured by the sort of sunglasses that Sophia Loren might have dismissed as being dramatically oversized. She appeared to have been dressed by a Milanese couturier but, from what little expression Yeboah could see under the giant shades, seemed unconcerned about getting her clothes dirty. Yeboah's VW was, as usual, covered in dust.

His car was the only vehicle left at the top of the beach. The body wagon had rolled off to the morgue and the police car containing his three constables was disappearing in the direction of the city. Yeboah had allowed Smith and Dawson to leave to have their delayed lunch and he could see their hired Toyota in the restaurant's car park. He was well aware that, despite being MI6, they almost certainly had nothing to do with decapitating random members of the local community. However, their presence was intriguing.

As he approached the VW, the woman straightened and pushed the sunglasses on to the top of her head with a well-manicured forefinger. 'Excuse me, Captain,' she began, bringing into play the sort of thousand-watt-smile that Yeboah suspected was designed to make overworked policemen buckle. 'What can you tell me about the dead man?'

'And you are?' said Yeboah, managing to avoid the effects of the smile. He was weary already and the day was only half over. If he was going to buckle, it was more likely to be through overwork than a smile, no matter how high the wattage. It really was absurdly hot for November. He could feel his shirt sticking to his back but the woman seemed remarkably unaffected by either the humidity or the temperature.

He wiped an off-white sleeve across his sweaty brow and looked at her. For the second time in half an hour, Yeboah decided that he was looking at someone who was repaying the effort with interest. First the small, blonde Lucy Smith and now this taller, dark-haired woman who, even with the smile dimmed, was considerably more pleasant a sight than the headless torso he'd just had to examine on the beach. Or Saul Dawson for that matter. The woman's own brow, smooth, flawless and deeply tanned, appeared untouched by perspiration. Possibly throughout her lifetime, which Yeboah estimated to be between thirty and thirty-five years, although the general flawlessness could be taking a few years off. The face below the brow possessed a character that made her striking. There was something about those features that suggested to his own trained-if-tired detective's eye a mixed heritage. Some ancestry hailing from the more northern reaches of Europe perhaps. And the blue eyes – that would be the northern heritage – were mesmerising, now that they were not hidden behind darkened glass.

Designer clothes, flawless skin, a searchlight smile and mesmerising eyes notwithstanding, there was little doubt in Yeboah's mind about the woman's profession. She was clearly a journalist. And she'd not yet answered his own earlier question.

'I can tell you nothing, miss,' he said. 'A statement will be released to the press later today.'

'Of course, Captain.' She cranked up that smile again. 'But I have to get back to Jo'burg. Deadlines, you understand.' She smiled again and Yeboah, despite himself, experienced a momentary pang of regret that she would soon be leaving Cape Town.

'What's your name, miss? And what newspaper are you from?'

'The Daily Sun,' which answered only the second question. She eased herself off the VW and stood to one side, turning to look at the restaurant a little way up the road, into which Smith and Dawson had now disappeared. 'Can you at least give me any information about the couple who reported the body?'

Yeboah opened the car door but paused before getting in. 'Why are the Johannesburg papers interested in a small-time crime all the way down here?'

'Small-time?' The woman raised her eyebrows, a quizzical look on her face. 'Is murder a small-time crime in Cape Town?'

Yeboah considered that question. There were still far too many murders on his beloved Cape for his liking, and far too many for any specific homicide to attract the attention of *The Daily Sun*, which had more than enough violent crime on its own doorstep to send reporters down to the western Cape for an isolated homicide. But if they had dispatched this fascinating if nameless correspondent to the foot of the continent, why was she so keen to leave again so soon after the body had washed up on the beach?

More importantly, how had she known about it? Yeboah looked around. There were no other members of the press in sight for the very good reason that the press had not yet been informed.

Captain Temba Yeboah surveyed the cramped room within Cape Town's outwardly imposing red-brick SAPS Central Police Station where press briefings took place. It was three hours after the headless body had been washed up at Bloubergstrand, most of which Yeboah had spent trawling through photos of recently missing persons. So far without joy. As a captain, he felt that he really should have been assigned a constable to take care of that kind of thing.

The temperature had edged another three degrees towards boiling point and his already off-white shirt was now more off than white. He had at least remembered to give himself a squirt of anti-perspirant before attending the press briefing. The police had not yet acquired sufficient budget to provide air-conditioning in the briefing room; either that or the powers that be had decided that the local representatives of the fourth estate were not worthy of cool air. Nor, for that matter, were middle-ranking detectives.

There were about twenty members of the press present, but he knew them all and none of the motley crew in front of him looked remotely like a stylish female correspondent with mesmerising blue eyes from The Daily Sun. The squirt of anti-perspirant had been something of a waste then; he didn't care if any of the hacks in front of him could smell him and he could definitely smell one or two of them.

The local television station was also represented and its cameraman was annoyingly close to his table. Yeboah waved the cameraman back a few paces and coughed. The cough failed to bring the room to silence as it was silent to begin with, apart from the flapping of a few notebooks trying to summon up a semblance of a draft.

'Gentlemen,' said Yeboah, even though he could see no

one who answered that description. 'As you know, a body was washed up across the bay at lunchtime today. The body is of a Caucasian male, who we believe to be between the ages of forty-five and sixty. We are presently trying to identify the man.' He paused. The pause was immediately filled.

'Have you found the head yet?'

'Has a murder enquiry begun?'

'Who was he?' (This clearly from someone who had failed to understand the part where Yeboah had said they were still trying to identify the body.)

'Where did the murder take place? Bloubergstrand or here in the city?'

And finally, 'Is this part of a step-up in gang warfare?' It was an inevitable question. Recently, there had indeed been an escalation in inter-gang fighting. Probably linked to a tightening of the net on drug trafficking in the western Cape. With too few drugs to go around, the weakest gangs were being squeezed out by the strongest.

Yeboah tried to smile but only partially succeeded. 'No; yes; we don't know; we don't know,' he said. 'And we don't know.'

A knobbly, arthritic hand precariously attached to the thin arm of an elderly, grizzled man in a crumpled linen suit in the back row raised itself slowly into the air. Heads turned. This was JJ van der Grieke, alternatively "The Greek", although the closest he had ever been to the actual Greece was a ten-day break in a three-star hotel on the Mediterranean coast of Egypt just west of Alexandria. As far as anyone was aware, it was the only time he had left South Africa, which made it more of a surprise that he knew so much about what was going on in the great wide world. And what he knew about that was as nothing compared to what he knew about the goings-on in South Africa and, in particular, Cape Town.

The Greek had been lots of things over lots of years, but primarily and most relevantly, he was the senior reporter of forty years standing of Die Burger, the biggest Afrikaans paper on the Cape. When The Greek asked a question, everybody listened. Even Yeboah. Information could be a two-way street, and what JJ van der Grieke didn't know about what was happening, had happened or was likely to happen in Cape Town was not worth knowing.

'Captain,' van der Grieke began. 'Temba. How are your children? Has Nandi recovered from her flu yet? It is even more distressing when it is unseasonable, *ja*? Please send her my best wishes.' Yeboah didn't even begin to wonder how The Greek had known about his seven-year-old daughter's flu; he himself had only heard about it the previous day. He doubted if Omphile, his ex-wife, would have told him had they not accidentally bumped into each other in the Post Office.

'Nandi will be fine, Mr van der Grieke. Thank you for asking.'

'She is a tough one, your little lady,' continued the reporter. 'Takes after her *ma*, I think.' There were a few titters from the rest of the room. The unspoken message was that van der Grieke considered Yeboah to be less tough than was generally considered desirable in a police detective working in the suburbs and townships of the Cape. Yeboah ignored the barb and waited for the question. It often took The Greek a while to get to the point. 'Is the size of the body a clue to its identity?'

'Its size?' This was not something that had occurred to Yeboah.

'*Ja*. I understand the man was very short.'

'Most headless bodies are shorter than average.' The joke was past Yeboah's lips before he knew it. He swore inwardly. He knew from bitter experience that The Greek was a man of extremely limited humour. He looked at the photo on the table in front of him and attempted to repair the damage. Yes, now he came to think of it, the torso did seem rather on the short side. However, no photos had yet been released to the press so how the old bastard knew about the victim's size was a mystery. 'We are of course including this fact in our ongoing investigation.' Or would be now. He stood up. The ongoing investigation would be less ongoing if he didn't get out of here quickly.

'One more thing, *asseblief.*' Apparently the old bugger hadn't finished. 'I understand that you spoke to three people at Bloubergstrand.' How did he understand? Smoke signals?

'That is classified information,' said Yeboah, slightly smug about rolling out the cliché.

'Why? I think we should be told if Rebecca Erasmus is a suspect.' There was a murmur from the small throng of journalists.

Who the hell is Rebecca Erasmus, Yeboah thought.

'Also,' van der Grieke continued, 'It must be of some concern to the *polisie* that the body was found by two British spies.'

Yeboah sighed deeply and audibly. The Greek might as well have a desk next to his own.

_____ In which Yeboah suffers mild
paranoia, and JJ van der Grieke
drinks whisky


Temba Yeboah knew where he'd find the elderly reporter. It wasn't a secret. Rarely an early evening went past without JJ van der Grieke shuffling into the dingy interior of the Dockview Bar which, as its name failed to suggest, wasn't particularly close to the docks and certainly did not enjoy a view of them. Instead, it was tucked away in – or more accurately under – an uninspiring side street off a series of equally uninspiring side streets round the back of Signal Hill. This particular side street comprised warehouses, some no longer in use. But if you looked carefully you might spot a rusting metal sign with an arrow pointing downwards to mark the location of the Dockview.

Yeboah had been there before, albeit only once and it hadn't been an experience he remembered fondly. The memory of dozens of pairs of eyes, not openly hostile but blankly menacing all the same, staring at him, a lone, Black policeman, had not been comforting.

But needs must. Van der Grieke had tipped the wink to Yeboah as he'd stood slowly up to leave the press briefing an hour or so earlier and if that hadn't been enough, he'd crooked an arthritic finger in his direction. It hadn't been particularly subtle and, quite honestly, it had also been unnecessary. Yeboah needed to find out more about Rebecca Erasmus and it was plain that van der Grieke had things he wanted to get off his concave chest.

Yeboah made even more certain than usual that he'd locked his VW, not that he had any qualms about how effective the locks might prove against any car thieving operation. At least it didn't scream police car, although it whispered it loudly enough for most of the local population to catch the auditory drift. He shrugged on his jacket despite the still oppressive heat, walked twenty metres to the steps that led down to the plain wooden door of the bar, and entered.

A disquieting feeling of venturing into a severe discomfort zone hit him as he strolled, as nonchalantly as he could manage, up to the counter.

'Yes, Captain, what can I get you?' A huge barman loomed out of the gloom. The question had been asked in a not noticeably friendly tone but Yeboah, hunting for positives, thought it wasn't outrightly confrontational either. Perhaps he was being mildly paranoid. He wasn't sure if the barman remembering him was a good or bad thing. Maybe they kept mugshots of all current serving local police officers on a wall somewhere, possibly in lieu of a dartboard.

Yeboah didn't normally drink on duty. In fact he didn't drink much at all, but on this occasion, not wishing to invite ridicule, he asked for a Castle. He looked around as his eyes slowly adjusted to the semi-darkness but in fact it was The Greek who saw him first and edged over, gnarled fist wrapped lovingly round a whisky. Or a quadruple whisky, judging by the amount of liquid in the tumbler. Yeboah wasn't sure how the emaciated arm of the old journo could possibly have the strength to lift it to his lips.

'Come with me, Captain,' wheezed van der Grieke and pointed towards an alcove even darker than the main bar. He picked his way through the crowded room. If these were dock workers, Yeboah thought, there wasn't a lot of work going on at the docks. 'You want to know about Rebecca Erasmus,' the old Afrikaner continued once they were seated in the alcove, which contained a small table that may have been cleaned on some date in the distant past. However, Yeboah felt dirty enough already and he could always shower later.

'She told me she was a reporter from The Daily Sun. I didn't believe her.'

The old man chuckled. 'You may yet make a policeman. *Ja.*

You are right not to believe her. So, if she is not one of us, who is she?'

By "us", Yeboah assumed The Greek was referring to the massed ranks of the press. 'I was hoping that's what you're going to tell me. You seemed keen that we should meet.'

'Ah, *ja*,' said van der Grieke, wagging an arthritic finger on the hand not currently engaged in holding his whisky tumbler. 'But information comes at a price, *is dit nie waar nie*. I am a reporter and you are a policeman. We can help each other. A bit of *quid pro quo, n'est-ce pas?*' Yeboah was struggling to keep up with the switching between three living languages and one dead but he wasn't surprised; he knew how these things worked.

'What do you want?'

'Exclusivity, Captain. There is a story here. I do not yet know what it is but the fair Rebecca, two English spies and a headless torso on Bloubergstrand at the same time is no co-incidence. When you unravel the mystery, I would like to know it...' he emptied his glass in one smooth swallow, 'first.'

'I have to keep my colonel informed of progress first. You understand that.'

'Pah.' Van der Grieke waved a hand dismissively. 'You are not the policeman I think you are if you go running to Colonel Swart every time you find a clue.'

'Make your mind up, old man,' Yeboah said. 'Just now you implied I might one day make a policeman. And now you're showering me with compliments.' It hadn't been a shower exactly, more a single, tiny droplet, but never mind. 'You tell me who Rebecca Erasmus is and I'll pass on anything I can to you before I tell the rest of your pack. That's the best I can do. If not, no deal.' He stood up but van der Grieke waved him back down again before signalling to the oversized barman who immediately lumbered over with another tumbler filled to the brim with whisky.

'This is on you, Captain,' said The Greek. The *quo* was

already outnumbering the *quid* but Yeboah slid a note from his wallet and handed it to the barman. The chance of getting any change seemed slim. Unlike the barman himself.

The transaction did seem to have persuaded van der Grieke to open up. He looked around furtively, leaned forward so that Yeboah could get the full benefit of his whisky-breath and whispered, 'Rebecca was born out of wedlock. I do not judge of course.' Yeboah hoped not; this was the twenty-first century after all, and even when the woman was born back in the late eighties or early nineties on the conservative Cape, it would not have been considered entirely disreputable. The Greek continued. 'So, Erasmus is the lady's name but she might equally accurately be called de Kock.' He paused. 'And she works for the State Security Agency.'

Yeboah leaned back. 'So you're telling me that Erasmus is another spy, like the man and woman on the beach?' It seemed unlikely; surely spies were supposed to be unobtrusive. To come across two excessively glamorous female examples in the same place at the same time strained credulity.

'Captain, I have been in this business since long before you were born. I know everybody on the Cape. And one of the people I know is Rebecca's mother. You do too. She works in your police building.'

Yeboah thought. He couldn't think of an Erasmus in the Cape Town Police. And while de Kock was a common enough name, he could only come up with one person owning it within the Central Police Station: Brenda de Kock. That is to say, Major General Brenda de Kock, the Acting Regional Commissioner.

___ In which a car becomes lopsided,
    and an ineffective gunfight
    takes place

When Yeboah reached the deserted street, it took a little while for his eyes to accustom themselves to the bright early-evening sunshine after the gloom of the Dockview Bar. The day already felt overlong, overtiring and over-frustrating.

He was mildly but pleasantly surprised to find his car sitting where he'd left it a little way down the street. He could see that it was still in full possession of all four wheels and both wing mirrors and the sun was glinting off enough glass to indicate there'd been no smash-and-grab malarkey in his absence. There was something strange about the vehicle though, he decided as he drew closer. The passenger side seemed rather closer to the ground than the driver's side. So either the suspension had suffered a malfunction or... he paused and peered more closely through the windscreen. The grime and sunshine allowed only the half-certainty of a shadow inside the car. A large shadow. Judging by the lopsided gait of the VW, the large shadow was also a heavy one.

Yeboah grunted and continued his walk to the car. He wasn't surprised to find that the driver's door opened without any assistance from his key. He got in, made himself comfortable, clicked his seatbelt on and, only then, turned to the massively intimidating man sitting next to him.

'Where to?' asked Yeboah, starting the engine.

The man turned his head slowly in his direction. As he appeared to have no neck, this normally uncomplicated minor manoeuvre became a major logistical operation. When the man spoke, it was with a subterranean Afrikaans growl. 'Coetzee,' he said. Presumably his name, Yeboah decided. 'Ms Erasmus wishes to meet with you.'

'The feeling's mutual. As I said: where to?' Yeboah let in the clutch and pulled out into the empty street without signalling.

'Turn right at the end. Then I will let you know. I must inform you that this is not my idea.'

'I didn't think you looked happy.'

'I am never happy. What is there to be happy about in this shithole? Go left at the next junction.'

'If we're going to Green Point Park, you could have just said.' Yeboah glanced across at Coetzee, who merely grunted. 'You're secret service, I take it.' Another grunt. Robben Island appeared as a flattened greenish smudge ahead of them as they rounded a bend and approached Green Point Lighthouse. Without being instructed, Yeboah turned the nose of the VW left towards the promenade and there, leaning on a railing with her back to them, seemingly absorbed in the progress of two tankers a couple of miles out at sea heading south-west, was the same dark-haired woman he'd met on the other side of the bay six hours earlier. She failed to turn as they pulled up a few metres away so the mesmerising blue eyes weren't in view. He could, however, see that they were no longer hidden by the enormous sunglasses.

The scene, exacerbated by the unseasonal heat, was placid with only a few other people in sight and none closer than a hundred metres. Out of nowhere, the roaring of a powerful engine, amplified as it rounded the lighthouse behind them, broke the stillness. Rebecca Erasmus whirled around; the noise spelled danger in metre-high letters. The vehicle, an inevitably black BMW X-7 with similarly blackened windows screeched to a halt between Rebecca and Yeboah's Volkswagen.

Belying his bulk, Coetzee threw open his door and leaped out, pulling a gun and letting off a volley of shots at the three men who had just as rapidly emerged from the BMW. Yeboah, still in the Volkswagen and transfixed by the sudden change in the situation, couldn't see any of Coetzee's bullets hit their mark before two of the men from the BMW returned fire, forcing his neckless companion to take cover behind the Golf.

Rebecca Erasmus was legging it towards the lighthouse but the third gunman, taking careful aim, brought her down, as far as Yeboah could see, with a single shot to her left calf. Quickly, the man ran over to her, scooped her up and carried her back to the BMW where a gunfight continued to rage between Coetzee, Yeboah – who had recovered his wits and was firing through the side window of his car – and the two gangsters covering their colleague and Rebecca. They piled back in the BMW and pulled away, leaving tyre rubber in their wake.

Yeboah, unimpressed by the accuracy of the shooting from all the participants, including himself, stuck the Golf in gear and hurtled off in pursuit, leaving his giant, secret service former passenger alone on the battleground. Flinging the car around Green Point Lighthouse and out onto Bay Road, he could see the X-7 some way ahead of him, already turning left onto the main M6 towards central Cape Town. For some reason he'd never been able to ascertain, his official Police Golf was not equipped with either Blues or Twos, so with rush hour in full flow, he struggled to keep the BMW in view. He was finally and irrevocably held up at the roundabout by the Cape Town Stadium.

Yeboah wasn't a man for whom foul language came naturally but now he thumped his steering wheel in frustration and yelled 'Fuck!' at a couple of uninterested gulls perched on a bus shelter by his window. The gulls took off and, a few seconds after as the blockage at the roundabout cleared itself, so did Yeboah, considerably less quickly.

He took the right turn that he thought he'd seen the BMW disappear into but knew it was hopeless. Rebecca Erasmus was gone.

___ In which Sapphire is taken to
an airport, and Stella Fish hits
a car driver

When Sapphire Waters awoke, she was no longer in her bed but lying on the rear seat of a car. This information took a somewhat circuitous route before it reached her brain. When it did, she frowned and tried to sit up but found this difficult as her wrists were taped together and she was belted in. It was dark and through the side window she could see that it was still night. See. She could see, she realised. As usual, she had removed her glasses when she went to bed but she was wearing them again now. Without them, Sapphire's eyesight was batlike. Her short-sightedness was the main reason she'd been stuck behind a desk for the last two years. The fact that her kidnapper had not seen fit to leave the glasses behind was something to be thankful for. Not much, but something.

But what the bejesus was going on?

'Hello?' she called hoarsely.

'You're awake,' said a female voice from the front of the car. Sapphire was not entirely sure if she was awake or not, this could very easily be a dream. Or a nightmare. With effort, she shuffled her legs sideways and managed eventually to sit up. There were two people in front of her but a combination of high seatbacks and the darkness inside the vehicle meant she couldn't see enough of them for recognition. Between the two heads, an almost deserted motorway was illuminated by the car's headlamps and a lightening of the sky above the horizon suggested that dawn was not far off. Her brain was beginning to crank into gear.

'What's going on? Who are you?'

The person in the passenger seat turned to look at her. Despite the gloom, there was enough light from the instrument panel for Sapphire to recognise the woman from the funeral, the woman who was not Julia Gulliver but who Sapphire herself had identified as an ex-member of the CIA, Stella Fish.

'What the fuck?' she yelled and started struggling against the tape around her wrists.

'Calm down, Ms Waters,' said Stella Fish. 'You'll do yourself an injury. We're nearly there.' At that moment, an indicator began clicking and the car slowed before the driver steered it off the motorway and up a slip road.

'Nearly where? Where are you taking me?' But an answer arrived almost immediately as the car turned through some gates and Sapphire caught a passing glimpse of a sign that said "Airport". She hadn't caught the name but that, for the moment, was irrelevant. If Stella Fish and her companion were intending to put Sapphire on a plane, it really didn't matter where it was leaving from. Where it was going to was more important.

They drove past a cluster of airport buildings and the headlamps lit up a small sleek jet, unmarked except for the compulsory number on the tail fin. The driver switched off the engine and opened the car door, prompting the interior light to come on. Sapphire saw that the driver was young, Black and female. Almost certainly the same person who, at the funeral, had driven the grey Vauxhall into which Stella Fish had climbed.

**This** grey Vauxhall, she realised, as the driver opened a rear door, unclicked the seatbelt and indicated that Sapphire should exit the car. There seemed little point in staying where she was, especially as she could see, as the sky slowly lightened, that Stella Fish, now standing a few paces behind the younger woman, had a small gun in her hand. It seemed a pointless precaution; Sapphire had her wrists taped and she was hardly an action-woman anyway. As she edged her way along the seat and put her feet on the grass preparatory to trying to stand up using just her stomach muscles to do so – muscles ill-equipped for the task – Stella Fish took a step forward and swung her gun hard at the side of the young driver's head. The woman toppled silently to the ground.

Sapphire was appalled. 'What did you do that for? She's your driver!' she yelled from her position half in and half out of the Vauxhall.

'Yes, but she's not my pilot. While I have nothing personal against Ms Nkunde, our interests no longer coincide. She'll be fine apart from a headache and if it turns out she needs medical attention, Rochester Airport staff will provide assistance when they arrive shortly. Now stand up, please.' Sapphire had very little choice but to comply. With some difficulty, she stood.

'Up the steps please, Ms Waters.' Stella Fish was being extremely polite, despite training the gun on her. Even if Sapphire had had two free hands, she doubted she'd be a match for the older woman. Once inside the aircraft, she was directed to one of two seats facing each other immediately behind the cockpit. The cockpit was empty.

'You mentioned a pilot.' she said. 'Where is he?'

'He? How very sexist. He would be me. Now sit down.' No please this time. A knife appeared in Stella Fish's free hand. 'Hold your hands out.' Sapphire obeyed and the tape around her wrists was cut quickly and efficiently. 'Fasten your seatbelt.' When she looked up from the buckle, the gun and knife had disappeared. 'Now, Ms Waters, I'm going to trust you to stay where you are and not do anything foolish. We'll be taking off and if you're a good girl, you'll remain unharmed. If you're not, either I'll have to knock you out like poor Ms Nkunde, which would be painful for you, or the aircraft will very likely crash, which would be terminal for both of us.'

Sapphire couldn't spot a flaw in the argument. For one thing, even in the unlikely event of her being able to overcome the older woman, she was well aware she couldn't fly a plane. And it was clear that Stella Fish was not planning to kill her. This was all linked somehow to Charles Gulliver's death and despite having no field experience, Sapphire **was** still MI6.

She knew her job was to see whatever this was through and find out what the hell was going on.

'Where are we going?'

Stella just smiled. 'Make yourself comfortable and I'll be back to have a chat in about twenty minutes once I've got this bird airborne.'

___ In which Sapphire thinks of
a letter, and wonders who she is


Sapphire wasn't keen on flying at the best of times and this flight wasn't the best of times. The plane took off and she spent the next twenty minutes trying to think things through before Stella Fish, true to her word, returned to the cabin.

One of the things Sapphire thought about were their likely destination and how best to conduct herself. Knowing that Jason Underwood was planning to re-recruit Dawson and Lucy, she'd spent some time reading up on them. Now, she decided she'd try to live by the mantra, "What would Lucy do?". Although, she suspected, somehow, she'd do a Dawson.

'Autopilot,' said Stella as she took the seat opposite.

'You don't say?' said Sapphire. Judging by the contempt on Stella's face, the attempt at sarcasm à la Lucy may not have worked. 'We're going to Cape Town, aren't we?'

'It's a long journey,' said Stella, answering the question by not answering it. 'You can take your seatbelt off. Feel free to move around. Make yourself comfortable. We're well stocked with food and drink. Even alcohol. G and T's your tipple of choice, I believe. I won't partake of course. Can't have the pilot getting drunk.'

'If we're going to South Africa,' said Sapphire, 'why is this plane American?'

'And what makes you think that?' Stella's eyes narrowed.

This is better, thought Sapphire. She doesn't know that I know that she's ex-CIA. She started to feel more Lucy-like. 'It's obvious. N.'

'N?'

'The international code letter for the USA,' said Sapphire. The tail number had started with it. She knew about international aircraft codes; she'd gleaned quite a lot of arcane knowledge while bound to her Vauxhall Cross desk.

'I always knew you had brains.'

'What do you mean, you always knew I had brains? I've never met you.'

'Oh but you have. You just can't remember, that's all. It was a few years ago, although that's not the reason you can't remember. No matter, we have ways of bringing your memory back. For example, you think you work for MI6 but, I'm sorry to break this to you, you don't.' Stella rose and returned to the cockpit.

Sapphire felt less than Lucy-like. What the hell had she just been told? That she didn't work for MI6? Yes, she did. She could distinctly recall the gruelling interview process and the two boring years sitting behind a desk because her vision wasn't good enough to even apply to go on the active list. Bloody eyesight! Then suddenly, her appalling visual acuity hadn't mattered after all and Underwood had plucked her from her desk, seemingly at random, to give her this huge promotion including Access To Pretty Much All Areas at the Cross. Did that mean that Jason Underwood and Stella Fish were secretly working together? That didn't make any sense, but no less sense than Sapphire herself not knowing who she really worked for.

She got up to stretch her legs and investigate the galley. Returning to her seat holding a large gin and tonic (as Stella had suggested), she found her captor was also back in the cabin and had opened up a laptop. She didn't even glance up as Sapphire walked past. Sapphire understood about autopilots but surely someone was needed to stay in the cockpit to keep an eye open for trouble and an ear open for air traffic calls? The fact that Stella considered that unnecessary was, to say the least, disquieting. Unless there was a second pilot all along. No, Sapphire could swear the cockpit had been empty when they'd boarded the aircraft. She decided to keep quiet. It seemed hardly likely that Stella Fish would deliberately put her own life in jeopardy, whatever her plans for Sapphire.

The plane continued its long journey south. All Sapphire could see through the window was unbroken cloud. She settled down with her drink. She realised that Stella had never confirmed in so many words that South Africa was indeed their destination. It could be a lie and Sapphire would have no way of knowing until they actually arrived. And given that she'd never been further south in her life than Paris, maybe she wouldn't know even then. Hopefully there'd be a flat-topped mountain in sight when they landed to give her a clue.

She found herself drifting off. As she did, the uneasy thought that she might not, after all, be an MI6 officer kept rattling around inside her head. It was absurd. This entire situation was absurd. But if true, then what else of the life she was living was also a lie?

*The knock on the door of our hotel room would have been unwelcome even if it was Room Service. But Room Service would knock more politely. This was a much more official-sounding knock. It held serious shades of peremptoriness.*

*'Is that Room Service?' called Saul from the bathroom. He obviously didn't have an ear for official-sounding door-knocks. As he also didn't have any clothes on, it fell to me to answer the door.*

*'I doubt it,' I said. 'Apart from anything else, we've only just had breakfast.'*

*I peered through the eyehole. Definitely not Room Service. Not unless Room Service dressed themselves in police navy-blue at this hotel and I was pretty sure that wouldn't be a good marketing ploy. They'd certainly lose a star they could ill afford to lose. I sighed inwardly. I'd been hoping, following The Headless Body Incident, we wouldn't be bothered by the local cops again. We only had two more clear days before our meeting with Rebecca Erasmus. The police at the door meant we could probably wave goodbye to one of the two. I opened the door.*

*'Ms Lucy Smith?' asked one of the unsmiling policemen. I thought I remembered both him and his equally taciturn colleague from the beach, where they'd had their hands full with a body-bag of headless corpse. Maybe Cape Town police had a recruitment problem.*

*'That depends on what you want,' I said unhelpfully. 'There are some vineyards north of here with my name on them.'*

*'They'll still be there this afternoon,' he replied. 'We need you to accompany us downtown.' It seemed unlikely he was offering to take us shopping so I assumed he*

meant to the police station. Dawson joined us, now mercifully semi-clothed, in as much as he had dragged some shorts on.

'Hi guys,' he said cheerfully. 'What gives? Found out who the dead bloke is yet?'

'I am not at liberty to say, sir. I was just informing your wife...'

'Not yet,' Saul interrupted.

'We need both of you to accompany us downtown, sir.'

'Downtown?' said Saul. 'Pet Clark fan, are you?' The quip disappeared down a deep hole but a failure to elicit a response didn't faze Saul for a moment. 'I'll just pull on a shirt then,' he said. 'What's the temp like today? Struck lucky with the weather, haven't we?'

Not with much else though, I thought, resignedly stuffing passport and credit card into a waist pouch and strapping it on. Dead body on the beach and another one at home. And I didn't even agree with him about the weather; I'd have been happy with low twenties.

---

I expected to be greeted by Captain Temba Yeboah when we were shown into a small, spartan room on the third floor of the Central Police Station in "downtown" Cape Town, but instead a short, grey-haired woman in a uniform bedecked with lots of gold trim stood up from behind a desk and indicated we should sit. There were two upright chairs in front of the desk. Mine was possibly the least comfortable chair in which I'd ever sat.

'Thank you for coming,' she said. The words were polite but her expression grim.

'Not sure we had much choice,' I replied shortly. 'Being arrested wasn't in the brochure.'

'You haven't been arrested, Ms Smith. You're free to go

*if you wish, but before you decide, we have a proposition to put to you. You might care to hear it.'*

*We? I'd not noticed anyone when I'd subtly scanned the room. I looked around, startled, and Saul did the same, the only difference being that he managed to upend his chair.*

*Picking himself off the floor, Saul said, 'I didn't see you there,' to somebody, but I was none the wiser until I felt a faint shift of air. A male outline appeared from my periphery. A man, slim, of Asian appearance with a truly forgettable face and wearing a grey suit that blended with the walls, moved past me and perched himself on the corner of the desk.*

*Saul righted his chair and sat down again, displaying not the slightest embarrassment. 'Perhaps you'd like to tell us who you both are,' I said to our hostess, 'before we decide whether to stay and listen to this proposition.'*

*'My name is Major General de Kock,' the woman replied, 'and this is Mr Patel.' Even his name failed to stand out from the crowd. Mind you, being called Smith I was hardly one to talk. She continued, 'Mr Patel is the Deputy National Commissioner of Police. He has kindly flown down from Pretoria to join us.' Something about the way she said "kindly" suggested the opposite.*

*'You're not trying to pin the murder of that guy from yesterday on us, are you?' said Saul.*

*'I believe you have recently been working with a gentleman called Charles Gulliver,' said Patel in a voice so low I could hardly hear it from four feet away. 'A gentleman who I am informed has recently been killed in a car accident.'*

*'What exactly are you doing in Cape Town?' added Major General de Kock, cutting in.*

*It seemed a strange question to ask, bearing in mind she'd already said they had a proposition for us. It was* time to come clean – up to a point. 'As you already know, Mr Dawson and I work for MI6. We have a meeting booked with a senior officer at your State Security Agency on Tuesday. That being so, we're really not in a position to discuss anything about our presence in your country until that meeting has taken place and only then if our contact wishes to share that information with the police.'

'May I ask who your contact is?' said de Kock.

I was just deciding whether we should give her that information when Saul made the decision for me. 'A lady by the name of Rebecca Erasmus.'

'I thought as much.'

'You know her?' said Saul, sounding surprised. I wasn't; there was no reason why senior police officers should not know who their counterparts in State Security were.

'Rebecca Erasmus is my daughter, Mr Dawson.'

Now that did surprise me. What Patel said next surprised me even more.

'We know about your meeting,' he whispered. 'However it will not be taking place. Rebecca Erasmus has been kidnapped. And the unfortunately decapitated gentleman you found at Bloubergstrand has been identified. His name was Andrew Gulliver.'

Lucy wasn't wholly surprised that Andrew Gulliver was dead. That had always seemed the likeliest outcome, but for his to have been the body they'd found in the sea was preposterous. The chances were astronomical, unless…

'It was planted,' said Dawson. 'The body, I mean.'

Patel breathed his question: 'Why do you think that, Mr Dawson?'

'There was a boat,' said Dawson, 'I mentioned it to Captain Yeboah. It came in quite close then suddenly turned tail and shot off back towards Cape Town. The captain didn't think the body had been in the sea very long but MI6 knew about Andrew Gulliver's disappearance last Monday. There's no chance he'd been drifting around aimlessly for four days before bumping into me, so he was killed and dumped into the sea on Saturday. From the boat we saw. Deliberately targeted at us.'

'Someone wants us arrested for murder,' Lucy finished.

'I'm not sure we can infer that,' the Major General said. 'But I'll get an update on the search for the boat from Captain Yeboah.'

'How did you know we were due to meet Rebecca?' Lucy said. 'Mother and daughter thing?'

'She keeps a diary. The SSA weren't keen to give us access, or at least, Rebecca's colleague wasn't. But Mr Patel here pulled strings. Why were you meeting Rebecca, Ms Smith?'

'Because of the Gulliver connection,' said Lucy. 'MI6 thinks Charles was murdered and we now know Andrew was too. We have an interest in this case.'

'But it's not your jurisdiction.'

'I think you'll find it soon will be, if your security agency wants us to help find the killers.' She paused. 'And is that what **you** want? Is this the proposition that you've failed to expand on?'

'Correct,' whispered Patel. Lucy and Dawson craned forward. 'You've been sent here to stick your fingers into our affairs. The South African Police Service does not take kindly to foreign spies setting foot outside their own embassy and treading on our toes, even if it is with the cooperation of our own State Security Agency.'

'You don't get on, do you?' said Dawson.

Patel ignored this. 'Your contact at the SSA has now disappeared and without her to back you up, we have every right to put you on the next plane back to London.'

'But you're not going to.' That was Lucy.

'No,' said Brenda de Kock. 'I would like you to help us recover my daughter. And find out who is behind all this.'

'What were they working on?' said Lucy. 'Rebecca and Andrew Gulliver. He was a lawyer, wasn't he?'

'We don't know,' said Brenda. 'Something important though. Andrew Gulliver was born in the United Kingdom but had been a naturalised South African citizen for over thirty years and was, as you say, a lawyer. A senior civil servant in the Department for Home Affairs, to be exact. We know he was working closely with Rebecca but don't know about what. Rebecca has now disappeared and Andrew's murder, as you can imagine, is of great concern.'

The presumption being that most murders aren't, thought Lucy. She supposed that when they were stacking up at the rate of eight a day, there had to be some sort of triage system. 'And despite all that, your State Security is keeping you at arm's length?' she said. 'Why?'

'Politics, Ms Smith. Where the police cannot go perhaps MI6 can. South Africa is still a relatively poor country in need of foreign aid. Our political system is beholden to those nations with deep pockets, an insatiable need for our natural resources and the ability to ride our tumultuous ways. Those nations are fewer than one might think. So when they show up and flip open the cheque book, questions don't get raised. Not even by the police. Not even after one of our own gets murdered. But you, maybe you can open doors we cannot. And of course, you will not only be helping us but yourselves too.' She drummed her fingers on her desk and looked at them.

'There's something else, isn't there?' said Dawson.

'Yes,' said Brenda de Kock. She paused. Dawson and Lucy waited. They'd almost forgotten about Patel but he was still there, right in front of them, perched on the corner of the desk, casually swinging a grey leg.

'Did Rebecca want to talk to you about her father?' Brenda said eventually.

'We didn't come all this way for a family chat,' said Dawson before remembering they were talking to Rebecca's mother.

'What about her father?' said Lucy.

'Rebecca's father is – was – Charles Gulliver.'

—

They'd been known as the Poison Dwarfs at Mount Road Police Station, Port Elizabeth, back at the start of the nineties. Charlie, all five foot two of him and newly arrived on a year-long secondment to the South African Police Service, and Bren, a whole inch and a half taller. 'What's it like up there in the clouds?' he'd asked when he first slapped eyes on her in the canteen a week after arriving from a wet England.

Bren had been slow to allow herself to be attracted to this short, smiley Brit. She was fiercely ambitious and unhappy at barbs such as the poison dwarf one and queries about whether sex was legal between two people of stunted growth. Especially as they hadn't actually had sex. Yet. But Charlie, who had developed a sense of humour as an initial defence against the verbal arrows of heightist and would-be bullies, had also been brought up in a one-bedroom flat in Brixton. He knew how to handle himself, not necessarily with a close adherence to Marquess of Queensberry rules. After a few days of jokes from their fellow officers, Bren was aware that the nastiest of the barbs stopped suddenly. And almost without her being aware of it, she and Charlie found themselves walking hand in hand on the beach at sunset and sharing fish dinners in idyllic beach-front restaurants up the coast.

Bren had written to him three months after his return to drizzly England at the end of his secondment to say (a) that she was now engaged to an industrialist named Willem de Kock and (b) that he might wish to start sending some paternity money across when their daughter was born in a few months' time. It would never have occurred to the upright, by-the-book Brenda Erasmus, soon to be Brenda de Kock, to try to pass off the forthcoming child as her fiancé's. And that had apparently been fine with Meneer de Kock.

Sapphire woke up to find she was lying on her back on a bed in a small, white-painted room. Sunshine was streaming through the window to her left. She was fully clothed although her spectacles had been removed. When she tried to sit up, she found she couldn't. Her wrists were strapped to low hand-rails, also white-painted, that ran down either side of the bed. She had a pounding headache and her body felt clammy and queasy. The room appeared to be largely empty but she could dimly make out the blurred outline of a small table beyond the window. As bile rushed to her throat, she leaned as far over as she could and threw up. The throwing-up took quite a while, leaving a generous puddle beside the bed. Most of the sick hit the floor but a dribble landed next to her on the bed. She couldn't have cared less about that and certainly wasn't concerned about who might have to clean the floor.

She yelled. Repeatedly and rather deafeningly. She wasn't quite sure what she was yelling. It might have been 'Hey!' or 'Help!' or something altogether incoherent. Whatever it was, it brought no response. All she could hear were birds singing outside the window, through which, from her position prone on the bed, she could see nothing but blue sky. At least it looked blue; even the sky was blurred.

She tried shouting again. This time she put more thought into it. 'Come here, you fucking bastards!' Almost before the sound of her voice faded away a lock clicked and a door opened. Her bloody awful eyesight meant that the person who walked into the room was only a blur and the first blur was followed by a second, larger blur. Blur One came closer and took the clearer shape of a man. Blur Two stayed by the door which he (or maybe a large she) had closed behind him (or her).

'Who the fuck are you and where am I?' Sapphire shouted. The first man took a deft half pace to the side to avoid flying spittle, sidestepping into the pool of vomit Sapphire had deposited. His foot went from under him. He had looked quite distinguished, as much as outlines could be, at first sight, white, in late middle age with a full head of greying, fair hair and wearing a doctor's white coat. He looked less distinguished lying on the floor covered in puke. Blur Two moved closer but, not wishing to become a second recipient of Sapphire's gastric deposit, stopped short of assisting the first man to his feet. Sapphire could now see that this second person was also male, but younger and bigger. Perhaps the older bastard's bodyguard.

'Serves you right! What the fuck is going on? Why am I handcuffed? What is this place? I want to see...' Sapphire stopped, suddenly realising that she had no idea who she wanted to see. In fact she had no recollection of anything.

Even her name.

Sapphire was shaking, sweating profusely and panting. Her head was thumping. What the hell was her name? She had no idea. The older man rose to his feet and wiped his hands down his previously white coat. The back of the coat was liberally smeared and his hands added two smears to the front. Sapphire really had been very sick. The man looked extremely cross. His younger colleague's face was expressionless but he might have been trying very hard not to laugh.

'You OK, Doc?' the younger, bigger man asked in what Sapphire thought was a New York accent. Brooklyn. The thought of America prompted some memory recall: America, aircraft... Stella. Stella who? Or what? Wasn't Stella a beer? Stella Artois? Or was that a character in 'Allo 'Allo? The fog thinned ever so slightly. The second name wouldn't come but Stella was the woman who'd flown her to... wherever this was. She could remember Stella's name but not yet her own. She fought to get her brain working but the fog inside was too thick. The fog outside too: everything was still a blur. There was one thing though. The big bloke had referred to the older guy as "doc" so her first instincts there had been correct.

'I'm all right, Claxton.' The doctor sounded testy. He spoke in a plummy, quasi-upper-class English accent. Whoever these people were, they seemed to be part of something international. Sapphire now had one more name: Claxton. In some strange way, knowing that calmed her. She found her headache was diminishing and her breathing coming under control. Maybe a second name would calm her further. Most doctors' coats had a name badge on them. She looked but this one didn't. Unless that smear of sick was covering it.

So she tried the direct approach.

'Who are you, you bastard? Why am I chained to this bed and where are we?' she asked. 'Oh, and perhaps you'd be letting me know what my name is. I appear to have forgotten. I imagine you'd be having something to do with that.' She was surprised to note how in control she now felt, even if she couldn't move, couldn't really see and didn't know her own name. Now that she could hear herself talk, she was surprised to discover that her voice had an Irish accent.

The doctor looked at her thoughtfully. 'Interesting,' he murmured. He seemed to have recovered his poise following his foray into the pool of vomit. 'Neither name? That is most unusual.'

__ In which a man falls on a bed,
   and Sapphire recognises a Glock


Sapphire fought to retain her equanimity. Neither name? Did he mean Christian name and surname? It hadn't sounded that way. That was doubly worrying but she found herself replying, still in that Emerald Isle lilt, 'Or maybe I can. Maybe I'm just not letting on.'

What was she saying? She had no idea. 'However,' she found herself adding, 'I'm genuinely not knowing your name, Mr Probably-Not-A-Real-Doctor, and I'd quite like to be finding out before I do you a considerable amount of damage.' Where the hell had that come from? Despite not knowing who she was, she was pretty sure she wasn't in the habit of going around threatening to damage people, even people responsible for chaining her to a bed.

And on that score: 'Key please, Claxton,' the doctor said, holding his hand out. The younger man reached into an inside pocket and extracted a small key which he passed across. As he did so, Sapphire noticed the blur of a gun in an under-arm holster. This did not surprise her, nor did the fact that the gun suddenly appeared in his hand as the older man bent to open the padlocks on the straps holding her to the bed's handrail. It was almost as though they considered her dangerous. 'Now then, my dear,' the doctor said in what he may have imagined to be a soothing tone, 'please continue to lie still. Claxton would not wish to shoot you.'

Sapphire found herself agreeing with this assessment. There's no way Claxton is going to be pulling that trigger, she thought. The Stella woman hadn't gone to all this trouble to fly her halfway around the globe to South Africa just to kill her at the drop of a bit of puke. Wait a minute! South Africa! Yes, that's where they'd been going. Knowledge was slowly beginning to return. Maybe her own name – or names – would be next.

As they were unlikely to want to harm her, and with no deliberation, she swung herself bodily sideways as the straps fell from her wrists and kicked the gun out of Claxton's grasp. It skittered across the floor and clattered into the opposite wall where Sapphire lost sight of it. By that time she was off the bed and kneeing the now-weaponless heavy in the midriff. He doubled over and Sapphire took a step to one side – adroitly avoiding the vomit on the floor – clasped her hands together and rabbit punched the big New Yorker on the back of the neck. As he fell forward he cracked his head on the metal bedframe and ended up sprawled, unconscious, in exactly the same spot that Sapphire herself had just vacated.

Meanwhile the doctor was stumbling across the room in an attempt to grab the gun, or so Sapphire assumed. She couldn't see the weapon herself but it seemed a bad idea to let the doctor – who presumably had better eyesight than her and knew where it was – obtain the pistol. She hurled herself on to the man's back and crooked her right arm around his neck, hard, holding it firm with her left hand clamped to her right wrist. Exerting more pressure on his windpipe, she heard the fleshy sound of ligaments tearing – she was pretty sure she hadn't broken his neck – followed by a cry of anguish. The man started falling to the floor under her weight. She slid off his back and let him complete his journey to the floor and back into the pool of sick, where he lay writhing and panting, desperately trying to loosen his collar with a hand now covered for a second time in vomit.

Sapphire didn't stop to wonder where her fighting skills had come from because she was now standing next to the small table she'd first noticed from the bed. And sitting on the table were her glasses. She put them on and the world – well, the room at any rate – swam into focus. She spotted the gun lying in the corner. She bent and picked it up and found herself knowing exactly what make it was (a Glock 19), how many rounds it held (fifteen) and how to make it go bang. She had no idea how she knew all this.

She didn't make it go bang but looked around with her newly-enhanced vision to determine the extent of any remaining threat. The Yankee goon was still unconscious on the bed with a bump the size of an ostrich egg now disfiguring his already far from figured face. She turned to the doctor who was lying, gasping, on the floor. She bent down and pointed the Glock between his eyes, which widened with fright. He stopped gasping. Whilst it seemed likely that his neck was giving him pain – ligament damage will do that – it would be nothing to the pain of a bullet in the head. At least, Sapphire assumed that would be his thinking process.

'You and I are going to be needing a little chat,' she whispered.

He may or may not have been about to pour out his life-story or, more helpfully, her life-story, when Sapphire heard a key turn in the lock. She spun round on her haunches, as the door opened and Stella Fish entered the room.

Before Sapphire could bring the gun to bear – before she'd even worked out whether she **needed** to bring the gun to bear – Stella Fish calmly said, 'Nemesis,' and Sapphire blacked out.

*After our meeting with Major General Brenda de Kock and her shadowy boss Mr Patel, we needed a morning's sojourn to Table Mountain. Following the cable car kerfuffle, we arrived at the top. The gunwoman then disappeared into the mist that was draped like a blanket over us. Saul and I gave chase.*

*With her male companion just a broken body at the foot of the mountain with Saul's bullet in his balls, she was our only lead. It occurred to me that there had to be a serious leak within the Cape Town Police Department if these two had been sent to kill us so soon after yesterday's meeting.*

*We didn't find the woman but at least Saul got to see his dassie. Several of them. The scruffy little rock hyraxes were fucking everywhere, emboldened by the mist. So emboldened that Saul, in attempting to clamber up a twenty-foot pile of rocks to see if he could get above the mist to catch a glimpse of our quarry, received a nasty bite on his left pinkie finger. 'Cute but with seriously sharp gnashers,' he observed, half-scrambling and half-falling down the rockpile.*

*Whilst not completely unsympathetic, I wasn't about to let him know that. 'You and your bloody dassies!' I said, stepping back smartly to avoid his plunge towards terra firma.*

*'Bloody finger, you mean.' He held up the digit in question. I laughed and passed him a tissue.*

*'I hope it fucking hurts.' I made a fake grab for the finger. He yanked it away with a grin.*

*'There's no sign of her,' he said. I hadn't expected there to be. The mist stretched endlessly out into the distance along the great flattened summit of the mountain and,*

if she was a local, she'd know all the best places to hide. We worked our way carefully back towards the restaurant and square twin-towers of the cableway building half a mile away. Well, hopefully towards them. We couldn't actually see them in the mist so at any time we could have been about to step off the mountain into thin air.

We made it safely back though. In our absence, no more than half an hour, a crowd had gathered at the top of the cableway. Two of the crowd were wearing uniforms, and not the green of the cable operating company but the dark blue of the Cape police.

'Mr Saul Dawson and Ms Lucy Smith?' said the larger of the two stern-faced policemen. If they weren't the two who'd taken us to the meeting with Patel and Brenda de Kock yesterday, they were hewn from the same stone. One of them stepped up to Saul. 'I am arresting you on suspicion of the murder of Mr Daniel Nkunde. You have the right to be informed of the charges on which you are being arrested. Most importantly you have the right to remain silent, to be informed promptly of such right and the consequences of not remaining silent. Any information uttered or willingly given to an officer may be used against you in court.'

That was quick, I thought. Too quick. The only witness to the man's likely death was his female accomplice last seeing vanishing into the mist. And Daniel Nkunde? They had a name for the man already? That was a mighty rapid piece of discovery and identification.

A dozen tourists, who'd been on the next car up the mountain and hadn't bargained for this unexpected sideshow, were thoroughly enjoying the spectacle. The policemen, however, did not suggest they were capable of enjoyment and displayed an admirable level of efficiency in relieving me of my purloined weapon and handcuffing the pair of us. Not behind our backs though, which I thought slightly unprofessional as they were dealing with a coldblooded killer and his moll.

I tried mentioning Brenda de Kock's name but the two officers gave no indication that they were aware who she was. Hopefully, she'd be at the Central Police Station when we arrived and could sort this out. We were escorted back to the cable car, which was waiting, empty and patiently, for our arrival. As we emerged from the lower station into the blinding sunshine, the mist by now just a fading memory, at least down here on the ground, I spotted a man skulking in the shadows. He wasn't that hard to spot; he wasn't much smaller than Table Mountain. It seemed inconceivable that such a noticeable slab should not also be noticed by the two policemen but, size or not, I guess they took him for just another sightseer, and there were plenty of those around. But I wasn't so sure.

'Get in,' said cop Number One as our small party reached the white police car with its broad blue and yellow stripe along the side.

'I do not think so, gentlemen. These people are with me.' The voice seemed to come from the bowels of the earth, so deep was it. The man-mountain had emerged from the shadows, casting his own on the pair.

Number Two Policeman spun round at the sound of the voice and raised his gun in the general direction of the man's sizeable midriff. The gun seemed to trump the size advantage as the walking boulder had no visible weapon himself.

'Stand back, sir,' said the policeman grimly. The man-mountain didn't stand back. Instead he took a deliberate pace forward. Either he hadn't seen the officer's gun or he considered it an irrelevance.

Meanwhile, the first policeman opened the rear door of the car and repeated his invitation for us to get in, emphasising the invitation with a push in the small of my *back. I'm never happy if somebody pushes me so I took it as reasonable provocation to shove back and as my foot was on the door sill, my shove gained added impetus. It sent cop Number One crashing into the back of Number Two, who in turn crashed into the unyielding bulk of the goliath, losing his grip on his gun in the process. The gun whirled into the air and was caught by, wonder of wonders, Saul, despite the hindrance of the handcuffs. He'd always said he was a cricketer.*

*I thought about attempting to relieve Number One of his own gun but before I could try, our rescuer picked us both bodily up, one under each massive arm, and hurled us into the back of the cop car. He then squeezed his bulk magically into the driver's seat and we were off, with the two coppers struggling to their feet. Number One still had his gun and managed to loose off a small volley of shots before we vanished behind an airport bus.*

_ In which Hansie Coetzee discusses
pistols, and Dawson and Lucy
visit a vineyard

'Good catch, mate,' said Lucy as they disentangled themselves on the rear seat of the police car.

'Thank you. I always think it's best to arm oneself in these situations. You should try it yourself.' Dawson sounded self-satisfied. He was less so when she casually plucked the newly acquired gun from his hand and started checking it for bullets, unhindered by the fact that she was wearing handcuffs. The gun was a Vektor SP1 containing nine rounds and, looking up at the back of their rescuer's virtually neckless head, Lucy considered putting one of the rounds in it. Despite the fun of unarresting themselves from the two policemen, it probably hadn't been the wisest course of action. 'Stop the car, big boy,' she said.

'Not yet,' Big Boy grunted. 'And please stop pointing that gun at my head, Ms Smith. It's making me nervous. Your reputation precedes you. We will all crash if you shoot.'

'And?' countered Lucy. 'We have seatbelts.'

By now the car was heading out of the eastern suburbs of Cape Town at a speed close to seventy miles an hour. It wasn't a particularly straight road either. Dawson looked behind them. No one chasing them as far as he could see.

'Slow down, fella, and tell us who you are,' he said quietly, 'or you won't need a bullet in the head to crash the car. I presume you think those guys weren't police.' He looked around him. 'This certainly looks like a cop car. I should know, I've been in one or two.'

'My name is Lieutenant Hansie Coetzee, and you are right, Mr Dawson, we do not wish to attract unwanted attention.' He eased his foot off the accelerator and Lucy lowered the gun in response.

'Driving around in a police car at any speed isn't exactly screaming anonymity,' she said. 'So, what Dawson said, *Meneer*. We're listening and the gun is too.'

'What sort of pistol is it?' said Coetzee, apropos of nothing.

'A Vektor.'

'*Ja.* And that would not be suspicious anywhere else in the Republic. Vektors are South African and standard police issue. Not here on the Cape though. Our police are old-fashioned. They carry Berettas, 92s or PX Storms.'

'I wouldn't say the evidence is conclusive.'

'Their uniforms were not quite correct either. There has been a change in manufacturer recently. The old firm was linked to corruption and the contract deemed illegitimate. The two local politicians who awarded it are now in prison.'

'On Robben Island?' asked Dawson.

'Robben Island has not been a prison for nearly thirty years. And the two politicians have not been re-employed as museum curators. You should visit the island. It is historically important and, personally, I do not understand what you can achieve here apart from getting in the way. I believe your holiday should remain exactly that. However, I have my orders.'

'I think the holiday ship sailed when the locals started pulling guns on us,' said Dawson, struggling with the analogy.

'And who do you take your orders from, Lieutenant?' said Lucy. 'If it's the genuine police, then you're going the wrong way.' They had left the eastern suburbs of Cape Town behind them and were heading into wine country. A sign indicating that the town of Stellenbosch was ten kilometres ahead flashed past.

'I think we saw enough vineyards yesterday,' said Dawson. Once they'd left the meeting with Patel and Brenda de Kock that is.

Coetzee grunted but then added, 'You will see. Very soon. We are almost there.' Abruptly he slowed and turned the police car down an unmarked, single-track road to the left a few kilometres short of Stellenbosch. After a series of further turnings the big Afrikaner pulled up outside a large, attractive white-painted bungalow with a red roof. There were several vehicles parked on the gravel forecourt. Some of them were pale green vans bearing the name Middelste Vallei Winery. The name fitted the location. Gentle hills rose all around the estate and the lower slopes were covered with vines.

'Very nice,' said Lucy, shimmying out of the car, still holding the gun and completely unhindered by the cuffs. 'But unfortunately we're not tourists any more. What's here apart from wine?'

'I think the wine would be a good starting point though,' said Dawson. 'I'm parched after all this excitement. Turns out that shooting bad men, running about on mountains and stealing cop cars is thirsty work.'

'Do not worry, Mr Dawson. I am sure that refreshments can be provided.' Easing his massive body out of the driver's seat, Coetzee produced from an inside pocket a thin, curiously-shaped metal implement, similar to those Dawson had been shown on the MI6 lock-picking course he'd attended earlier in the year. It was a matter of seconds before the lieutenant had removed the cuffs which he tossed onto the back seat. 'Follow me,' he said and trudged off around the side of the bungalow, through a long arbour liberally festooned with trailing vines.

To the rear of the building was a raised terrace enjoying a magnificent view northwards across hundreds of acres of vineyards. A few comfortable-looking garden chairs sheltered under parasols were grouped around a table next to a small swimming pool. A pair of ice buckets gleamed invitingly on the tabletop.

Two people stood up from the table as Coetzee, Lucy and Dawson appeared. One was a middle-aged Black man with receding hair and, as if to make up for that, a substantial beard. The woman with him was white but deeply tanned and probably, Lucy thought, in her mid-thirties. Her brown hair was cut quite short, expensively so in Lucy's opinion, and she was wearing a white summer dress that did little to disguise the tan. She pushed a pair of oversized sunglasses on to the top of her head with a forefinger as the trio drew near. Lucy, who rarely took much trouble choosing her clothes, was suddenly acutely aware that her own jeans and t-shirt had just survived a climb on to a cable car and a half-hour scramble across part of Table Mountain.

She was also acutely aware of something else. She stopped short and Dawson nearly cannoned into her. 'What the hell?' he said.

'What the hell indeed,' Lucy echoed.

While she and Dawson had never met Rebecca Erasmus, they had been shown photos. Apparently Coetzee's boss was not so kidnapped after all.

__ In which Stella pours tea,
    and Sapphire rejects
    an escape attempt

Sapphire regained consciousness. She was lying on a sofa in a comfortably furnished drawing room with French windows to her left. They opened on to a wide lawn which headed down towards a stand of trees swaying gently in the breeze. The trees were unfamiliar. South African, she supposed. In the distance she could make out the blue-grey outline of a range of mountains. None of them had a flat top, so wherever they were in South Africa, it might not be Cape Town. Wherever it was, it was a very pleasant view. It was also a very clear view, despite the fact she was again not wearing her glasses. She held her hands – which were unrestrained – up to her face to make doubly sure of this miracle.

Stella Fish rose from an armchair opposite, moved to a side table and poured two cups of tea. 'Contact lenses,' she said.

'I can't wear contact lenses,' said Sapphire, confused. 'They make my eyes swell up.'

'Ah, well, maybe we have access to resources that are not at MI6's disposal. Your eyes look fine. How do they feel?'

Sapphire had to admit her eyes felt great, much better than the throbbing inside her head. Stella moved across with a cup of tea. Sapphire carefully swung her legs to the floor and sat up. She took the cup from the older woman but looked at it warily.

'How do I know this isn't poisoned?' she said.

'You don't. You do, however, need to drink something. You're dehydrated and it's a bind bringing in all the equipment to get fluid into you intravenously. Particularly as Dr Norton is not too enthusiastic about coming close enough to you to administer it. Nor Claxton for that matter.' The names meant nothing to Sapphire. Stella returned to her armchair and took a sip from her own cup. 'You see?' she said. 'Perfectly harmless. You saw me pour both cups from the same pot but I can get you a glass of water if you prefer.'

'No, you're right,' said Sapphire. 'I am thirsty. I'll have the tea.' She took a mouthful. The tea was just as Sapphire liked it. 'You didn't ask me if I wanted sugar.'

'Why would I do that? I know perfectly well you don't take it.' Stella drank some more, looking at Sapphire over the rim of her cup. 'By the way, what's your name?'

'My name? My name's Sapph...' Sapphire stopped short. She was Sapphire Waters and she worked for MI6. Her whole history came flooding back to her, including her current assignment with Lucy Smith and Saul Dawson; Gulliver's funeral with the woman opposite her posing as his sister; and then the flight to South Africa, where she must now be, on the executive jet with American markings. She stood up, her half-full cup slopping tea over the saucer on to an African-themed rug.

Stella put her own cup on the table beside her. 'Sit down and finish your tea, my dear,' she said. 'You're making the room untidy.'

Sapphire stayed standing. The French windows were wide open and she could be through them in two steps, away down the lawn and into the trees. While there was no indication that Stella was armed, if she did have a gun on her, then Sapphire would be a sitting duck. Technically, a running duck. There could be any number of other people in the house as well. And even if she did make it to the trees, what then? She was in South Africa and South Africa was a big country. She could be anywhere and she knew without checking that she had no money, no wallet and no phone on her. Nothing in her training suggested she could evade capture for more than a few minutes.

The only thing in her favour was that she could see and

she was unconvinced that the contact lenses wouldn't soon be making her eyes swell and close.

Another thing she remembered was telephoning CIA headquarters in Langley, Virginia to enquire about Stella Fish and being told reluctantly and after a three-minute gap in the conversation, that she no longer worked for them. If that was true, who did she work for now? Maybe Sapphire had been lied to. Maybe Stella still was with the CIA. The American plane might be a clue there and who but the CIA would have access to resources that were beyond MI6? Although Sapphire had never heard that ophthalmological expertise was one of the CIA's core strengths.

There was something else too. Sapphire was part of the SIS, however frail a part that might be, and hadn't been taken on a whim. Which meant that whatever game Stella was playing it was inextricably linked with Charles Gulliver's death and the disappearance of his brother here in South Africa.

As on the plane, she found herself thinking: What would Lucy do? Lucy, she decided, wouldn't be running away. So she sat back down on the sofa. Her tea was beginning to get cold but she finished it anyway.

'Good,' said Stella. 'One more question and then we'll have dinner. You must be hungry.' Sapphire realised she was. And still thirsty too. The tea had barely touched the sides. 'Can you tell me what you can remember between falling asleep on the plane and waking up on this sofa?'

Sapphire thought but nothing came. As far as she was aware, there **was** nothing. It was as Stella had suggested. A combination of exhaustion, worry and gin and tonic had sent her to sleep on the flight south and then she'd woken up in this room.

'What day is it?' she asked eventually.

'Sunday.'

Sapphire worked things back in her mind. She'd gone to bed in her flat on Thursday night. They must have taken off from Rochester Airport early on Friday morning. She'd fallen asleep no more than three hours into the flight. But, unless Stella was lying, it was now late on Sunday afternoon.

'Are you saying I've been asleep for two whole days?' she asked slowly.

'More or less,' said Stella.

Stella led Sapphire along a carpeted corridor to a small dining room where a po-faced young woman with shortish, dark-blonde hair and a full figure served them a plain and unpalatable three-course meal. Sapphire did not often eat as much in one sitting but she really was very hungry and ate as if her life depended on it, despite not being able to identify much of the fare in front of her. If Stella Fish (who ate sparingly, her nose wrinkling with distaste at every mouthful) was telling the truth, she'd been asleep – drugged – for over two days. It certainly felt as if she hadn't eaten in that time. Thinking back, her last food could have been the two chocolate biscuits she'd eaten mid-evening Thursday. It was a wonder, all things considered, that she felt as good as she did, headache notwithstanding.

With food inside her, Sapphire decided it was about time she started to earn her recently increased salary. 'Did you kill Charles Gulliver?' she asked.

It took a while for Stella to answer, but that was not an admission of guilt, more because she was having trouble swallowing something completely unchewable which she'd inadvertently put into her mouth. 'No, of course not,' she said eventually.

'So why were you at the funeral posing as his sister?'

'Because I was expecting somebody to show up.'

'Who?'

'You, my dear.'

'Me? Why?' Sapphire had been at the funeral but had been at pains to stay out of sight so that she could take photographs. Stella Fish had been looking for her but had not seen her. Sapphire was briefly proud of that fact but then realised that it hadn't done her much good; here she was anyway.

'You'll find out in the morning,' said Stella. 'I wasted the best part of three more days tracking you down so we need to get you started on your duties as quickly as possible. Unfortunately, Dr Norton's pride has been damaged and he's taken to his bed, otherwise it would have been tonight. It can't be helped.' There was that name again, Norton. It continued to mean nothing to Sapphire.

'Why am I so important to the CIA?'

Stella pushed her plate away with most of her food uneaten and eased herself up from the table. She laughed humourlessly. 'Time for bed,' she said.

And that was the end of the conversation. Sapphire still had no idea what was going on, nor who Stella Fish really was and who she worked for. Despite the English accent, Sapphire thought Stella was almost certainly American and, remembering the abstruse conversation with Langley, was beginning to think she wasn't an ex-CIA agent but a current one. But what would the CIA want with her, Sapphire?

The only other question she **had** received an answer to was the confirmation that they were In South Africa (although not exactly where) and that there would be a full briefing session about Sapphire's duties in the morning. Duties? What did that mean? She'd asked if she could contact Jason Underwood. The answer had been unequivocal: no. All would be explained in the morning.

'You need sleep, my dear. We all do.'

All? Thus far, Sapphire had seen no one but Stella and the stocky young woman who'd served dinner, although the mysterious Dr Norton was already in bed, and there was also someone named Claxton. As for the server, she hadn't been particularly good at her job, but Sapphire assumed that neither waitressing nor, judging by the terrible food, cooking, were her primary occupation within the CIA. Or whatever this was. Something about her suggested she might spring to life should Sapphire decide to make a run for it.

Sapphire surprised herself by agreeing that a good night's rest would be helpful. She may have been asleep for over forty-eight hours but it didn't seem to have done her much good. Her head felt thick and a jugful of cold water drunk over dinner hadn't really improved the dryness of her mouth. Stella escorted her up a flight of stairs and along a passage to a bedroom, complete with an en suite shower. The bed looked extremely inviting.

That wasn't what caught her attention though.

On the way, with Stella a couple of paces ahead, the softest of coughs had prompted Sapphire to glance to her left towards a door that was slightly ajar. She'd been surprised to see the waitress standing there, half hidden by the door.

The young woman had smiled at Sapphire, winked and put a forefinger to her lips.

Sapphire, continuing past without breaking stride, considered that, if the wink and the signal to keep quiet constituted a message, it probably wasn't a request for her opinion of the meal (Quantity 5 Star, Quality 1 Star). It was another curiosity to add to the pile: Who was the waitress and what secret was Sapphire supposed to keep?

_ In which Dawson enjoys some wine,
   and a man with a beard bows


'Well, that was easy,' said Dawson. 'We've found you. Job done.'

'You're a quick healer, Ms Erasmus,' Lucy added as they reached the table. 'We were told you took a bullet to the leg a few days ago.' There was no sign of a scar on either of the woman's tanned legs. 'We were also told you'd been kidnapped. I could ask you when you were released but I suspect there's more to it than that.'

'Yes,' said Dawson. 'Tell us all about this so-called snatch of yours.'

'You might want to re-word that,' Lucy said.

'Sit down, please,' Rebecca said. 'You too, Hansie. Have a drink. The wine is excellent. We make it ourselves.' She waved a hand to indicate the surrounding vineyards. It was an unnecessary wave; Lucy was pretty sure she knew the purpose of vineyards. The so-far unintroduced bearded gentleman with Rebecca poured three glasses of white wine from one of the chilled bottles. The pouring was expertly done but Lucy doubted he was employed as a sommelier.

'Thank you, Mr...?' she said.

'My name is Dlamini, Ms Smith. Jacob Dlamini.' He spoke with a pleasant, low, slow voice. Lucy was aware that Dlamini was one of those prolific names that aren't necessarily genuine, rather like the one she'd grown used to calling her own, so he may not have been telling the truth.

'Talking of names,' said Dawson to Rebecca. 'Do you prefer Erasmus or de Kock? We've been speaking to your mother.'

'Erasmus, please. As my mother no doubt informed you, Willem de Kock is my stepfather. You are, I imagine, now aware who my natural father was.'

'So you could equally be called Gulliver,' said Lucy.

'As you could equally be called Joanna Leigh Delamere. But

you prefer not to be. It's all a matter of personal choice, isn't it?' She smiled, a row of perfect white teeth in a wide mouth. Lucy smiled back. It was becoming increasingly obvious that calling herself Lucy Smith was pointless given that every international intelligence service apparently knew her real name.

'Excellent wine,' said Dawson. 'Sauvignon?' Lucy noticed he was already halfway into his glass while she was still getting herself properly comfortable in the shade. She took a sip. Unquestionably a Sauvignon of some variety. She couldn't remember Dawson ever previously displaying much knowledge of wines: he was more a pour it, drink it and don't ask too many questions kind of bloke.

'So how come the State Security Agency is moonlighting as wine growers?' she said.

'The SSA is not moonlighting,' said Jacob Dlamini in the same slow, measured tones. 'As Rebecca has already intimated, we are not the State Security Agency. Indeed, that organisation is not officially aware of our existence.'

Dawson had by now drained his glass but had nevertheless been paying attention to Dlamini's brief speech. 'They're not very good at their job if they don't know you exist,' he said. 'Especially as at least two of you work for them. Not to mention the fact that you have a stolen police car sitting out front.'

'It is not a police car, as I have already told you, Mr Dawson,' said Coetzee. 'In any case, it has been removed.' Maybe by some sort of telepathic communication; Lucy hadn't heard Coetzee or anyone else giving such an order.

'So what do you guys do that State Security can't?' asked Dawson. 'And what do you call yourselves?'

'We grow wine, Mr Dawson,' said Dlamini, with a butter-wouldn't-melt expression. 'The SSA do not do that. Their budget is not large enough.' Lucy supposed this was a joke. 'And you know what we are called. This is the Middelste Vallei Winery.'

'Of course,' Lucy said. 'You and Becky spend all your working days out in the fields picking grapes while young Hansie here tramples them in a giant vat in the back room. Pull, as they say, the other one.'

'You are of course correct. Middelste Vallei is both a working vineyard and a winery with full production of several varieties of red and white wine. Several of our products have won awards, including the excellent Sauvignon that you appear to be enjoying so much, Mr Dawson. But it is not only that.'

Rebecca Erasmus opened a second bottle and replenished Dawson's glass. She held the bottle towards Lucy but she placed her palm over her still full glass. If she'd had little idea what was going on before this latest development, she needed her wits about her more than ever now, and suspected she'd need to make up some shortfall in that department from Dawson as well. He was now well into his second glass of wine.

'We employ a complete staff of some fifty full- and part-time workers,' said Rebecca. 'Jacob and I are registered with the CIPC as directors of the company. It is all completely official and above board.' She smiled her wide smile again. 'You're right in one respect. I have neither the time nor inclination to tramp the fields and bring in the harvest myself, although Jacob here has been known to do so.'

'It is an excellent way to relieve stress,' said Dlamini. 'And what we are doing can be very stressful.'

'As for Hansie here, we prefer his feet to be used to stamp upon more, let's say, undesirable things than grapes,' added Rebecca, continuing to smile. Coetzee didn't smile. He hadn't touched his wine. More of a lager man, maybe.

Lucy couldn't match the wattage of the other woman's smile so didn't try. 'Thanks. But you could have just given us the brochure. So what's it a front for?'

'And how did you get rid of the bullet wound in your leg?' added Dawson.

'Ah, yes,' Rebecca said, reaching down and stroking her left calf. There was no bullet wound. 'My men were firing blanks. And I acted a little.'

'Your men, yes,' Lucy said. 'So, why the staged kidnap? To confuse the police, I imagine. Which is why Hansie here made sure Captain Yeboah was present.' Major General de Kock had run through the sequence of events at Green Point Park as related to her by Yeboah. 'Your mother did mention how surprised the captain was that nobody got hit in the gunfight.'

Coetzee grunted. 'Everybody was firing blanks,' he said.

'Even Yeboah? I don't think that's his recollection.'

'He did not know. I switched his gun in the car.'

'Hansie is rather more dextrous than his size would lead you to believe,' said Rebecca. 'I needed to fake my own disappearance in order to stop others from attempting to remove me. I believe that, like Andrew Gulliver, I was considered to be a threat to others' plans.'

'Right,' Dawson said. 'Now we're getting down to the nitty-gritty.'

'That is not an expression that should be used in Africa,' said Rebecca. 'It is a corruption of *nigritique*. The French colonists called their African slaves *"la population nigritique"*. The Cape was colonised by the English and Dutch, of course, and not the French, but you would nevertheless make few friends should you use it in a local bar.'

'I apologise for my colleague,' Lucy said. 'When he dies, I'm donating his brain to medical research so that they can determine how many mistakes it's possible to make in a single lifetime.'

Rebecca continued, the million-watt smile still in evidence. Lucy looked from her to Dawson mid-quaff and momentarily wished she was gay. 'We have invited you to Middelste Vallei to help us, so you need to know what we are doing. We are a little short-staffed at present.'

'I'm not sure we were invited, exactly,' Dawson said. 'And

what about the fifty staff you just mentioned? And the fake kidnappers?'

'Do you know what is happening in the republic in January?' Rebecca asked.

'No,' Lucy said.

'Yes,' Dawson said. He'd stopped drinking wine and was now fully focused. 'There's a presidential election. I'm guessing you'd quite like to see the right winner. Perhaps that right winner is sitting at this table.' He looked at Dlamini who bowed his head slightly.

Lucy was moderately astonished. She'd taken Dlamini at face value as the likely head of whatever shadowy outfit Rebecca and Hansie were mixed up with. Much more of this and Dawson would be claiming to be the brains of their partnership. Not that she'd mind − it was quite hard work being the brains **and** the brawn.

Rebecca nodded. 'Regrettably, there are others who have different intentions. Intentions that would be quite disastrous for South Africa. I believe you are familiar with this lady.'

Rebecca opened a small clutch bag sitting on the table and extracted a photograph. She handed it to Lucy, who looked at it and passed it wordlessly to Dawson. 'Yes,' he said, 'although that's no lady. You may know her as Gao Chang but as far as we're concerned, this beauty's called Songsung Rong, China State Security's finest in assassination and espionage.'

___ In which Colonel Swart is choleric,
and Brenda de Kock and Temba Yeboah
go for a walk

Major General Brenda de Kock did not usually accept unsolicited phone calls at work, especially on a Sunday, but the caller told the switchboard operator that he had information regarding her daughter's disappearance. Despite it being classified information that the chief even had a daughter, the well-trained operator sensed it was more than her job was worth not to put the call through.

Brenda took the call. 'Who is this?' She wasn't in the mood for idle chit-chat.

'Be at the Rhodes Memorial at three o'clock if you do not wish to receive some distressing mail in the next couple of days. Come alone. Do not wear uniform.' The caller rang off.

'Tell me you put a trace on that call,' de Kock demanded, marching into the comms room thirty seconds later.

'Yes, ma'am. Public telephone kiosk at Signal Hill.' There was a touch of smugness about the way this information was delivered.

'And we have a squad car how far out from the kiosk?' The staff looked at each other. Maybe not that well trained after all. It was too late now, the major general realised. 'Never mind,' she said. Never had the phrase, "never mind" sounded so much like, "get your things, you're fired". But Brenda was a realist; there was no formal manhunt for her daughter, who, twenty-four hours on, had not officially been reported missing. She couldn't expect her level of urgency to be shared by her junior staff.

There was no urgency in Patel's voice either when she spoke to him two minutes later. 'What are you going to do?' he asked softly.

'I'm going to be at the Memorial at three.' What the hell did he expect her to do?

'Do you want backup?'

The caller had told her to come alone. 'Can you be discreet?'

'Discreet is my middle name.' Brenda de Kock could well believe it.

———

The call Temba Yeboah received was a peremptory summons from his boss, the reliably irascible Colonel Swart.

'My office, Captain. Now.'

Temba was used to working on a Sunday. As a police detective, his days regularly blurred into each other. He was often unsure what day of the week it was. It was the principal reason why his marriage to Omphile had fallen apart. This, however, was not a problem that afflicted Colonel Swart. Temba had never known the colonel to work on a Sunday. He had no idea what activities his boss pursued instead but they did not involve pursuing criminals. Swart did not look like a golfer so perhaps he spent his Sundays kicking cats. Temba had nearly fallen off his chair in astonishment when he'd heard the colonel's voice on the phone.

If irascible was Colonel Swart's default setting, then it had been ratcheted up several notches to choleric when Temba entered his office. Through gritted teeth, Swart explained that not only had he been ordered into the office by Deputy National Commissioner Patel, who was down here on the Cape fucking up the place when he should be fifteen-hundred kilometres away fucking up Pretoria, but that he'd told the colonel to go and act as discreet, unseen support to Acting Regional Commissioner de Kock who was about to go on some fool's errand at the Rhodes Memorial.

Temba thought that the words Swart, discreet and unseen were unlikely bedfellows, so it came as no surprise to hear that it would be Temba himself undertaking the job, leaving the colonel to go home and resume his cat-kicking responsibilities.

It was twenty past three. Brenda de Kock had been at the Rhodes Memorial for over half an hour and no one had approached her. Why not? The inference had been unmistakeable: if she wasn't there, she could expect to receive one of Rebecca's body-parts through the post.

She looked around again. The Memorial was crowded. It was a popular place and on a warm Sunday the tourists and locals were out in force. She'd spotted Captain Temba Yeboah as soon as she'd arrived. He was trying hard not to be spotted, doing his best to blend into the crowd, but despite the jeans and scruffy t-shirt he was wearing, he was no Patel. Brenda was surprised Patel had deputed the task of keeping an eye on her to the captain. Maybe the Deputy National Commissioner was somewhere there as well. If so, Brenda knew she'd never spot him – unless he wanted to be spotted.

This was ridiculous. She and Yeboah were both wasting time. He had other things to be getting on with, such as finding Andrew Gulliver's killers. But then, that investigation was inextricably linked to Rebecca's kidnap so...

Something caught her attention. Three people were behaving unusually. It wasn't so much what they were doing as what they weren't doing. Visitors to the Rhodes Memorial were generally either looking at the spectacular view eastwards across the Cape or upwards at the statue of a horseman in heroic pose who had spent the last hundred and ten years busily engaged in contemplating the same view. These three, two men and one woman, were doing neither. In fact, Brenda was sure she'd caught them out of the corner of her eye staring at her. And now they were walking off along one of the paths leading upwards from the rear of the Memorial into the trees at the foot of Devil's Peak. She saw the woman glance back as they disappeared.

Brenda had seen her face before, and almost immediately

she remembered it. She possessed a near faultless memory for faces, particularly criminals' who had crossed her path. This woman was a small-time crook named Asha Mbaso.

Brenda came to a decision and headed towards Captain Yeboah, who saw her coming and scanned about for a means of escape before realising how ridiculous that would be. 'Are you armed, Captain?' she said when she was close enough not to be overheard.

'Er, no, ma'am.' Temba's reasoning had been that he was in civilian clothes and that it was too warm to wear a jacket so, having nowhere to conceal a gun, he'd left his police-issue Beretta 92 in his car at the far end of the car park.

Brenda de Kock was not impressed. Despite being in civilian clothes herself, she **was** armed. It would have to do. 'Come with me,' she said and strode off towards the path the woman and her two male colleagues had taken. 'And listen carefully.'

'You realise this could be a trap, ma'am,' Temba said after she'd outlined her suspicions about the three people they were following, particularly Asha Mbaso.

'Of course it's a trap. Which is why I was told to come alone. It's also why two weapons would have been better than one.' They had left the crowds at the Memorial behind them now and Brenda pulled out her own Beretta. 'But we're talking about my daughter's safety. I'm not sure where these people are leading us but I'm not running away.' She glanced at him. 'I'm not ordering you to come with me, Captain.'

As she said it, she realised she'd done exactly that, but before she could apologise, a bullet thudded into an umbrella pine a foot from her head.

As it happened, Discreet was neither Patel's first nor second name. His mother, a dear old soul who had always pined after the Indian motherland she had long since left behind and above whose mantelpiece hung a portrait of her hero, Gandhi, had named her son Mahatma in his honour. At the age of five, he had discovered that Gandhi's name had actually been Mohandas, Mahatma being merely a title thrust upon him by his followers, which translated from the Sanskrit as "the great-souled one". This error had been pointed out to him by various unkind children at primary school. Patel, despite being slight even then, had withstood the bullying stoically but was stuck with the name. He would not have described himself as great-souled but as soon as he was old enough to decide, he began referring to himself by his initials, M K. The K, inevitably, stood for Karamchand, Gandhi's middle name. His mother had got that one right.

Patel knew full well that the first thing Colonel Swart would do on being instructed to shadow Brenda de Kock was delegate downwards, and it took no great imagination to predict that the industrious Captain Yeboah, the only actual detective in the police station at the time, would be the person deputed by the colonel to do the job for him. And that suited Patel who, under instruction from his paymasters to remove the Acting Regional Commissioner from the game, didn't want the most irritatingly studious and thorough policeman on the Cape investigating her disappearance. So he would also have to disappear.

Patel was at the Rhodes Memorial himself to see his team begin their mission. He witnessed de Kock talking to Yeboah from a distance of twenty metres but his ability to blend into the background with the casual expertise of a premier league chameleon meant he could have been ten metres closer and they still wouldn't have noticed him. He made himself comfortable and awaited his team's return.

—

'Now would be a great time for Patel's discreet surveillance to start making itself less discreet,' muttered Brenda de Kock as she and Temba crouched in the thick undergrowth surrounding the now bullet-scarred umbrella pine. Two more shots were fired as the pair scrambled for cover. Then nothing. Thirty seconds passed. Brenda was busy trying to find somebody to point her gun at. Temba, who was manoeuvring himself sideways to get a view in the direction the bullets had come from, said, 'Patel? The Commissioner? You think he's here somewhere, ma'am?'

'I'm sure of it.'

The view Temba eventually achieved was not encouraging. Instead of an open vista containing a gunman somewhere in the middle-distance, he parted a small stand of long grasses to find himself staring at a black, size eleven boot from a distance of six inches. The boot had its twin next to it and a little further back was a pair of grey Nike trainers, also size eleven. Temba Yeboah, as an experienced police officer, prided himself on being something of an expert on shoe measurements.

Size eleven boots can be quite hefty and Temba discovered very quickly that this applies doubly when one of them is placed on your head. The size eleven boot started grinding his face into the undergrowth. The undergrowth was dry, as was the ground from which it sprouted; Temba found the experience becoming very painful very rapidly. The pain was exacerbated when he received a wholly unwarranted kick in the kidneys. Luckily the kick was from one of the less hefty Nike trainers but even so, Temba hoped it wouldn't be repeated. It wasn't, and he heard a voice telling him to get up. He would have liked to comply but the voice issuing the command hadn't told its own size-eleven booted foot so Temba remained pinned to the ground. A second voice repeated the instruction, this time accompanied by the unmistakeable click of a gun's safety catch being released.

'For fuck's sake, I'm trying,' he shouted. Or at least, that was his intention. What he actually said was 'fufezzemtering', but that was more than enough for Brenda, hiding a few metres away, to understand that he'd been caught. The commotion, the click of the safety catch and the two commands from Boot Man and Nike Man to get up had also been clues she couldn't help but notice.

Instructing a prone man to get up while simultaneously pinning him to the ground with your foot on his head could be seen by some as a lack of basic intelligence. It certainly seemed that way to Major General Brenda de Kock. An additional clue to the two men's encouragingly high levels of dimness was that they had clearly seen and shot at two people – Temba and herself – a few minutes earlier. However, they had only captured one and yet appeared to have lost all interest in the movements of the second.

She couldn't believe it was this easy. She stood up, pointed her gun at the two men and said calmly, 'Drop your weapons.'

The two men didn't comply. They turned to face this forgotten second person who was rudely interrupting the enjoyable footwork they were employing on Temba, mouths hanging slackly open and guns now pointing anywhere but at the woman holding the Beretta 92, the business end of which was arcing between Boot Man and Nike Man. Brenda, who had come second in her latest weapons training programme, was confident in her ability to execute a couple of headshots from a distance of five metres if either of the men showed any inclination to put up a fight.

Which they did. The one with his foot continuing to rest on Temba's head tardily started to swing his own weapon around towards Brenda, so she shot him between the eyes. Temba, a few feet south of the bullet, caught a slash of blood across the face but was so glad that the size-eleven pressure on his cranium had been relieved, he didn't care. Nike Man, who had presumably spotted that his colleague was now dead, was so stupid that he repeated the unsuccessful manoeuvre that had led to his mate's demise. Brenda shot him too. Reluctantly, it must be said, as she would have preferred to ask at least one of the two a few questions. But there was still the third person, the woman, if she and the captain could find her.

Or if **she** could find **them**.

Asha Mbaso materialised from behind another umbrella pine a few metres away. 'You really should not have done that, Major General,' she said. 'Mr Patel will be most displeased.'

_ In which Sapphire has breakfast,
and an arm is broken

The next morning, Sapphire was woken by a phone ringing
next to her. She tried to ignore it, turning away from the noise
and snuggling back under the duvet, but it kept ringing. Eventually, sighing deeply, she pushed herself to an upright position, rubbed her face and eyes and reached for the phone.
She remembered she hadn't removed the contact lenses that
Stella Fish had insisted she was wearing and yet, even after a
full night's sleep, there was no discomfort from her eyes and
she could still see, despite the dimness of the room. She did,
however, have a headache which stretched from the back of
her head to her neck. She realised that her head had been
aching ever since she'd arrived but this was of little immediate
concern. She had more important things to worry about.

'There you are,' came Stella's voice. Quite where else she
had expected Sapphire to be was uncertain. 'Breakfast will be
served in the dining room in fifteen minutes. Please do not
keep me waiting. We have a busy morning ahead of us.'

Sapphire lay thinking for a moment before easing herself
reluctantly out of the extremely comfortable bed and padding
across the soft carpet to the bathroom. There was a small,
mirrored medicine cabinet over the basin. The mirror told her
new twenty-twenty vision that she was a mess and when she
opened the cabinet, hoping to find some paracetamol for her
headache, it was empty. She stood under the powerful shower
for ten minutes – Stella and breakfast could bloody well wait
– and slowly came to.

Again she put herself in Lucy's shoes. Underwood had
given her a full dossier on the woman, as well as Dawson.
Lucy Smith's dossier was quite impressive, her skill set especially. And while Dawson's value to the intelligence service
appeared, on paper at least, to be flimsier, she'd noted the

phrase "hidden depths" underlined in green.

'Who are these people?' Sapphire could remember asking. Underwood had, at the time, not given a straight answer. He rarely did. She'd found his obfuscation rather exhilarating. Twenty-four deskbound months with MI6 had never made her feel much of an intelligence agent but Underwood's wired-in secrecy had changed all that. Only now, when Sapphire was questioning everything about the operation and the CIA's (or whoever Stella was working for) current, obscure interest in her, did it occur to her to wonder if Underwood was up to something more ... sinister.

Back in the bedroom, Sapphire realised the clothes that she'd been wearing since Thursday morning had been removed and replaced with a white blouse and sky-blue, summer-weight trouser suit. There were bars on the window. That didn't matter as she hadn't been planning to jump out of it. Besides the door was unlocked.

Downstairs in the dining room, the dinner table had been pushed back against one wall and breakfast – cereals, eggs, toast, coffee and juice – laid out. There looked to be enough food for a small army but the eggs were hard and greasy and the toast rather paler and more rubbery than one would normally expect. Certainly cooked by the same Master Chef as last night's dinner.

Glancing around as Stella said, 'You're late,' Sapphire saw there were two other people in the room. One, sitting on a leather sofa, was a middle-aged man with greying, fair hair, smartly dressed in a dark suit. Standing beside him was a big guy in his mid-twenties with watchful eyes and a tell-tale bulge under his left armpit. Both men were looking warily at Sapphire. People didn't often look at her warily, especially armed men possessing an air of physical capability. It was odd, especially as she recognised neither of them.

'Have some breakfast and then we'll get started,' said Stella, indicating the groaning table. Sapphire poured herself a cup of coffee but found that, despite the probability of last night's nearly indigestible dinner being her only meal in the last three days, she wasn't especially hungry. However, she decided that she ought to be fortified for whatever was going to happen after breakfast. Ignoring the greasy eggs, she plucked two slices of flimsy toast from a rack, found butter and marmalade, and picked up a knife. So Stella trusted her with a knife, she thought, smiling to herself. But then bluntish cutlery wouldn't be a match for the gun under the younger man's jacket.

'Aren't you going to introduce us?' Sapphire turned to Stella with a slice of toast in her hand and nodded at the two men, who had neither moved nor spoken but kept staring at her with watchful expressions. She noticed a small smile cross Stella's face.

'You don't recognise these gentlemen, then?'

'Should I?'

Stella made a noise that might have indicated satisfaction and the man on the sofa nodded once. 'This is Dr Norton,' she said. The man in the suit nodded again. He obviously knew his own name even if it meant nothing to Sapphire. 'And his, er, colleague, Mr Claxton.' Colleague is one way of describing the younger man, Sapphire thought, bodyguard might be another. 'Dr Norton will be assisting us this morning.'

The expression on Dr Norton's face suggested that he considered his role to be rather more important than merely assisting. 'Assisting in what?' Sapphire said, swallowing a last mouthful of toast. 'It's about time I knew why I'm here. And I would like my personal belongings back.'

'Of course,' said Stella, smiling. 'I agree it's time.' She failed to specify exactly what it was time for but glanced at the young man, who reached under his jacket and produced an automatic pistol just as Stella said: 'Nemesis.'

At which point, Sapphire felt the room swim.

The swimming sensation was only a momentary experience. When the room stabilised, Sapphire didn't recognise her surroundings. She looked around for no more than a second, dispassionately taking everything in. The three people in front of her she recognised but no names came to mind. A middle-aged woman, behind whom stood a muscular young man holding a pistol and, sitting on a sofa against the wall, leaning forward, hands together and lips pursed, an older man.

The woman spoke. 'How do you feel?'

Sapphire did not reply. She was evaluating her position. Her own name had evanesced but that, for the moment, was of no concern. She felt calm, in control, her breathing shallow and regular. The man with the gun posed the most immediate threat. She would need to disable him first, acquire the weapon and take charge of the situation before doing anything else.

Without warning, she took two quick paces forward, placing the middle-aged woman between herself and the young man holding the gun. Sapphire shoved her bodily into the man who was fatally slow to reorient his shot. He staggered back under her weight and they toppled together onto the older man on the sofa. Sapphire, moving without conscious forethought, grasped the younger man's elbow and wrist with both hands, brought her knee up abruptly and snapped his forearm in one motion. He let go of the pistol with a cry of pain. It was a Glock 22 she noted, plucking it from the air and shooting its former owner in the head. His cry was instantly extinguished.

Sapphire pointed the Glock at the woman, who said, 'Nemesis,' and the room went black.

*'How are you getting on? Do you have any beach reads. I've heard Gulliver's Travels is good. My copy in Cape Town went missing.' Underwood's voice was as annoyingly meas-ured as usual.*

*'Well, actually,' I said down the phone, 'I'm afraid your copy is lost. Pulped even.'*

*'How unfortunate.' He didn't skip a beat. 'What about my copy of Rebecca? Also missing?'*

*As codes go, this wasn't quite in Enigma territory but I played along. 'No. It appears your Rebecca went missing of its own accord but we found it again.' Actually, that didn't make much sense. I wasn't very good at this game and I had no idea how I could come up with a secret codeword that would indicate Rebecca was hobnobbing with the favourite to be the next president of South Africa while on the run from the Chinese.*

*Saul leaned towards the phone. 'I think we'll carry on with our holiday now, boss.'*

*'Not yet, I'm afraid. I have another book for you to track down.' There was a pause. Maybe he was running out of appropriate titles.*

*'What book?'*

*'We appear to have misplaced my guide to precious gemstones.'*

*Oh for fuck's sake. Enough was enough. I put the phone on speaker. 'What? You mean Sapphire's disappeared?'*

*'I am not confident this is a secure line, Lucy. Watch what you're saying.'*

*'We're not trying to solve a cryptic crossword. I think we need it straight.'*

*'And if we're calling it like it is,' said Saul, 'you ought to know, there was a bit of a to-do on Table Mountain*

*earlier this morning. I may have shot a bloke called Dan-iel Nkunde.'*

*'Nkunde?' It sounded as though this was not the first time Underwood had heard the name.*

*'Yes, you might find this hard to believe but Dawson probably saved my life.'*

*'No probably about it, dearest,' said Saul.*

*I ran through the Table Mountain incident and our sub-sequent trip with Lieutenant Hansie Coetzee to Middelste Vallei winery, where we still were. Andrew Gulliver was dead, and the SSA officer who'd been leading the investi-gation into his disappearance, Rebecca Erasmus, gone to ground. I finished with the news that the possible next president of the republic was currently preparing an early lunch for us all, and confirmed that Songsung Rong was definitely involved in whatever was going on.*

*'So this is political,' said Underwood. 'I had a nasty feel-ing it might be. I think you'd better come home. HMG is not going to get involved in another country's political processes.'*

*'It's never stopped them in the past,' Saul said. 'And it doesn't seem to be stopping China now.'*

*'What about Sapphire?' I said. 'What's happened to her?'*

*'We have reason to believe she may be in your vicin-ity.'*

*Vicinity? Only Underwood could talk like that. 'South Africa, you mean. What makes you think she's here?'*

*'Because she and Stella Fish took off from Roches-ter Airport in a private plane a few hours before you left Heathrow.'*

*'And you know this how?' said Saul.*

*The answer was typically oblique. 'The staff at Roch-ester Airport found an unconscious woman on the runway when they arrived at work at eight o'clock Friday morning.'*

'So we need to get Fish out of Waters,' said Saul.

'Or the other way round,' I added. 'Who was the unconscious woman?'

'The local police arrived but when she woke up, the woman claimed diplomatic immunity.' I raised my eyebrows at Saul, hoping that Underwood would get around to giving us a name before we died of old age. 'She said she was with the CIA but had no documentation to prove that, so Kent police took her away and called my office. I travelled to Maidstone in person to interview her.' He made it sound as though he was even less enamoured at having to travel to Maidstone than he was going to Stallford for the funeral. 'When I arrived, she'd gone.' As if Maidstone wasn't bad enough, it had been a wasted journey.

'Gone?' said Saul. 'Maidstone's cells not very secure?'

'I doubt if they put her in a cell, Dawson. But no, two gentlemen from the American Embassy – with appropriate ID and paperwork – got there before me. I was less than happy, as you can imagine, but the police didn't have much choice. As I say, diplomatic immunity.'

'What's her connection to Stella Fish?' I asked. Through the window, I could see two white-jacketed Middelste Vallei staff by the pool laying out the lunch that Jacob Dlamini had prepared.

'Now that we have a clear idea what she looks like, we know she was Stella Fish's driver at Gulliver's funeral,' Underwood said. 'And since we know that, it calls into question the CIA's denial that Fish is an ex agent.'

'Speaking of the CIA, have you heard back from your mate, Melhuish?' I asked. It had been four days.

'No, I haven't. We think he's in Cape Town though.'

'In our vicinity?' I couldn't resist. 'So, basically, everybody's in Cape Town but you want us to come home.'

'As I say, Lucy, now that we know it's a political matter,

I cannot let you meddle further.' I wouldn't call what we'd been doing "meddling".

'And what about Sapphire?' said Saul. 'You expect us to just pack up and leave her?'

'She's a trained intelligence agent. She can look after herself.'

'She can pour coffee and use a camera,' I said. 'I'd hardly call that trained.'

'I'll make sure the embassy keeps an eye out for her.'

The conversation was becoming pointless. 'We'll book a flight then,' I said. Saul looked daggers at me but I put a finger to my lips. 'Just out of interest, you haven't given us the name of the CIA woman Stella Fish knocked out. Might be useful in case she turns up here.'

'Oh, I think she's already turned up,' said Underwood. 'Her real name is Kaya Rabada. However, she was travelling in the UK under the name Kaya Nkunde. It appears she may have been going through the wars. Not only did Stella Fish knock her unconscious on Friday morning but as you've just told me, you killed a gentleman with the same name today. I'd say it's a fair bet that Kaya Nkunde was the lady with him. The one you punched on the nose, Lucy, and then allowed to escape.'

## In which Coetzee is unenamoured,
   and Lucy taps her foot

'You can go home if you like,' said Dawson as they made their way outside to the terrace by the pool, where Rebecca Erasmus, Jacob Dlamini and Hansie Coetzee were sitting at a laden table. 'I'm going nowhere. We have to find Sapphire.'

'What was it about the finger I put to my lips that you didn't get?' said Lucy. 'Of course we're staying and of course we're going to find Sapphire. Who the hell's going to keep you in Bourbons if we don't? Also, I'm quite keen to discover why two CIA agents pulled a gun on us in the cable car this morning.'

'And MI6 have instructed you to return to the United Kingdom?' said Dlamini when they had finished recounting the conversation with Underwood. 'Perhaps Lieutenant Coetzee should speak to your Mr Underwood. As one Secret Service to another.'

Coetzee didn't seem too enamoured by the suggestion. 'Ms Erasmus is the senior officer,' he said. 'I do not have the authority to speak to MI6.'

'It doesn't matter. We're not going anywhere.'

'Will you not be dismissed if you disobey orders?'

'Probably, but it wouldn't be the first time.' Dawson laughed and helped himself to some food. Lucy found she wasn't particularly hungry. She also stayed away from the ever-present wine on offer, instead pouring herself some orange juice.

Dlamini said, 'I am confused. I was not aware that the CIA had any interest in this election.'

'We're not certain. But just to be clear,' said Lucy. 'You have no one secretly backing your campaign? No red-white-and-blue envelope get slipped under your door?'

'My party is my only backer, Lucy. And we hope, the people. The transition from apartheid has not gone as smoothly as we had hoped, not helped by one or two, shall we say, less than savoury presidents following Mandela. I intend to make corruption a thing of the past. Not everyone is delighted with my goal and some seek to put another in my place. Now this Stella Fish you spoke of, the woman you believe has your colleague, she is not CIA?'

'According to them, she's not anymore. They could be lying. I think our first call after lunch needs to be to the CIA's Anthony Melhuish, their Head of Station on the Cape.'

'If you can find him,' said Rebecca. 'Even I don't know what he looks like. Forgive me for returning to my original task: how is this going to track down Andrew Gulliver's killers?'

'Stella Fish, the CIA, Sapphire's disappearance, Andrew's murder – it's all connected. Besides, you know who killed Andrew,' said Lucy. 'You showed me her picture: Songsung Rong, Gao Chang or whatever she's calling herself now. If she didn't chop Andrew's head off herself, she issued the order.'

'There is no proof,' said Coetzee. 'Gao Chang is an official in the Chinese Consulate. She has diplomatic immunity.'

'We're not big on proof,' Lucy said. 'We work more on assumptions. And this is what I assume: we know Rong was in England when Charles Gulliver was killed. I have no doubt she killed him. He was in my car so maybe she got the wrong person – she and I have personal history – but maybe it **was** Charles she was after. Maybe Andrew passed him some information as a failsafe because he knew the Chinese were closing in on him. And therefore on you too, Rebecca, which is why you faked your own kidnapping. You daren't leave Jacob's side because you know full well that the Chinese don't want him as president and will do anything to stop that from happening. You need our help and I repeat, we're not going anywhere. So, a question. If the Chinese don't want you to be president, Mr Dlamini, who **do** they want?'

'Jacob,' said Dawson, secretly pleased that he could call a future world leader by his given name, 'I think we're happy to accept that you're whiter than white...' Lucy winced but Dlamini just smiled, '...helped by no international leg-ups, as it were, but at least one of your competitors has no such compunction. So as Lucy says, which one?'

'I understand what you are saying, Dawson,' said Dlamini, 'but I am not prepared to cast any aspersions on the honesty of my opponents.'

'Jacob might not be but I am,' said Rebecca. 'I can't say I'm sure about any of them but one name stands out. A man called Lugay Phukuntsi. Well, I say a man...'

—

Two hours later, Dawson and Lucy were at the South African Security Agency headquarters in Wale Street, where it was housed in a building that proclaimed itself the Department for Human Settlement. They were with Coetzee, who believed that the best way to find Underwood's CIA man, Melhuish was through Kaya Rabada, AKA Nkunde.

Coetzee knew how to track her down. 'Her best friend used to work here,' he said. 'A young woman called Asha Mbaso. Mbaso was convicted of burglary and went to prison briefly. As you can imagine, she was dismissed from her job at the same time. By Ms Erasmus.'

'And this Mbaso woman was friends with Kaya Rabada?'

'Ja. It was odd that the opposition was consorting with petty criminals.'

'Opposition?' said Dawson. 'The CIA?'

'Of course.'

'Does that make us opposition too?'

'Ja. But as long as Ms Erasmus wants you here, then I will accept the situation.' He turned his massive bulk towards the door. 'Wait here. I will extract Mbaso's records from the personnel files. She is no longer in prison so she can lead us to Rabada and from Rabada to Melhuish.'

'And Melhuish to Fish to Sapphire,' said Lucy.

'So Asha Mbaso is a known lowlife,' said Dawson after the big Afrikaner had left. 'And Rebecca sacked her. Asha's not going to be too fond of Rebecca then, is she?'

'Hardly a motive for murder though. And if it's Rebecca she's got the beef with, why would she kill Andrew Gulliver first? And where does that leave us vis-à-vis Charles?'

—

Ten minutes passed. Lucy had reached full foot-tapping mode. 'I've had enough of this,' she said. 'What's he doing? Having another lunch?'

'He's a big lad. I should think he needs a lot of nourishment.'

'He's only gone to get a file, for Christ's sake.' She crossed to the door and tried the handle. The door wouldn't open. 'What the fuck? He's locked us in.'

'Probably.'

'Why would he do that? Doesn't he trust us?'

'Of course he doesn't trust us. You, particularly. You're getting a reputation as being, oh, I don't know... a little hotheaded?'

'Fuck off,' she said, punching him on the arm. 'If I was as laid back as you, nothing would get done.'

At that point, the lock clicked and Coetzee re-entered. He was accompanied by a tall, heavily tanned, white man in late middle-age with receding brown hair. The man looked unhappy and slightly dishevelled. Lucy glared at Coetzee but shook the newcomer's outstretched hand. She'd give him thirty seconds, she decided. Politeness could only stretch so far.

'Ms Smith, Mr Dawson,' said the man, speaking Home Counties English with a trace of something else. Lucy always noted accents. It was an interest that sat comfortably alongside her multilingualism. This time, however, she couldn't immediately place the trace of something else. This increased her annoyance. 'My name is Melvyn Gilbert. I'm very pleased to meet you. I am the Assistant Deputy Director of Domestic Intelligence.' That was a mouthful, Lucy thought. If Gilbert had to announce himself to visitors on a regular basis, it was a wonder he found the time to get any work done. 'Likewise, Mr Gilbert,' she said, miraculously keeping her impatience in check.

'Lieutenant Coetzee informs me that you wish to use the Agency's resources to track down a foreign agent.'

'That's right. A young woman called Kaya Nkunde or Kaya Rabada. She may be able to help us find a missing colleague of ours. Also, she pulled a gun on us this morning. We're told she's CIA so I'd quite like to have words with her.'

'I think you may have your wires crossed, Ms Smith. Kaya Rabada cannot possibly have been the woman you encountered on Table Mountain. My understanding is that she's in the UK.'

'She certainly was three days ago,' said Dawson. 'But it sounds like you're unaware that somebody invented air travel a few years back.' He was uncharacteristically short on good humour. 'We just want to have a little chat with her. Hansie thinks we can find her through her old pal, Asha, who used to work here.'

'I'm very sorry but we can't help you,' said Gilbert, running a hand through his thinning thatch. 'MI6 have no jurisdiction in South Africa and the lieutenant tells me you have already been instructed to return to London. I really think that would be your wisest course of action.' He held his hands up apologetically. 'Now, if you will excuse me, I have somewhere I need to be. Lieutenant Coetzee will escort you from the building.'

He left. This time the door remained unlocked.

___ In which Brenda de Kock and Temba Yeboah
    visit a bar, and meet two fat men


Asha Mbaso led Major General Brenda de Kock and Captain Temba Yeboah at gunpoint to a second car park a couple of hundred metres from the Rhodes Memorial. It was a car park that neither local police officer had previously been aware of, a fact which was almost as embarrassing as being captured.

Mbaso's reference to Patel meant it was no surprise to Brenda to find him waiting for them, together with three other men. Two of the men were sent back up the mountain trail in a 4x4 to recover the two bodies. Patel ushered Brenda and Temba into the rear of an unmemorable, grey Mazda and took the wheel himself. The third man climbed into the front passenger seat and Asha Mbaso slid in alongside her captives. They set off down the lower eastern slopes of Table Mountain past the University of Cape Town and on to the M3 expressway towards the city.

'Where are we going?' asked Brenda.

Patel remained silent as they left the main commercial area behind and headed towards Signal Hill. Signal Hill, where the phone call instructing Brenda to go to the Rhodes Memorial had originated. Signal Hill, where Captain Yeboah had lost the van in which Rebecca had been whisked away from Green Point.

She tried again, an edge to her voice. 'Where are we going, Mr Patel?'

'Don't worry, Major General,' said Patel, softly as always. 'Somebody wishes to talk to you. This is fortunate for you. Otherwise it would have been you who died on the mountain today rather than my two men.'

'Who are you working for, Mr Patel?' Brenda had met Patel in person for the first time only that morning. She was curious about how and why a respected senior police officer with a favourable reputation had gone rogue.

'Or are you not Mr Patel?' said Temba who had also never previously come into contact with the Pretoria-based Deputy National Commissioner of Police.

'You think I've disposed of Patel and undergone rapid constructive plastic surgery on my face to impersonate him? Your thinking is unimpressive, Captain. So much so that, if it were not for the fact that today's events mean I am forced to resign from the police service, I would seriously contemplate demoting you.'

The car travelled along High Level Road around the north of Signal Hill, not far from Green Point. Brenda was familiar with this part of the city, but then they plunged left into a maze of back streets with which she was not familiar. She had been doing her policing from behind a desk for several years and couldn't remember the last time she'd ventured into this downbeat part of Cape Town, a jungle of roads giving off the whiff of a forgotten past, full of warehouses and small industrial units, many boarded shut but a few still in use, although closed today, Sunday. She soon lost her bearings. She realised she needed to get out of the office more.

Finally the Mazda turned into a road largely indistinguishable from its neighbours and stopped at the top of a short flight of steps leading down to a plain wooden door. Above them, a rusted sign proclaimed the place to be the Dockview Bar. Brenda had heard of the Dockview but never been there. She recalled it to be a well-known hangout frequented by the sort of citizen she would not care to visit alone. Journalists, for example. She had other, larger, more junior male officers to do that sort of thing. One of them was sitting next to her but Captain Yeboah was not really in a position to offer much protection.

Asha Mbaso, who'd remained silent throughout the journey, stepped out on to the pavement as soon as Patel brought the car to a halt, and indicated that Brenda and Temba should follow. The afternoon was drawing on and the quiet street was in deep shadow, shrouded by the towering warehouses opposite the bar. Patel took Brenda by the arm with a smile. 'Down here, Major General,' he murmured.

With Temba close behind and Mbaso and her male colleague bringing up the rear, Patel led Brenda gently down the steps to the unmarked door which was opened from the inside as they negotiated the bottom step. Standing just inside the dim doorway was a huge man who had a certain proprietorial air about him, suggesting that he might be the owner of the Dockview. The interior of the bar wasn't much brighter than the shadowed street outside. The man stood to one side to let them through. Even so, there was only just room for them to squeeze past his stomach in the cramped anteroom to reach the bar proper.

This too was darker than any bar Brenda had ever been in and at first she failed to recognise the person sitting in a necessarily large chair in the centre of the room. The man who'd let them into the bar may have been oversized but he was a midget, at least from side to side, when compared with the man in the chair. His huge upper body was draped in a bright yellow shirt that shone like a beacon through the gloom. Brenda had seen smaller bedsheets. She still had Patel's hand, almost unnoticeably, on her arm but she stopped in astonishment as the man's features came into clear focus.

'Mr Phukuntsi,' she said. 'This is a surprise.'

'Welcome to my office, Major General. It is a pleasure to meet you again. You will forgive me if I don't rise.' Phukuntsi spoke in an unexpectedly high, sibilant whistle, as if all the air in his body was being funnelled through one tiny hole. His head looked disproportionately small sitting atop the mass of his torso. His eyes were so deep-set that they were almost invisible. Altogether a disconcerting sight.

Brenda's mind raced. She didn't share Phukuntsi's pleasure and couldn't fathom what he was doing there. Lugay Phukuntsi was an allegedly immoral Member of the National

Assembly whose election three years earlier had been mired in controversy, given that his main competitor had died. Phukuntsi was regularly in the newspapers, rarely in a positive way.

So, here was Phukuntsi, a well-known if dodgy politician sitting in the Dockview, a well-known if dodgy bar. All in all, an unappetising match, if not one to suggest that the situation Captain Yeboah and she found themselves in carried any mortal danger. If one disregarded the fact that Patel had said how fortunate they'd been to come down from the mountain alive and that it had not been his decision.

Phukuntsi's then? Did he even make decisions all by himself? And if not him, then who?

And what the hell was the connection between Phukuntsi and Patel?

'What's going on, Patel?' She turned to the slight man next to her.

'The National Assemblyman and his, let us say, sponsors are concerned about the good captain's current investigations, Major General de Kock. They would like him to stop, which is why they requested that I involve myself in the matter, even at the expense of my own career.'

'That's not going to happen,' said Temba.

'I'm afraid, Captain, you are not in a position to make that call,' sighed Patel. 'In addition, they wish to know exactly where your daughter is, Major General, and are confident you will tell us.'

That's also not going to happen, thought Brenda. She had no idea where Rebecca was.

'Well, that was helpful,' said Saul.

I was seething. 'You're supposed to be on our side, Lieutenant,' I said to the giant Afrikaner. Hansie Coetzee shrugged his monolithic shoulders. 'Perhaps we'd better ring Rebecca to see what she thinks.'

'That would be inadvisable. Calls made from within this building are monitored. And please keep your voice down, Ms Smith.'

'We're on our own then,' said Saul. 'We're looking for four people.' He always claimed to be good at maths. 'First, Sapphire, MI6's gem,' and he held up one finger. 'Second, Melhuish, an American spook so spooky no one can see him.' Another went vertical. 'Third, our lengthy old pal, Songsung Rong.' Up with the third. 'And fourth, Kaya, who appears whenever she wants to kill us.' All four fingers were now fully extended.

'Five. You're forgetting this Asha woman, Kaya's bestie.' I said. To help him, I unfolded his thumb.

'I'm forgetting nothing.' Once again, Saul was being assertive. It was slightly disconcerting. It wasn't his machismo that attracted me to him but I supposed I could get used to it. 'I'm prioritising,' he continued. 'Asha Mbaso, as a small-time crook, was just a means to an end, so if Hansie here can't get us her contact details, let's move on up the list.' He tucked his thumb back under. 'Sapphire's number one and I can't see how we're going to find her without talking to this CIA chap, Melhuish.'

'What about Rong?' I said.

He laughed. 'I don't think we need to worry about her. If she knows you're in South Africa, dearest heart, she'll find **you**.' He was right. I couldn't wait. 'So, Hansie, any suggestions?'

*I could almost see the cogs whirring inside Coetzee's massive head.*

*'Come with me,' he said and chugged off down a dreary corridor and into a small room with a printed sign on the door saying, "R Erasmus, Senior Investigator". The room contained two untidy desks and not much else apart from a whiteboard, scrubbed clean, on one wall.*

*'You don't get to have your name on the door then,' Saul said undiplomatically as Coetzee moved to one of the desks and started poking around in the least organised drawer I'd ever seen. A grunt was all the reply he received, thankfully. I'd have been considering a punch on the nose but I'd already realised that the monolithic Afrikaner possessed phlegmatism – was that a word? I wasn't sure but it fitted – in spades. Whatever he was searching for in the overfull drawer was eluding him. Several sheets of paper, some plain, some typewritten and some containing indecipherable scrawls, fluttered to the floor, followed by half a dozen paperclips, many of them bent and useless.*

*After a minute or so Coetzee grunted again and held up a small booklet. 'Map,' he said.*

*'A map,' I said, deadpan. 'That's the best you can do?'*

*He ignored me and, moving some of the rubbish on the desk to one side with a hand the size of a shovel, spread the map out. He pointed a square forefinger. 'Here,' he said. 'There is a bar. Dockview. Try there.'*

*'And what will we find there?'*

*'Thieves, reporters, other pieces of filth. Maybe answers if you ask the right questions.' He paused and looked at us with his usual lack of expression. 'Maybe not. But it is the best suggestion I have.' There was another pause. 'Are you armed?'*

*It was possible he'd forgotten about the fake policeman's Vektor SP1 that Saul had caught in the kerfuffle at the foot of Table Mountain and, as I'd not found any reason to give it to anyone else, was safely stowed in a pocket of the cargo pants I'd put on this morning. I was trying to decide whether honesty was the best course of action when Saul said, 'Can you supply us with guns?'*

*Geen, said Coetzee shortly and the subject was dropped.*

*'What about transport?' I asked. 'Do you have any pool cars?'*

*Geen. At least Coetzee didn't beat about the bush. 'You have a hire car.'*

*'Yes, but it's in the car park at Table Mountain.'*

*'It will no longer be there. The police will have impounded it.'*

*'The real police or those two fake ones whose car you stole?' asked Saul.*

*'We're wasting time,' I said. 'How about the car you brought us in, Lieutenant?'*

*Coetzee grunted again. 'I need my car.'*

*'Taxi then,' said Saul. 'Where's the nearest rank?'*

*'You will find taxis outside the cathedral.' He jerked a thumb towards the window. 'But they will not take you to the Dockview. They consider it too dangerous.'*

*I was beginning to get exasperated. No, scrub that. I'd been exasperated ever since we'd set foot in Cape Town. 'Has anyone ever told you how truly unhelpful you are, Coetzee?' I asked.*

*Ya, he replied and, for the first time, I detected a hint of a smile breaking cover. 'Frequently. You should walk. It is only about five kilometres. Or catch a bus. You will find the bus stop in Strand Street, just over there.' Again the large thumb jerked towards the window. 'Take the Fresnaye bus but get off before you reach there. Ask for Albany Road and head towards Signal Hill on foot. You will find the bar here.' A finger landed on the map but it* was such a large finger that it was difficult to see exactly where he was pointing to. It covered a couple of blocks. However, it looked like it was all we were going to get. I gathered up the map and gave it to Saul who had bigger pockets than mine. Also, I had a gun in mine. 'You have phones?'

'Sure,' said Saul, pulling his own out and waving it about unnecessarily.

'Call this number if you encounter any problems.' Coetzee scribbled a number down on a sheet of paper and handed it to me. 'Only serious problems, you understand. You are professionals.' He glanced at Saul as if to check for any hidden signs of professionalism. 'It would be better if you memorised this.' I already had, so tore the paper up into tiny pieces and threw it into a bin under the desk.

Saul looked concerned. 'Shouldn't I have memorised that too?' he asked.

'How long would that take you?' I raised a quizzical eyebrow.

'I don't know. Not too long, probably.'

'I've got it.' I tapped my head for emphasis. 'Now, let's get going. We've got a bus to catch.'

The three of us made our way downstairs and parted on the pavement in the mid- afternoon sun. 'Where are you off to, Hansie?' Saul asked. Coetzee simply grunted, turned away and strode off up the street. He really did need to work on his communication skills. I also noted that while he'd said he needed his car, he wasn't taking it.

'Where's this bus stop?' Saul started to pull the map out of his pocket but I stopped him and pointed to a road almost opposite.

'Loop Street,' I said. 'If we head down there, we'll find it at the far end.' At least I'd been paying attention to Coetzee's instructions.

___ In which Stella and Dr Norton
discuss programming, and Sofija
and Guna Sesks laugh


'For God's sake, Stella,' said Dr Norton, struggling up off the sofa from under the lifeless body of Claxton. 'What the hell did you think you were doing? She's a fucking weapon. You can't just set her off without warning. This is what happens when you do.' He indicated his dead colleague. 'And look at what happened yesterday. She went berserk without any of us even saying Nem... that word. She would have killed us all.'

'No.' The woman glanced without emotion at Claxton's body, then looked down consideringly at Sapphire's unconscious form. She bent and retrieved the Glock 22 from the carpet where it had fallen, clicked on the safety and pocketed it. 'You're wrong. You know perfectly well that she's only programmed to kill under two circumstances. After all, you did the programming. Firstly, in self-defence and secondly, of course, at the right time when she sees – '

'How the hell can you be sure that "self-defence" wouldn't mean killing everyone in the room, not just the person with the gun? This isn't black and white. There are any number of unknowns. I've told you it's too soon to put into practice. You're playing with fire, Stella.'

'We have no choice. The election is only a few weeks away. This has to be done now. Tonight. At the rally. Before the movement builds and becomes unstoppable. We have no alternative.'

'And what about Claxton?'

'He was expendable. Hired muscle, nothing more and not very good at that. Witness his performance yesterday.' She refrained from passing mention of Norton's own, sick-covered performance. 'We could have used any of the boys. Or the cook. In fact, especially the cook. She's dreadful. Having her shot would be a mercy killing.' She paused. 'Except that it had to be someone with a gun in order to provoke Nemesis and the cook isn't armed. Her only weapon is the so-called food she produces.'

Norton blanched visibly at her use of the name Nemesis and glanced sharply down at Claxton's red-haired killer lying on the floor. To his relief, she was still unconscious and the Glock was out of harm's way in Stella's pocket.

The cook, listening from an upstairs room via a tiny transmitter, chuckled softly. She was in fact very much armed and she had to agree that her faked *résumé* contained rather more culinary stars than her actual cooking warranted. Next to her, her almost identical twin, identically dressed and also listening in, grinned. 'She right. I glad I not eat your food, sister,' she whispered.

'I cannot be good at everything,' the cook replied softly. 'It is why God invented pizza.'

In the room below, Norton was speaking again. 'Talking of the cook, where did she come from? And where is she now? She will have heard the shot.'

'You're right. A couple of the boys can deal with her. She's only agency. In a few days, we can tell them she just left without warning. Agency staff disappear all the time. Go and fetch them. They can get rid of this too.' She prodded the lifeless body of Claxton with an immaculate black court shoe.'

'What about Nem... Waters?' said Norton.

'We'll chain her to the bed again for the time being. Carry on, Doctor, and go and get the boys. Time's a-wasting.'

Norton shrugged and left.

Upstairs, Guna Sesks switched off the transmitter and looked at her sister, Sofija. 'It is time to make yourself scarce, sister,' she said. 'We do not want them realising there are two of us.'

'What must I do?'

'Go and find your friend, Dawson. He will be pleased to see you, I think.'

'I not so sure. He think I after his girlfriend.'

'True, but she is not after you. She prefers men. Well, Dawson anyway.' They both laughed softly. 'You must leave the house and drive off quickly and openly now, pretending to be me, before Stella Fish discovers you are not me and has you killed.'

'It you she want to kill, Guna. Because you poison her with your terrible cooking.'

'This is also true. But there are better ways to kill her than with bad food. Anyway, this is my job. You are just helping during your holiday instead of lying on a beach somewhere.'

'Ugh. I not like lying on beaches. It boring and I look like whale. Very attractive whale but definitely whale.'

'I am pleased you are here. My boss will be too. He may even pay you when I tell him.' They laughed again. 'You go and find Dawson and Lucy and tell them about the rally tonight and Stella Fish's captive killer woman.'

'What rally?' Sofija paused. 'Actually, sister, I not know what rally is. I thought it was car race.'

'No. English is a silly language. It needs more words. This is a political rally at the football stadium at Green Point. All the candidates for president will be speaking.'

'Why can't we speak Russian or Estonian? English very hard.'

'Even Stella Fish might be suspicious of a Russian cook. No, we must keep talking English. My boss insists and he pays the money. Anyway, your English is improving, sister.'

'So I warn Dawson and Lucy that this woman might kill next president? But we not know who she is.'

'They called her Sapphire and Nemesis is some sort of trigger word. We know this.'

'Do not say Nemesis too loudly, sister. She might kill you too.'

'That is not likely. However, there is another problem. We do not know **which** next president the Nemesis woman is set to kill. Five candidates are speaking at the rally.'

'Why we not just kill Stella Fish and killer robot now?'

'I am under instructions not to start a bloodbath.' Guna shrugged. 'It is disappointing. Anyway, my boss will want the Sapphire woman back alive, of this I am sure. Go now, sister. I will hide and bide my time. They will think you are me and that I have therefore left the house. They will not follow. The wimpy doctor will want the men around him to provide protection from Nemesis killing machine when she wakes up. You need to hurry. They must not catch you before you drive away.'

'Should I kill them if they do catch me?' asked Sofija. She had a hopeful look in her eyes.

'No, you must not. No bloodbath, as I said. Anyway, you have no gun and there are still four of them left now that Claxton is dead, sister.'

'What is your point?' They nearly collapsed into a fit of giggles before Guna pecked her sister swiftly on both cheeks, pushed her out of the door into the upstairs corridor and disappeared rapidly through a second door in the opposite wall.

_ In which Dawson ties a shoelace,
   and doesn't get run over by a bus

Dawson had lost contact with Lucy. He'd bent down to tie a shoelace and when he straightened up she was nowhere to be seen. She'd been striding out ahead of him, keen to get to the bus stop and either hadn't heard or had ignored him as he called out, 'Hang on a sec, Luce,' when he'd noticed the errant lace.

What with his shoelace being the unwitting cause of his losing Lucy, Loop Street was somewhat ironically named. It was busy with traffic and pedestrians, both shoppers and office workers. Dawson called again, stepping into the street to attempt to see round the scrum of people. 'Hey, Luce, where are you?' There was no response and still no sign of her. A horn sounded behind him and he jumped back on the pavement.

Edging into a gap between two buildings, he pulled out his phone and called her. The call seemed to connect but all he could hear was static and then he was cut off. That wasn't promising. As for the number Hansie had given them, that was in pieces in the waste paper basket back in the Wale Street office – and in Lucy's head, a fat lot of good now. Worried, he reviewed his options. There was really only one, to carry on down Loop Street to the bus stops in Strand Street. Either Lucy would be there, waiting for him, tapping her foot impatiently, or she wouldn't be.

She wasn't there.

Dawson hurried along the line of covered bus stops, five of them, two with buses about to depart and surrounded by dozens of passengers, hanging around or getting off or on. None was Lucy and neither of the two waiting buses was going to Fresnaye. Somehow his redoubtable fiancée had been abducted from under his nose in a busy city centre street. How could that possibly have occurred? This was Lucy, after all. She'd have put up a fight. She had a gun for Christ's sake. She'd be fine, he decided and if he did succeed in riding to her rescue like some sort of beige knight, he'd more than likely make the situation worse. He grinned ruefully at the thought.

'What is so funny, idiot?' asked a voice from behind him.

He jumped, slipped on the edge of the curb and almost fell under a bus pulling out on its way to Newlands. Dawson had no time to think about whether he'd rather be watching cricket at Newlands than being run over by a bus in central Cape Town, having just lost his fiancée, when a powerful hand gripped him by the back of his collar and hoisted him back on to the pavement.

'How many more times I save your life, idiot?' said the same voice.

Dawson knew he was dreaming. Just to be certain though, he turned round to check. He found himself staring into the familiar but completely unexpected, round and ruddy face of Sofija Sesks. Quite what the Estonian Security Agent, last seen boarding a plane back to Tallinn, was doing in Cape Town, he had no idea. He did know that her presence wouldn't be coincidental though. In the circumstances, he thought he did remarkably well to summon up the *sang froid* to respond, 'I think it was your turn.'

'You still funny. Still also idiot.' Sofija laughed and hugged him, following which Dawson surreptitiously checked for broken ribs.

'I might regret asking this,' he said, 'but what the fuck are you doing here, Sofija?'

'I here to help obviously,' said Sofija. By now she had Dawson's right hand firmly in her left and was hurrying him up Strand Street. Experience told him escape was futile. Trying to disengage himself from her grip would rank very high on a long list of things he would find impossible to do. Mind you, apart from Lucy, he could think of no one he was more pleased to see at that precise moment. Sofija, the odd stray pedestrian bouncing off her solid body, continued. 'You lose things and I help find them for you. This nice of me, yes?'

'What am I supposed to have lost?' he panted. She was setting quite a pace.

Sofija stopped suddenly. 'You not know?' she asked, peering up at him with a serious expression from under the shock of untidy dark-blonde hair that he remembered so well. 'Come in here and I remind you.' They were outside a small café. 'You get coffee, I find table,' propelling him towards and nearly into the counter running along one side of the establishment.

'You not lose money too, I hope?' She laughed and moved off to find a vacant table. Dawson thought there was every possibility she might forcibly empty one if there were none unoccupied but when, carrying two cappuccinos, he found her a couple of minutes later it looked like physical persuasion had proved unnecessary. She'd found a secluded table near the ladies' toilet.

'Good view here,' she said, indicating a couple of attractive young women emerging from the restroom, and laughed again. She clearly hadn't lost the propensity to find even the most mundane things – toilets, coffee, Dawson, casually killing foreign agents – funny.

'Tell me,' said Dawson, 'what's the Estonian government's interest in all this?'

'All what? You will need to fill me in. But not in sexy way, you understand. I not into that as you know. And is nothing to do with Estonia. I am on holiday.'

'Holiday? Really?' South Africa was an unlikely destination for a relaxing holiday, as he and Lucy had discovered.

She shrugged her wide shoulders. 'Working holiday then. I freelance now. Helping my sister.'

'Your sister?' Surprises were coming thick and fast. 'Fuck's sake. Guna's here too? Who the hell is **she** working for?'

'Ssh.' Sofija put a finger to her cappuccino-frothed lips then
licked it experimentally. 'Walls have ears.' She leaned forward
across the table, nearly knocking over her mug of coffee with
her left breast. 'Why I say that? Walls have sausages, not ears.
People have ears and there are many people here. But important thing is Guna and me both here to help.'

'Ah, yes, that,' said Dawson. 'Remind me what I'm supposed
to have lost.'

Sofija sat back again. 'You forget your fionky, maybe? Even
you not that much idiot.' Dawson was still trying to work
out what a fionky was but Sofija carried on regardless. 'Also,
someone else, another woman.' She looked around cautiously
but nobody was paying them the slightest attention. 'Woman
called Sapphire?' she whispered. 'We think you lose her too.
You very careless. Well, good news. We find her for you.'

Dawson couldn't quite believe his ears. It was if a genie had
materialised out of thin air in Strand Street to grant him three
wishes. Well, all right, just the one wish so far and it was hard
to imagine Sofija squeezing herself into a lamp. 'You know
where Sapphire is?' he asked.

'Ssh,' she said again. 'Keep voice down. Yes, Guna watching
Sapphire woman. But is something you need to know...'

Dawson interrupted. 'What about Lucy? Where's she?'

'I tell you about Lucy soon. She look after herself. Now I am
telling you about Sapphire woman before you open big mouth.
Is why I here. Not just to see your face again. Guna is with her.
She in house south of hill.' She waved a hand vaguely around
her. Dawson guessed that by hill she meant Table Mountain.
'Old CIA lady have her. She very strange.'

'Who's very strange? Sapphire or the old CIA lady?' Sofija
was presumably referring to Stella Fish, although calling her

old was stretching it; she probably wasn't more than fifty. Was she suggesting that Stella was still with the CIA? Jacob Dlamini had been unconvinced by the Americans' possible involvement. The CIA was pretty much the only international intelligence agency Dawson and Lucy hadn't crossed swords with this year. He wondered if they'd get a prize if they reached the full set.

'Sapphire woman strange. She robot.' Robot? Sofija, whose English was patchy, had a tendency to mix her words up but Dawson couldn't imagine what she meant by robot. 'They do something to her brain, I think. I serve dinner. Guna cook. They think we one person.' She laughed. 'Guna very bad cook, but we listen. We not know detail but Sapphire shoot man at breakfast when Stella woman call her Nemesis.' Getting Sapphire's name wrong seemed a thin excuse for her to kill someone, Dawson thought.

Stella it was then. 'So Stella is still CIA?'

'No, I say old CIA. You listen please. Or you come to sticky end. Even I might not save you. Guna have eyes on Sapphire so I come to find you to tell you about rally.'

'You mean ex-CIA, not old. And rally? What, a car rally?'

'Not car rally, idiot.' Sofija had conveniently forgotten that she'd originally thought the same thing. 'Talking rally. Tonight. At football ground. Sapphire will kill someone if you do not stop it.'

'Me? How? And who is she supposed to be killing?'

'We not know. One of the presidents.'

It was far from the first time the Estonian agent had talked apparent gibberish in front of Dawson so he gathered together all his experience of deciphering her. "Talking rally". "One of the presidents". And then it came to him. Some sort of political rally. 'Jacob Dlamini?' he asked.

'If you say so. Guna say there are five. We not know which one. Maybe you right about Jacob Dalmatian. Perhaps you spot him and save him.' Her look suggested that the thought was a novel one.

'Five?' said Dawson. 'Well, that muddies the waters.' He winced at the unintended pun but it washed over Sofija's head. But first his fiancée. Ah, fionky. 'You said you knew where Lucy was.'

'No, I not say that. You not listening. I say you lose her and I help you find her.'

'OK, thanks. Do you have any idea where to start looking? We were heading to the Dockview Bar near Signal Hill so perhaps we should go there.'

'We go where car go. If car go to bar, yes, we go there. If not, no.'

'Car?' Dawson was still finding Sofija's conversational branch lines hard to follow.

'Yes, car. I creeping up on both of you to say boo and make you jump but when I get close enough, you looking at ground while Lucy forced into car by two men in black suits.'

'So why are you here now drinking coffee with me and not following the car?' Having spent fifteen minutes listening to Sofija's confusing news, including the unlikely information that Sapphire had killed somebody, it now seemed to Dawson that it had been fifteen minutes they could have better spent chasing the car containing Lucy.

'I cannot run as fast as car. Even in city. And Lucy able to look after herself. You, less so.' Even Dawson had to admit this was true. 'Anyway, I brush up against car just in time and stick transmitter to wheel arch. We go and find it now.' Dawson was mildly surprised that the car had managed to survive its brush with Sofija.

'Going back to Sapphire...' he started but she interrupted him.

'No, you not listen, idiot. We not going back to Sapphire. Guna in charge. She look after things there.' Dawson reflected that Guna looking after things might very well result in several more deaths in a short space of time.

'No, no, I didn't mean that,' he said. Even now he was unsure when Sofija was pulling his leg. 'Explain about Sapphire. They've done something to her brain? What do you mean? You called her a robot.'

'I not sure. But she two different people. Sometimes she Sapphire woman, ordinary, although with funny hair, and some-times killing machine. As I say, Guna think they use her to assy... what is word? kill, one of presidents, your Dalmatian perhaps.'

'Assassinate,' Dawson murmured. A thought occurred. 'So if Guna is with Sapphire, why doesn't she just grab her from Stella Fish.'

'Guna has orders. Also house full of men with guns. Not as full as before Sapphire shoot one but still full.'

Dawson wasn't sure that a houseful of goons with guns would necessarily prevent Guna doing whatever she wanted; he'd seen her in action before. And orders from whom, he wondered. As far as he was aware, Guna worked for the Russian SVR. This was turning into quite the party. He let it go for now and jumped up. 'OK, let's go find ourselves a car and a fionky.'

'Hello, again, Kaya,' I said, pulling myself upright on the rear seat of the car where I'd been unceremoniously dumped. I dusted myself down. It was far from being the first vehicle I'd been thrown into this year. It was becoming a trifle boring. 'I think you may have forgotten somebody.'

'Mr Dawson? He's not who I was told to collect. Just you. Even for us, it would be hard to scoop two people up off the street in the middle of the city – although I did think you'd give us more trouble.' Kaya Rabada, AKA Nkunde, was sitting in the front passenger seat, looking at me over her shoulder. I couldn't see any obvious damage to the nose I'd hit this morning so either she was a quick healer or I was out of practice. Next to her, the driver was expertly weaving the car through the traffic.

I was furious with myself. All I'd done was glance behind me when I'd heard Saul call out, 'Hang on a sec, Luce,' and half a second later I was face-down on the less-than-sweet-smelling seat of the car. I was beginning to question my professionalism. Mind you, it had taken two of them to grab me and they were a pretty big two as well. Both the driver and a second man squashed uncomfortably close to me on the rear seat were fairly bulging out of black suits and both wore dark glasses. These two might as well have had CIA stamped on their foreheads in three-inch letters. That they'd kidnapped me in a busy city centre street with no problem at all suggested they might prove troublesome should I decide on either fight or flight.

I still had the Vektor though, with its nine rounds up the spout, and in any case, neither fight nor flight was on my mind. We'd set out to find Kaya and here she was finding us – well, me at any rate – as if by magic. Hopefully, she'd lead me to the mysterious Anthony Melhuish and if so, she'd have saved me a bus fare.

I was interested to know why it was just me getting the chauffeur-driven treatment and not Saul. If Kaya thought Saul was unimportant, maybe her information on him was out of date. I wondered how much longer people would carry on underestimating him. I was pretty confident that he would get himself to the Dockview Bar as we'd planned sooner rather than later and, if Coetzee was correct about the place providing some answers, he would find them and use them to track me down.

I was assuming that these three weren't taking me somewhere to eliminate me, but I couldn't be 100% certain. The last time I'd seen Kaya, I'd punched her on the nose and Saul had shot her companion, Daniel Nkunde. If Daniel had been CIA as well, killing him would probably make them quite cross. And if he had been Kaya's brother, she might be quite cross too.

I moved away as far as I could from the bulk of the silent, black-suited bloke on my left and looked around at the passing cityscape. I knew Cape Town about as well as I knew the inside of Kaya's head. I pulled my phone out. Saul had tried to call me (of course he had) but I hadn't heard the phone ring. 'No calls in this vehicle,' said Kaya. 'They get blocked.' Intriguing.

'Tell me about Daniel,' I said to Kaya. 'Would I be right in thinking he wasn't your brother and that he wasn't working for you lot? If so, what were you doing with him in the cable car this morning?'

Was it really only this morning? Time flies when you're having fun.

Kaya laughed. It made me blink. So far, I'd only seen her scowl. 'You're half right,' she said. 'Actually, he **was** my brother. It's why I was chosen to infiltrate Patel's little operation. That and the fact that I knew Asha Mbaso as well.'

That was quite a lot of information all at once but one thing in particular had my head whirling. 'Patel?' It was a common-enough name but I had no doubt who she was talking about. 'You mean the little grey police chief down from Pretoria? What operation?'

'We've had our eyes on Patel for quite a time. We've suspected for a while that he's been working for the Chinese and him turning up on the Cape at this particular time pretty much all but confirms those suspicions.'

This is getting murkier and murkier, I thought. Just how I like it. 'Forgive me for saying so, Kaya, but you don't seem too upset that we killed your brother this morning.' I was using the Royal We. It was of course Saul who'd done the actual killing.

She laughed again. 'You saved me a job. Daniel was a psychopathetic dick. I've spent twenty-three years hating his guts. His death wasn't in the plan at the point that Mr Dawson killed him, but he's no loss.'

Despite the skill of the driver, we didn't seem to be making much progress through the city-centre traffic. 'Where are we going? Dawson and I were heading for a place called the Dockview Bar.'

'Not there,' Kaya said. 'Maybe later. My boss wants a word first.'

'Melhuish?'

Before she could answer – if she was intending to answer – the car swerved right and down a ramp into an underground car park. 'Everyone out, said Kaya. Her two colleagues, just extras in the melodrama, had not uttered a single word during the journey.

We were to switch vehicles. There was an identical car, unremarkable, grey, shabby, parked a few metres away. The switch was undertaken with little fuss. I was hurried *across the short distance from one to the other, one of the Men in Black holding me firmly by the upper arm. As much as I resented being manhandled, I had no intention of trying to escape and Kaya Rabada should have realised that by now. If I'd wanted to wave my three escorts goodbye, it wouldn't have been that difficult; I still had the Vektor in a pocket of my cargo pants and couldn't help thinking that if the CIA hadn't bothered undertaking even a rudimentary search, then the agency was going downhill.*

It occurred to Dawson as he and Sofija left the coffee-shop that she'd shown him no tracking device. 'How do we know where the car is?' he asked.

'We go to car,' she said. Even with all the practice he'd had in Sofijanese, it continued to be like wading through treacle.

'Yes, the car.' He tried to be patient. He knew he'd get there in the end. 'How do we find it?'

'I think you more idiot than you were before,' said Sofija, sounding exasperated. She strode off down a side street. 'Lucy in car. We follow in car. As I tell you, I cannot run as fast as car. Anyway, tracker in car.'

So that answered that. Two cars. Dawson was just about to ask where she'd left the car containing the tracking device when she turned into a small car park. A grubby black Kia was parked askew across two spaces up against a wall. There was a ticket fixed to the windscreen which Sofija tossed away.

'Get in,' she said, opening the driver's door.

'You don't believe in paying for parking then,' said Dawson getting in alongside her.

'Not my car,' she said. He quickly pulled on his seatbelt – Sofija not bothering with hers – as the Kia shot off with a jerk that nearly threw him through the side window.

'Tracker in here,' Sofija said, leaning across and opening the glove compartment, taking her eyes off the busy street for a full five seconds in so doing.

'Watch out!' shouted Dawson, alarmed, as they briefly mounted the pavement before bouncing back on to the road. Miraculously, no pedestrians or other vehicles were damaged during this manoeuvre. The red light on the tracker indicated that the car containing Lucy was stationary and no more than half a mile away. Thank God for that, Dawson thought. There must be a fifty-fifty chance they could reach the location without Sofija mowing anyone down.

'They still in city,' said Sofija, leaning across and looking at the tracker too, this time for no more than three seconds. 'I not expect that.' Half a minute later, she mounted another pavement, deliberately this time, stopped and turned off the engine. 'We walk from here.' She took the tracker from Dawson and got out.

'Are you just going to leave the car here?' said Dawson as he squeezed out onto the bare foot of pavement between him and the wall of the building next to them.

'Yes,' she said. 'It belong to old CIA woman. Maybe it have diplomatic plate. We find other car, maybe faster one, if we need to.'

They were in a quieter part of the city now, away from the main thoroughfares and the tracker was pointing towards a nondescript office building a little way up the street. There was no sign of any car but a ramp led down into what Dawson presumed was an underground parking garage beneath the building. As bold as brass, Sofija walked up the street and started down the ramp. Dawson followed.

'Are you armed?' he asked. He'd seen no sign of a weapon and it seemed foolhardy to walk into a lion's den without at least one gun.

'Of course not.' She grinned at him. 'I only waitress, I told you. And on holiday. Why would I have gun?'

The underground car park at the foot of the ramp was nearly empty but an elderly grey Ford Mondeo was parked close to, and half-obscuring, some lift doors. Sofija grunted in satisfaction. The tracker started bleeping loudly as they neared the vehicle. Sofija switched it off. As they rounded the Mondeo, Dawson glanced inside. It was empty.

Sofija stopped suddenly as the lift doors came into full view. Dawson was busy congratulating himself for not cannoning into her when she muttered, 'This not good.' It was clear what she meant; the doors had a cross of red and white sticky tape poorly affixed across them. Nevertheless, perhaps hoping that the tape was some sort of chimaera, Sofija pressed the lift button firmly with her thumb. Dawson reflected that in his experience, when Sofija pressed something it tended to stay pressed. The fact that the button didn't pop out again when she removed her thumb tended to reinforce this theory. The doors stayed resolutely shut.

'It broken.' she announced after a couple of seconds. The red-and-white tape had been something of a clue in this regard. Whilst it didn't actually have the words "Keep Out" printed on it, doubtless that was the impression it was intended to give.

'Stairs,' said Sofija, sounding undaunted, although her earlier 'this not good' was likely to be a more accurate reflection of her feelings. She looked around but it was Dawson who saw the stairs first, half hidden behind a dirty pillar.

The stairwell smelled like the hordes of hell had defecated in it and looked no more pleasant but they headed upwards anyway. When they reached the ground floor, the reception area they entered didn't as much scream "Welcome" as "Fuck Off". They looked at each other and wordlessly separated. Dawson heard various crashes and bangs coming from the direction Sofija had taken but doubted that they signified anything more than her version of a search. It took less than two minutes to establish that the building was empty. Possibly condemned. If not condemned before Sofija started searching it, then definitely so now. Anyway, it didn't contain Lucy.

'They switch cars,' said Sofija, leaning against a grubby wall. 'I not think of that.'

'Idiot,' said Dawson. He was ten feet away so felt relatively safe.

She looked at him and grinned ruefully. 'This true,' she said. 'I am in good company.'

___ In which Kaya Rabada makes tea,
and Lucy knocks a chair over


Kaya hadn't confirmed that they were going to see Jason Underwood's CIA contact, Anthony Melhuish. She didn't have to. The expression on the South African woman's face told Lucy she'd hit the nail on the head. Where that particular nail was going to be hammered next she had no idea.

The second part of the journey hadn't taken very long at all, just a few minutes before the replacement car swung off the road into a restricted parking area. A high, metal gate slid shut behind them. Lucy allowed herself to be hustled inside a bland sixties-built office block to a set of lift doors; it seemed polite to continue giving the two black-clad heavies something to justify their existence. At a word from Kaya, the men left and just the two women rode the elevator up to a bland corridor with bland doors which probably, Lucy thought, opened into bland offices.

Kaya stopped outside one of the bland doors, which bore no name or number, and knocked. 'Come,' a voice called from inside. Kaya opened the door and motioned for Lucy to precede her into the room. The reason for the two car journeys being comparatively brief was apparent to Lucy as soon as she saw the man who was standing behind a tidy desk in what was indeed the blandest of offices.

She'd last seen him in Wale Street less than two hours earlier. Without knowing exactly where in Cape Town they now were, Lucy worked out that the total time spent travelling meant that Wale Street could hardly be more than two or three miles away. Melvyn Gilbert was no longer the slightly unkempt, harassed and embarrassed Assistant Deputy Director of South African Domestic Intelligence who'd forbidden Lucy and Dawson access to the SSA's personnel files. The air of authority he now gave off was almost palpable.

'Mr Gilbert,' said Lucy, advancing to the desk, shaking his proffered hand and sitting on one of the chairs in front of the desk. 'Or should I say Melhuish?' Kaya took the other chair. 'How nice to see you again. You've been telling porkies, haven't you?'

Melhuish laughed. 'Of course, Ms Smith. But then, so have you. So has virtually everybody you've met. It all rather adds to the fun, doesn't it?' The Home Counties accent of a couple of hours earlier had disappeared and the "trace of something else" that Lucy had failed to identify was now fully up front and centre: New Hampshire, she decided.

'Does South African Security know you're a fully paid-up member of the CIA?' she said, then immediately answering her own question. 'Of course not. So, what's going on? And is there any chance of a cup of tea while you explain?'

'Tea? Of course. Where are my manners?' He glanced at Kaya who rose unasked and left the room. She might be a gun-toting CIA agent but she was also a woman so tea-fetching duties – of course – fell to her.

Lucy nodded towards the door as it closed behind Kaya. 'This is a little confusing, Mr Melhuish,' she began.

'Anthony, please.'

'Whatever. The first time Dawson and I met Kaya, she pulled a gun on us. I don't take kindly to people pulling guns on me, so why should I take kindly to her now? And therefore, by association, you.'

'You certainly deserve an explanation about that.' Melhuish leaned forward on his desk, steepling his fingers and pursing his lips. 'You've gathered by now that Kaya is a CIA agent reporting directly to me on this, er, project that you have become involved in. Rather coincidentally, actually. I found it strange that it should be you and Mr Dawson who found Andrew Gulliver's body at Bloubergstrand.'

'Somebody wanted us to find it. The body was dumped from a passing cabin cruiser.'

'Really? Darn tricky, the Chinese. You've got to hand it to them.'

'Kaya has already said she's not too concerned about her brother's death. I'm sure Dawson will be relieved to hear it.'

'Yes, indeed. I doubt if family Christmases *chez* Nkunde were harmonious affairs. Still, her animosity was useful. As was the fact that she used to be pals with another of Mahatma Patel's little organisation, Asha Mbaso. And, as Kaya's a fairly recent recruit, she was able to pose as driver in the UK to another lady you might be aware of, by the name of Stella Fish.'

'I think Stella might be aware of her now, bearing in mind she hit her over the head with a gun a few days ago.'

'Yes, that was unfortunate but it doesn't matter.'

'Did you really just call Patel, Mahatma? Who does he think he is, some sort of chosen one?'

'He's undoubtedly some sort of greedy one. I doubt if he's a dedicated commie, just a dedicated believer in a luxury retirement.'

'Which you intend to make sure he doesn't get.'

'Up to a point, yes. For some reason, we Americans are getting an increasingly poor press, so we don't want to be seen disposing of senior local policemen, whichever insalubrious bed they've chosen to sleep in. I was rather hoping you might be able to help us out.'

'Are you suggesting that I'm some sort of gun for hire?' Lucy, seriously angered, jumped to her feet, her chair crashing to the floor. Kaya, re-entering the room at precisely the wrong moment with three mugs of tea on a tray, did exceptionally well not to fumble them.

'Ah. You sound upset,' said Melhuish, rising rather more calmly to his own feet. 'Your record suggested you might relish the, er, opportunity. I apologise if I've offended you. Please, sit down again and drink your tea.'

'Did you ever speak to Jason Underwood?' said Lucy, righting her chair and taking a mug off Kaya's tray.

'Who?'

'Jason Underwood of MI6. My boss.' Melhuish's face was blank. 'Never mind.'

Interesting, thought Lucy. Either Melhuish or Underwood is lying. Why would that be? It could be trivial but, trivial or not, it was a question for another day.

'You asked about the incident in the cable car,' said Melhuish. 'I'm sorry about that.' He smiled. 'I seem to be doing a lot of apologising. It was both fortunate and unfortunate that when Patel was told to, er, eliminate Mr Dawson and yourself, he instructed Daniel and Kaya to do it together. We believe it was meant to be a test of her loyalty.'

'It was certainly unfortunate for Daniel,' said Kaya.

'What do you mean, fortunate **and** unfortunate?' interjected Lucy.

'Well, fortunate for you because it meant that Kaya would be trying, somehow, not to let you be killed. Unfortunate for us because that, in turn, would reveal Kaya as a, er, fifth columnist. As it turned out, thanks to Mr Dawson, Daniel had no opportunity to tell anyone.'

Lucy paused and took a sip of tea while she thought back to the series of events on the cable car. Now she considered it, she had overpowered Kaya and taken her gun much more easily than she might have expected to, MI6 training or not. Kaya had then crashed into Daniel Nkunde, sending him toppling out of the window, from whence he'd clambered on to the roof of the car only for Dawson to shoot him. On reflection, there had been no obvious reason for Kaya to cannon into Daniel; Lucy couldn't remember pushing her, although it had all happened very quickly.

'I'll buy that.' Lucy turned to Kaya. 'But why the theatricals afterwards? I assume you were pretending to be scared. And why did you run? When we reached the mountain?'

'Theatricals?' said Kaya. 'You thumped me on the nose, you bitch. It fucking hurt. I thought it was broken. I wasn't acting, I was seriously dazed.' She was smiling as she said it though.

'She ran away because she was under instructions not to

reveal herself to you,' added Melhuish.

'And because I thought you might hit me again. You're tougher than you look.'

'Moving on,' said Melhuish, leaning back in his chair with a relaxed air, mug of tea in hand. 'This is a rather complicated set of circumstances you and Mr Dawson have fallen into, isn't it? Things have jumped forward so it's about time we got you on board. There are things we know and things you know and I always feel a touch of *rapprochement* is for the best.'

'And is this *rapprochement* going to include Dawson?' Lucy asked.

'Yes, but not directly. Mr Dawson has met up with an old friend. Not, admittedly, an old friend that we are officially employing but no matter. And I don't want to put all my eggs in one basket.'

'What old friend?' Captain Temba Yeboah, maybe? Hardly an old friend though.

'Lady by the name of Sofija Sesks,' said Melhuish.

'Sofija?' Lucy was so astonished she nearly dropped her mug. 'Fuck off. Why would she be here?' It wouldn't be because she was after Dawson's body.

'Not our idea,' said Melhuish, shrugging. 'Her sister insisted.' Lucy could feel her mouth droop open. She had no words. 'I believe you've met Guna. When she insists on something, I've found it's usually wise to take a pragmatic approach.'

Lucy was glad she was sitting down. She drained her tea as she waited for some sort of useful response to emerge in her brain. Melhuish and Kaya stared at her. She felt rather like a specimen in a laboratory. Eventually words formed. 'Guna Sesks,' she said slowly, 'lately of Russian Intelligence, is working for the CIA. You. Have I got that right?'

'Exactly right, Ms Smith.'

'So... what? She's turned traitor, has she?'

'Oh, no, I wouldn't go so far as to say that,' Melhuish demurred. 'She resigned from the SVR soon after your little exploit in Estonia. They were happy to see her go. I believe the Russians thought she was becoming, er, uncontrollable. Guna herself considered she might be forcibly retired if she didn't leave of her own accord. She contacted Langley and my director thought the agency might find some use for her. He gave her to me.' He paused. 'The sister, Sofija, was not part of the deal but Guna said she couldn't do what we needed her to do without her help. There was something about cooking. We're not exactly overrun with agents on the Cape so when Guna intimated that her sister was on annual leave and, it seems, bored, I agreed to let her help. Of course, if Sofija becomes too troublesome, we can always do something about that.'

'Really?' said Lucy. 'To use a well-worn cliché, you and whose army? You've just said you're understaffed. You might find understaffed becomes no staffed.' She considered. 'There are a lot of people working for more than one master, aren't there? You, for example, Mr Melhuish. One minute you're, what was it? Assistant Deputy Director of Domestic Intelligence for the South African State Security Agency, and the next the local CIA head honcho. And what's with the accents, by the way? I'm guessing the current New Hampshire one is genuine but why the plummy Home Counties English when you were pretending to be South African?'

Kaya spoke. 'He can't do South African, Lucy.' Melhuish looked momentarily rather cross. 'Lots of Englishmen work down here. Andrew Gulliver for example. Something about the climate attracts them. Anyway, you're no stranger to working for two masters yourself.'

'Me?' Lucy said. 'Which two would that be?'

Kaya started counting on her fingers. Maybe maths wasn't her strong point. 'MI6 and...'

She was cut off by Melhuish. 'I believe you've met a gentleman called Jacob Dlamini...'

But he too was cut off – by an explosion deep in the heart of the building.

___ In which Melhuish thinks about the
Fish who swam away, and brings in
reinforcements


The CIA had known that some sort of assassination attempt was on the cards when Stella Fish had abruptly vanished. Stella Fish, Senior Scientific Officer, a title that didn't actually mean she had much of a scientific brain herself but more the sort of organisational nous to bring together other more scientifically-orientated brains in potentially beneficial experimental operations. Beneficial to the Agency that is. And ultimately to the wider United States, not that that was a given.

Then Stella became the fish that got away. Where she'd swum off to was not immediately apparent. While not forgotten, netting Stella was not a top priority. When she'd vanished, she had been the second in command of a hastily discarded, ill-thought-out CIA hypnosis programme designed to create a small band of untraceable killers. Only two subjects for the experiment had been found before the abandonment of the project. One, a Mexican student, had accidentally died on the operating table, and no sooner was he cold than the feet of some very senior Washington officials became equally cold. The programme was cancelled with immediate effect.

But that left the problem of what to do with the second subject, a young Irish woman with no family who had inconveniently decided **not** to die on the operating table. Against all protocol, certain senior figures within the CIA, including Anthony Melhuish, who should have known better but didn't much like the idea of peremptorily dispatching the innocent to an early grave, decided to go ahead anyway. She'll never be needed, they decided. But always good to have a backup. Just in case. With the world the way it is, you never knew...

So the Irish woman, who went by the quaintly fanciful but genuine name of Sapphire Waters, found herself working for MI6 in London. There was no one in MI6 who the CIA particularly wished to assassinate at present but hey, things could change and London was a hotbed of international skulduggery; you couldn't predict what measures might be required moving forward. Melhuish and his colleagues, determined to keep all this secret in case a US prison should start to loom large in their futures, failed to account for their rogue agent: Stella Fish.

Nor had they accounted for the erstwhile project's chief medical officer, Dr Henry Norton, who was provided with what he considered an unsatisfactorily meagre redundancy package. Dr Norton, it turned out, was a man who carried a grudge.

And Stella Fish was in possession of his phone number.

It wasn't until Sapphire in her MI6 guise phoned the CIA and asked about Stella Fish, the sister of a dead man, that Anthony Melhuish started to take a serious interest. The dead man just happened to be the brother of a South African government lawyer they were keeping tabs on and who, coincidentally, disappeared shortly after his brother in England passed through the pearly gates.

The alarm bells truly started to ring when Melhuish heard that Stella Fish had left England for the Cape of Lost Hope and that MI6 had managed to lose the young Irish ex-guinea pig. Oh shit, he thought. And instructed his own rogue – perhaps maverick would be a better term – ex-SVR agent Guna Sesks to hop on a plane to Cape Town sharpish. Not only did he lack a suitable alternative but he was wary of a possible future in orange prison scrubs.

Guna had been tasked with tracking Stella Fish and discovering exactly what she was up to. Fish's arrival in Cape Town in the company of the unsuspecting Sapphire Waters, only a few weeks prior to a South African presidential election, ratcheted the importance up several levels. And not just in regard to Melhuish's retirement plans.

Sapphire was the instrument of assassination. The questions remaining were where and when. And who.

___ In which Guna yearns for cooler climes,
   and Dr Norton is busy with
   a bandage


Guna Sesks found herself in an unusual position. She wasn't used to being outmanoeuvred, let alone outfought, but here she was standing with her hands in the air, four guns pointing unerringly at her. Her own weapon was pinned to the ground a few metres away by a black court shoe, having been removed from her jacket by a man who, in Guna's considered opinion, now deserved not to live much longer. While Guna had been confident in her ability to overcome Stella's gang of armed muscle at the correct time and given a modicum of forward planning, that time had not yet arrived and she was paying the price for her lack of attention.

However, she was still alive, surprisingly, and a fully breathing Guna, even unarmed, remained extremely dangerous – far more dangerous than either Stella Fish or her gang realised. Guna wasn't sure why she was still alive. Her abysmal cooking alone would have been reason enough for any self-respecting enemy to pull the trigger.

Somehow, she needed to turn the tables and get her mission back on track. Her new chief, Melhuish, would probably be disappointed if she were to get herself killed. The CIA might even withdraw the offer of the waterside condo in Florida that she'd been promised. And Melhuish would be even more disappointed if she failed to prevent the Sapphire/Nemesis woman carrying out the assassination that Guna was now certain Stella had her lined up for. While Guna was pretty sure that the rally at the Green Point Football Stadium was now the time and place, she had no idea which of the five candidates the target was to be. She couldn't work out why so many people apparently wanted to be the president of such a hot country. Maybe the condo in Florida was not such a good idea after all; Guna was beginning to yearn for the cooler, fresher climate of the Baltics.

That was for another day though. For the time being she had to avoid being dead as that would seriously hamper her chances of thwarting Stella's plans. Not that being captured and imprisoned would be much more helpful.

Guna had confidently – overconfidently, as it had transpired – expected Stella to assume that it was she who had left the building when Sofija had driven the elderly Kia away down the drive in a spurt of gravel and a crunching of gears. Guna hadn't instructed her twin to make a noisy getaway. She hadn't needed to; it was just the way Sofija always drove. And if Stella believed "the cook" had disappeared into town, maybe to buy ingredients from which to make even more disgusting meals, then there was no reason for Stella to think she was still in the house. It wasn't as if Guna had been wandering around in the open; she'd been content to carry on listening to conversations taking place in the various rooms in which she and Sofija had managed to hide tiny, unfindable bugs.

Stella Fish held up a tiny, unfindable bug between a manicured finger and thumb. OK, not unfindable then, thought Guna. Shoddy work by Sofija, obviously. She'd have to have words with her twin when she'd recovered the situation. 'I believe this may be yours, Miss Balodis,' said Stella icily.

'I not know what you mean,' said Guna in the halting, heavily accented English she'd been employing since arriving at the house as Galina Balodis, the agency chef from Latvia. 'I cook. I not know what you holding.'

'Leaving aside the fact that you **don't** cook in any accurate sense of the word, I presume you also "not know" what the gun is that Ralf has just removed from your jacket.' Ralf, thought Guna. She'd remember that name. Stella held up the pistol. 'A Glock. My old pals in the CIA use identical weapons. That's very interesting, wouldn't you say?'

Guna's Glock had been in the pocket of her jacket, which she had hung on the back of her chair. That had been careless but it could also give her a few more minutes. 'I not know what you mean, madam. It not mine. It planted maybe. By your man, Mr Ralf. He has Glock. All men have them. I see this.' She held her arms wide and tried to adopt a look of wide-eyed innocence that would have come more naturally to her twin. Even more naturally to Dawson. The latter thought made her mouth twitch.

Stella Fish noticed the twitch and nodded to Ralf who brought his own Glock hard down on the back of Guna's head. Guna's head was harder than average and it was covered with dense, albeit quite short, dark-blonde hair, but even so, she felt herself blacking out and her knees giving way. In two years' active service with the SVR she had managed to avoid being injured in the line of duty and she was momentarily annoyed that her reputation for efficiency had been demolished only weeks into her first assignment for her new American employers. Then unconsciousness overtook her.

She woke up with her wrists and ankles chained to the frame of a bed in a small, light room. Dr Norton was leaning over her putting the final touches to a bandage which had been wrapped around her skull. It was the same bed in the same room to which Sapphire had been chained the previous day and then again today following her shooting of Claxton. The still unconscious Sapphire had had to be moved to another room in order for Guna to be restrained.

Dr Norton, spotting that Guna was awake, stopped what he was doing and took a step back. He really was too nervous for his line of work, Guna thought, as he gathered unused bandages, tape and various other medical bits and pieces into a black holdall and scurried out of the room, locking the door behind him.

'Unbelievable,' said Guna softly to the empty room. 'Even now, they have not killed me. These people truly are amateurs.'

'What the hell was that?' I yelled, jumping up. Plaster was flaking from the ceiling of the office and fluttering gently to the carpet following the explosion from somewhere beneath our feet. Even as I said it, I knew what a fatuous thing it was to say: it wasn't a bloody firework, that's for sure.

'Kaya? Go check,' said Melhuish, turning to part the half-closed blinds behind him with his left hand. A pistol had appeared as if by magic in his right. 'Nothing out there,' he said. Kaya, her gun also very much in evidence, was now at the door.

'Can you open the door?' she said.

'It's one of my skill-sets,' I replied with a touch of sarcasm, and moved to join her. The initial explosion had been followed by silence. There were certainly no sounds of movement coming from beyond the door. It occurred to me I had no clue which floor we were on; I should have been paying more attention in the lift.

'You said you were understaffed,' I whispered in Melhuish's direction. 'Exactly how many people have you got here?'

'Including Kaya and me? Four. You've met the other two, Best and Cope.'

I could only hope that Best could cope with whatever had happened downstairs, or that Cope was the best they had. I shook my head; that was Saul-like thinking.

Kaya held up three fingers, closing one after the other, rather unnecessarily mouthing, 'Three, two, one,' as she did so. When she got to "one" I flung open the door and she leapt into the corridor, gun held firmly in both hands in a classic straight-armed pose. She immediately spun and looked the other way. 'Clear,' she barked and Melhuish joined me at the door.

'Quite a large building for just four people,' I said, not that I had any idea exactly how large it was.

'It's not our building,' said Melhuish. 'We're not big on infrastructure. We've just borrowed it for a while.'

'Perhaps you should have avoided sending out invitations to all and sundry to join you when you were doing the borrowing.'

'You won't find me arguing,' said Melhuish, 'but we've been here less than forty-eight hours. We move around all the time so how anyone's cottoned on to us this quickly is a question I'd like answers to once this is over.'

'What floor is this?' I'd decided that any leaks within the South African branch of the CIA weren't my concern. My priority was staying alive, what with the building breaking and everybody shaking.

'Third,' he said. As Melhuish was American, I reconfigured that to second.

'Top floor,' said Kaya, which clarified things a little more.

'Is there a roof?' I asked.

'Yes, but no way to reach anywhere else from it,' said Melhuish. 'In any case, I'm not in the habit of running away from something, especially when I don't know what that something is.'

'I think we're about to find out.' I'd just heard the sound of several pairs of heavily shod feet approaching at speed up the staircase, just past the lift doors ten yards in front of us.

The sound of the footsteps ceased suddenly and a hand appeared at floor level around the corner to the staircase. Kaya was quick to fire off a shot – just as the hand released something to roll along the corridor. The bullet hit the hand and there was a shout of pain as it was snapped hurriedly from view. Of more concern though was the something it had released; a thick, acrid smokescreen began to fill the passageway.

Immediately, I felt the back of my throat burning and my eyes started to water. 'Back in here,' I gasped, stumbling to the door of the office we'd just vacated. Kaya and Melhuish – despite his earlier assertion that he never ran away from things – followed and I slammed the door shut.

I heard the footsteps again, moving more cautiously up the corridor towards us. I imagined the owners of the footwear were equipped with some kind of gas masks but I had no idea how many of them there were and wasn't feeling inclined to hang around to find out. 'Window,' I said. I wasn't sure why I was taking charge – just natural instinct probably – but at least my voice was back in full working order. Melhuish, who was past fifty and nowhere near as fit as either Kaya or me, was holding a handkerchief to his face and spluttering.

I was already at the window by now and Kaya, half-supporting her boss, arrived next to me just as I discovered it was a sealed unit. 'I've locked the door,' she said, brandishing a key and then pocketing it.

There was no way of opening the window so I grabbed Melhuish's chair and hurled it at the glass. The chair ricocheted, nearly braining me and knocking me against the desk. I managed to half-catch it and repeated my attack on the window, this time not letting go of the chair. This second attempt was so successful that the window pretty much disintegrated; I lost hold of the chair which disappeared through the massive hole created and, gravity being what it is, it dropped out of sight. I hoped no one was in the street (although a falling chair might encourage someone to call the police) before a loud clunk from below window level prompted me to peer cautiously out. The chair had been caught fast by a fire escape I hadn't known was there.

A fire escape! Leaning further through the window, careful not to impale myself on broken glass, I glanced up and down. Down wasn't encouraging. Two men were standing on the ground thirty feet below me and they pointed up as soon as they saw my head poke through the window. That they weren't just pointing with fingers was quickly apparent as two bullets whooshed past me, one nearly chopping off my ponytail – a capital offence in my book – before clanging off the fire escape above me. I hurriedly withdrew my head as I glimpsed the two men start to climb the fire escape.

Kaya was guarding the door, gun again held firmly in both hands. She'd had to leave Melhuish to his own devices and he was leaning against a wall. His breathing was shallow and his face pale and sweaty; he really hadn't been in good condition if a few seconds of tear gas could have that effect on him.

'They're outside,' Kaya said quietly.

'That's good,' I said brightly. 'Far better than having them inside.' I wasn't entirely sure why I felt so upbeat but it wasn't just an act to encourage my new companions. I was genuinely beginning to enjoy myself. I'd grown into this action-girl lark during the course of the year. Even so, I was unsure why our attackers hadn't broken down the door. Maybe it was a security door. Or knowing we were armed, no one in the corridor wanted to be first to enter the room and take a bullet for their trouble.

I decided it was time to bring my own stolen Vektor into play and pulled it out of my pocket. 'Where did that come from?' said Kaya.

'You should try searching people when you lift them off the street,' I said cheerfully. 'You're lucky I'm an ask-questions-first kind of girl or you and your mates might not have made it as far as this current entertaining scenario.'

With Melhuish in no fit state to contribute to the defence of the office, I left Kaya to continue guarding the door and moved back to the window, gun raised. I was just in time to see a head appear above the level of the sill. As I pointed the Vektor at the man and pulled the trigger, I couldn't help but think that leading with your head wasn't the most sensible of options. There was a spurt of blood and the head disappeared soundlessly from view.

I must have killed him. It had been rather cold-blooded so I wasn't proud of myself. But needs must. By my reckoning there was still one attacker outside and alive on the fire escape and we had no idea how many of his colleagues were in the corridor outside the office waiting for the best moment to strike. Whichever way you looked at it, the three of us, including one increasingly sick-looking middle-aged bloke, were trapped. Kaya spoke urgently, stepping back from the door. 'More gas,' she said. She was right; tendrils of vapour were curling up from under the door.

And then I heard a familiar voice from the corridor. 'Miss Lucy Smith,' it said. 'Milady Delamere. British Imperialist Agent.' Songsung Bloody Rong. I quite enjoyed being referred to as a British Imperialist Agent. I'd add it to my CV.

Rong continued. 'We have unfinished business, the two of us. The gas will not kill you. Later on, you'll wish it had.'

_____ In which Lugay Phukuntsi looks
    at some lights, and a bottle
    of cognac disappears

Assemblyman Lugay Phukuntsi owned a house at the top of a steep, twisting, unmade road in Bakoven, seven kilometres south west of the city. The house backed on to the craggy, partly wooded western slopes of Table Mountain and was several hundred feet above sea level, where the air was clear and smelled of the ocean that he could see from his balcony.

Phukuntsi enjoyed living there, even if the property had been acquired for him by the Chinese government by way of several shadowy intermediary organisations and without his opinion on the matter being sought. He'd asked no questions; it was a lovely place to live. As he was a man of below average height but vastly above average circumference, his weight touching thirty stone, the steep approach to the house did him no favours. Luckily, a man named Karl Benz had been clever enough to invent the automobile in the nineteenth century and for more than two years, the furthest Lugay had trekked was from car to door or from armchair to fridge. Except on those inconvenient occasions when his political duties demanded he travel to Pretoria, which meant boarding an aeroplane. He was not a fan of the steps that he was required to climb to board planes, planes which he didn't entirely trust to stay airborne. This was an assessment shared by flight attendants when they saw his bulk approaching their aircraft.

Tonight, he'd have to be a little more energetic than usual. He wasn't looking forward to the rally at Green Point but it was the price you paid to live in a lovely house enjoying lovely ocean views. Not to mention the enjoyable prospect of becoming the next president of the Republic of South Africa. Money had also been promised in the future, an amount of money substantial enough to allow him to live in extremely comfortable retirement, as would befit an ex-president.

Being elected president had only been mooted earlier this year. In all honesty (something he veered away from most of the time), he wasn't entirely sure how he had even become a National Assemblyman. It started three years ago and was a means to an end. The end being to make himself wealthier by accessing opportunities that, it had seemed to him, came with a social strata not within reach of a small-time casino owner from Nyanga.

Deals were done and money had changed hands. To start with, this was mostly from his own hands into other hands. It was money he didn't necessarily have in the first place, but Nyanga was a place where people knew people who knew people. Suddenly he was a paid-up member of the South African Transformative Party and standing for election to the National Assembly. Even then, he hadn't expected to be elected, his policies widely dismissed as risible, or trussible as the current jargon had it. But a fortunate road accident a week before polling day had removed the ANC candidate from the fray and elected he had been.

At the time, he'd no reason to suspect any international influence at play. He had never been the brightest star in the firmament and it wasn't until a fortuitous (as he inaccurately believed) meeting with Mahatma Patel that Lugay Phukuntsi's political star began to ascend.

Patel had in turn introduced him to more people. People with influence. Lugay's shady past was gradually forgotten. His momentum became unstoppable and here he was, a few weeks shy of the presidential election, only a handful of points adrift of the favourite, Jacob Dlamini, in the polls. And that points difference would evaporate at the rally tonight, Patel had assured him on the drive back from the Dockview Bar to Bakoven yesterday. Rest up, he was told. Sleep well. Don't worry about our guests. Patel would look after them.

Tonight would be Lugay Phukuntsi's night.

Even now, he had no idea that it was the Government of the People's Republic of China pulling his strings. Phukuntsi wriggled uncomfortably in his groaning armchair. Now that the rally was nearly upon him, he was nervous. Patel had told him not to worry about Major General de Kock and the other police officer whose name he didn't know and didn't want to know. But their appearance at the bar had unsettled him, despite his outward bluster. And he knew that they were now somewhere in the building, brought this morning by the young woman with the cold, dark eyes. He presumed they were in the basement, which stretched deep under the mountain but which Patel forbade him from entering. That was fine by him. What Lugay didn't know couldn't hurt him.

He reached out a chubby paw for his Remy Martin cognac. There were barely two millimetres of liquid left in the glass. He grunted in disappointment and turned his head to locate the bottle but it was no longer on the side table. It had been spirited away silently by Patel, who was now standing behind him. Lugay's disappointment at the disappearance of the bottle of Remy Martin was compounded by the appearance of Patel and even more by his next words.

'No more after that, Assemblyman,' said the slight, grey spectre. 'We cannot have you drunk. You will need to be at your best this evening.'

'You said everything was done and dusted,' Phukuntsi grumbled.

'We must keep up appearances.' Patel's face revealed what he thought of the likelihood of Phukuntsi's appearance ever reaching acceptable levels of respectability. The gross ex-casino owner would not have been his choice. But he had received his orders a long time ago and was committed to seeing them through. His not to reason why, his but to... well, who knew in this uncertain world, but he had Cathay Pacific on speed-dial just to be on the safe side. He moved in front of Phukuntsi, blocking the politician's view of the twinkling lights of Camps

Bay. 'You have rehearsed your speech, I hope.' It wasn't a question.

'I can read,' grunted Phukuntsi. 'The speech will be fine. I have given speeches before. And anyway, it is irrelevant, yes?'

'Rehearse it again,' said Patel and turned to leave.

'What about our guests?' said Phukuntsi. He didn't really want to know but the words left his mouth unbidden.

'They are unimportant. Do not concern yourself with them.'

___ In which Brenda and Temba eat
pot noodle, and Asha Mbaso
thinks vengeful thoughts


Two floors below Lugay Phukuntsi's ocean view in a window-
less basement room, Major General Brenda de Kock and Captain Temba Yeboah sat on uncomfortable chairs silently await-
ing whatever fate Asha Mbaso had in store for them. Or rather,
whatever Mahatma Patel had in store for them. Neither Patel
nor Lugay Phukuntsi had yet made an appearance but at least
the two officers hadn't been left in darkness this time. Quite
the opposite. Overhead strip lighting bathed the small room in
a harsh, blue-white brightness.

They'd been brought here in a van after an uncomfortable
night on the floor of the stark back room of the Dockview Bar.
Blindfolded, they'd had no way of identifying what make of
van or deciphering the route. Temba had made a valiant but
ill-advised attempt to make a break for freedom and had the
cuts and bruises to show for it.

Once securely bound to the chairs in their new prison, the
blindfolds had been removed and they'd been left alone apart
from a single visit from a sullen Asha Mbaso, who had sloppily
spoon-fed them with some indescribable variety of pot noodle and allowed them a few sips of water. After she had left
the room, Brenda and Temba had spent some time fruitlessly
speculating on why they were still alive, given that they could
identify Phukuntsi, Patel, Mbaso and the two lugheads. No answers came to them.


—


On the other side of a triple-locked, solid-steel door, Asha
Mbaso sprawled lazily on a comfortable sofa, idly spinning
a small automatic pistol around a forefinger. She was busy

thinking. Patel had only just seen fit to inform her that her lover, Daniel Nkunde, was dead, killed on the Table Mountain cable car by the Englishman, Dawson. Asha, being a vengeful woman, came to the conclusion that somebody needed to pay for Daniel's death and as his actual killer was not currently available, there were two possible alternatives not ten feet away. They were both police. She hadn't forgotten her recent stretch in Pollsmoor Prison. Pigs. They would do.

Alternatively, there was the Chinese bitch, Gao Chang, who always looked contemptuously down her nose at Asha. Maybe her then.

Asha held no strong political convictions. She was neither pro- nor anti-communism. She was simply being paid to do a job and if a better offer came along or, as now, a personal vendetta, she would simply disappear. It was a big wide world and with her skillset, she wouldn't be out of work for long.

It seemed to her that it was time to make a move. She didn't much care for the oily Patel either and as for Phukuntsi, the man was a gross irrelevance. She toyed with the possibility of killing the two of them as well but decided, reluctantly, against it, pleasurable though it would be. Her future prospects would be hindered were she to bump off her employer. Word got out. The Chinese were exceptionally efficient at following up on that sort of thing.

The two police bastards in the next room would do. Later this evening, when Patel and the fat politician were at the rally.

___ In which Dawson hotwires
     an engine, and two doors
     are opened violently


For once, Sofija seemed unsure about what to do next. 'Sister kill me,' she muttered as they made their way back down the foul-smelling staircase. 'I let her down.'

'It's lucky you're only on holiday then,' said Dawson. 'She may be less upset than you think. Call her.'

'No phone,' said Sofija, looking unusually downcast, as they made their way back up the ramp from the car park into the bright late afternoon sunshine of the road above.

'I have a phone,' said Dawson, flourishing it.

'We keep radio silence.' She paused. 'Anyway, we twins. We know what each other think.' He suspected the radio silence excuse was just that, an excuse to avoid facing Guna's displeasure until the situation improved.

It was Dawson who first noticed that the Kia was not where they'd left it. Sofija was still looking at her feet. 'Problem,' he said and pointed at the empty pavement.

'This get worse,' said Sofija, stopping. 'Who take car?' She looked surprised and completely at a loss, for pretty much the first time ever in Dawson's experience. He was less surprised to find the elderly vehicle missing. Not wanting a punch on the nose, he decided not to mention that leaving the Kia on the pavement was liable to attract the attention of the city's parking wardens and it had probably been towed away. He doubted if even the most desperate of car thieves would steal it.

'Don't worry. If it's transport we need, I know where to find it,' he said, grabbing Sofija's wide shoulders and, not without some effort, turning her 180° and striding off back to the underground car park. He wasn't sure if she'd follow him – she wasn't the following type – but she did.

'*Voilà*.' He pointed to the grey Mondeo. 'Transport, *ma brave*.' Why was he talking French?

'This fine,' said Sofija. 'But no key.'

'No key, no problemo.' Now he was speaking pidgin Spanish.

During a training session on lockpicking with MI6's Kev the Key in the bowels of Vauxhall Cross, Kev had kindly provided tutelage on the art of hotwiring an engine. Dawson removed the plastic covering from the underside of the steering column and quickly created a small spark which prompted the starter motor into exuberant life.

'You not so much idiot after all,' said Sofija. Dawson couldn't remember her ever looking so impressed with him. 'But where we go now? We have no one to follow.'

Dawson could only think of one place. 'Lucy and I were headed to the Dockview Bar.'

'This no time for drink.' He risked a quick glance across at the stocky Estonian woman. She was smiling again. He pulled into a bus stop and consulted his phone to try and identify where they were and how to get to the Dockview Bar. The only directions Hansie Coetzee had given were to take the Fresnaye bus, get off at Albany Road and head towards Signal Hill.

'Well?' said Sofija, not looking quite as impressed as she had done a few minutes earlier.

He was just about to say he didn't know when there was a peremptory blast on a horn from behind him and he looked in the mirror to see a bus approaching and wanting to use the allocated stop in which Dawson had brought the Ford to a halt. 'Shit,' he said, but then looked in the mirror again. 'Bingo!'

'Bingo?' said Sofija. 'You say Dockview is bar, not bingo hall. Make up mind, idiot.' The not-an-idiot interlude had lasted mere minutes.

Dawson waved his hand in apology in the bus driver's

direction and eased forward a few metres. 'Look behind us, Sof,' he said. 'That bus is going to Fresnaye and we're going to follow it. Keep your eyes peeled for an Albany Road. Dockview Bar, here we come.'

'How I peel my eyes? They not oranges. You very confusing.' Dawson laughed at the irony of that statement. He was in charge, they were heading for the Dockview Bar and they were going to recover his girlfriend and, between the three of them (with Guna's violently enthusiastic assistance *vis-à-vis* Stella Fish) sort out this mess.

And then Lucy and he would have that proper holiday.

—

The Dockview Bar was shut.

Dawson banged on the scuffed, plain-wood door several times as hard as he could and, failing to elicit any response, allowed Sofija to try. She banged considerably harder but with the same result, or lack thereof. Dawson climbed back up the steep steps to the dreary, warehouse-lined road, and walked up and down for a short distance, searching for any signs of life or a back entrance. He found neither. It was some way past five o'clock. He didn't have an intimate knowledge of South African licensing laws but he reckoned that any self-respecting bar should be open by now, more so if it wasn't self-respecting.

He was gone no more than three minutes but when he returned, the door to the Dockview was open, a little lopsidedly, and an impatient Sofija was waiting for him.

'How did you open the door?'

He should have known better. 'It not as strong as it look,' said Sofija, shrugging as she pushed past the damaged door and entered a small lobby.

The lobby led through into the bar proper. Dawson liked pubs, indeed he'd spent a not insignificant proportion of his life in pubs and bars. He wouldn't want to be spending more time than he possibly could in this one though. It was dark, grimy and musty, containing a motley selection of tables and chairs that may have been trawled from the city's junk shops. When he walked across to the bar and leaned on it to see if perhaps anyone was hiding behind it, his hand stuck to the surface.

To one side of the bar counter, there was a door which led to the toilets and storerooms. Dawson took a step towards it, hoping to find somewhere to wash his sticky hand but he was still three steps away when it crashed open from the other side and a giant burst through it, sending him flying.

Dawson cracked his head on the corner of the counter and was immediately out for the count.

_ In which Lucy lands on a roof,
   and thanks a dead man


Lucy, inside the CIA's partially blown-up office block with Melhuish and Kaya, reviewed their options. It didn't take long. The
corridor contained a six-foot three-inch Chinese government
assassin with a chip on her shoulder and a swarm of goons to
do her bidding. The room they were in was filling rapidly with
gas. On the bright side, the huge hole in the window was, to a
degree, dissipating its effect. Outside the window was another
gunman and, as Lucy had just killed his mate, he too was likely
to be a bit chippy. If she could ditch the second thug and get
up on to the roof – or preferably down to ground level – that
would be a whole lot better bet than trying to charge out into
the corridor.

The other fly in this sticky ointment was Melhuish, who
was slumped on his haunches up against the wall, his breathing more and more ragged. He couldn't make it to the roof.
Kaya backed away from the door, gun still raised, and loos-
ened Melhuish's collar and tie with her free hand. 'He needs
medical attention,' she said. 'Gao Chang wants to kill you so
you must make a run for it through the window. She won't do
anything to us; we're CIA. It would cause too many diplomatic
issues.'

It sounded like a thinner than thin argument to Lucy who
was, after all, MI6 herself. But maybe killing MI6 agents didn't
tot up as many minus points as killing CIA agents. She found
herself wheezing almost as much as Melhuish. 'I hope you're
right. I'll go through the window and try to disable the remaining guard out there. Once I've done that, I'll come back
for you guys.' She reckoned she could double back over the
roof and down into one of the offices on the other side of the
building. Hopefully, an attack from the rear was not something
Songsung Rong would expect. Lucy didn't know how many

men the Chinese agent had with her but that was a bridge to be crossed when she reached it.

Kaya nodded and resumed her position facing the door. 'Good luck,' she said. 'Here, take this.' She passed her gun to Lucy. 'You might need more than eight bullets.'

'What about you?' Lucy was shocked. 'Keep it.'

'I've more chance of staying alive if they find me unarmed when they get through the door,' said Kaya smiling. 'And Mr Melhuish is in a bad way. I can't leave him and, you never know, they might take pity on him. Me too. I don't know what you've done to upset Chang but it's you she's after.'

'I may have sort of shot her a few months ago.' She took Kaya's gun. 'More than once.' She gave the young CIA agent a quick hug. 'Good luck yourself, Kaya.'

Lucy stepped to the broken window and looked cautiously out. She saw no one below her, either on the ground or on the fire escape. True, the office chair, wedged fast ten feet below her, blocked a chunk of her view and it seemed unlikely the man had gone home for his tea, but she had little choice but to take a chance. The roof was only a swift, short jump upwards from the railing four feet away. If not exactly a piece of piss, it would be less of a challenge than her clamber up the side of a cable car. Both she and Kaya had come a long way in a few short hours, albeit not geographically. Even so, as she leapt for the railing, she was thinking that jumping onto roofs was a gap in MI6's training that could do with being filled. She landed as planned with her right trainer firmly on the balustrade, knee bent, and in one smooth motion twisted and pushed off upwards, reaching with her free hand for the concrete wall around the flat roof six feet above the window. She was in mid-air when a bullet grazed her left shoulder, ripping a hole through her favourite green hoody and the t-shirt beneath. She experienced a sharp stab of pain but it didn't slow her down, and a second later her fingers curled over the edge of the wall. Then she realised that the shot had come from the roof itself, and here she was, with one shoulder stinging like buggery, hanging by the fingers of one hand, completely at the mercy of any second bullet.

Lucy glanced upwards but no head appeared over the concrete wall. Perhaps the gunman was running scared. She pushed the Vektor into the side pocket of her hoody, where it was less than secure. At least she was now hanging by two hands. If he was still up there, the shooter would now see both her hands, so unless he believed her capable of firing a gun with her teeth there seemed nothing to stop him leaning over for the *coup de grâce*.

Whatever the situation, she couldn't hang there for ever. With her left hand starting to go numb from the bullet graze on her shoulder, it would be only a couple of seconds before she landed back in a heap on the balcony outside the window she'd just exited. And that wasn't an option; she heard the door being broken down and Songsung Rong's voice instructing Kaya to lie on the floor. At least she hadn't been summarily executed.

Lucy gritted her teeth and using all the strength in her uninjured right arm and shoulder, twisted herself up, hooking a leg over the wall and then, after a quick gulp of air, hauling herself painfully up to lie flat on the roof. She tensed, waiting for a second, final bullet. But none came. She rolled over and found herself staring into the unseeing eyes of the man who, she presumed, had fired the shot that had so annoyingly ruined her hoody. How he'd died was a mystery she certainly wasn't going to solve lying around on the dusty surface of the roof, so she got to her feet. From an upright position she could see a knife protruding between the man's shoulder blades. That explains the how, she thought, but not the **how**.

Standing twenty feet away was a helicopter. She had no time to dwell on its unexpected presence before she heard a grunt and a snuffling. Slumped in front of an open fire door and half obscured by the helicopter, she saw a man in a black suit. She didn't know if this was Best or Cope but whoever it was, had done his absolute best to cope with the gunman on the roof. And succeeded. Whether he'd be alive to receive Lucy's thanks was a moot point as his black suit was in tatters and his face a mass of blood. If he'd been caught by the original bomb blast downstairs as feared, it was a miracle he'd made it up to the roof at all. Lucy hurried to him and knelt. He was only just alive and fading fast. There was nothing she could do except hold his head against her chest and murmur her thanks before he passed away.

As his eyes gave a final flutter, she heard, for the second time that afternoon, footsteps approaching at speed up a staircase. Holding Cope/Best's head in her lap, she had no time to react before Songsung Rong appeared in the doorway, a nasty little cosh in her hand. Lucy knew what was coming. She was unable to reach either of her guns and there seemed little point in trying to get to her feet: she'd just have further to fall.

She shut her eyes and waited for the blow.

___ In which two wolves go to
a better place, and Dr Norton
mixes up some drugs


Stella Fish had made a mistake. Well, two mistakes. Firstly, she hadn't killed Guna when she had the chance. If she'd known her cook was Guna Sesks and not the wholly fictitious Galina Balodis, she would have.

The name Guna Sesks was not entirely unknown in world-wide intelligence circles. She had the reputation of being something of a wrecking ball, one of the reasons Russian Intelligence had been keen to part company. They'd been so keen to part company that they'd sent six (to be on the safe side) Kevlared men, equipped with enough armament to bring down a small insurrection, to her apartment in the Moscow suburbs only to find it empty. Well, not quite empty. Guna had left a present in the form of two very hungry wolves which she'd managed to free from the Moskovsky Zoopark. Several minutes' fun and games ensued following the Kevlared men's forced entry to the flat. When the fun and games were over, both wolves were unfortunately dead but four men required urgent hospital treatment.

The second mistake that Stella Fish made, in order to accommodate the unconscious Guna, was to move Sapphire Waters from the room with the secure bed to a second room. It contained nothing more secure than a barred window and a locked door with a goon of limited intelligence outside. This was fine as long as Sapphire remained Sapphire and didn't morph once more into Nemesis.

And Guna knew the Nemesis codeword.

For a short time, the house settled down into a peaceful rhythm as they waited for the evening when Sapphire was due to attend the presidential rally, primed and ready to become Nemesis and, well, go off.

'I don't understand who took the Kia.' It was Dr Henry Norton speaking.

'Or why.' That was Ralf, who preferred his cars shiny, fast and German.

'This is why I didn't want Balodis killed,' said Stella, exasperatedly. 'We need to find out who her accomplice is and where she's gone. Why the fuck did you have to hit her so hard, Ralf?'

Ralf, who thought he'd hit the cook hard enough to ensure she never woke up at all, merely grunted.

Stella turned to Norton. 'Haven't you got anything in your black bag to bring her round, Doctor?' The doctor shared Ralf's opinion that it would be better if Galina Balodis stayed unconscious for as long as possible. Or for ever. After his unfortunate experience the previous day when Sapphire Waters had woken up chained to the same bed now occupied by the Balodis woman, he didn't want to risk something similar happening again. Even though the cook was unlikely to be as dangerous as Sapphire in her Nemesis *alter ego*. Or quite as sick.

But Stella was insistent that Norton try to revive Galina Balodis. The doctor had some Ritalin in his bag which probably wouldn't work but which meant he could at least tell Stella he'd tried. Despite her former position as Senior Scientific Officer in the CIA, Stella Fish had no idea what Ritalin was or looked like, so the substance Norton drew into the syringe he was preparing to inject the cook with was actually potassium chloride. A dosage to terminate a horse.

He returned grudgingly to the secure room and Ralf, who would have approved wholeheartedly of the doctor's choice of medication had he known about it, went with him and, taking no chances, led with his gun. Stella, also ignorant of the potassium chloride, stayed by the open door as befits a true leader.

The stocky cook was still unconscious, lying on her back, both arms strapped to the rails running down each side of the bed and secured by hefty padlocks. Her breathing was heavy and even. The bed, Norton knew, was firmly secured to the floor. He noted that the cook's arms looked unusually muscular for a female but then cooking did require a certain amount of heavy lifting. Full saucepans and the like.

Guna wasn't unconscious. She was acting. Her instructors back in Russian Intelligence had told her often that she should have been on the stage although, with her physique, not with the Bolshoi Ballet. She'd been awake for fifteen minutes. Her head hurt and her ego was bruised. These two things were making her very unhappy so she was pleased to see, through nearly closed eyelids, that company had returned and that the door had been left open.

There were, it is true, a few minor difficulties. One, both arms were padlocked to an immoveable bed. Two, the man who had hit her and would therefore have to be the first to die, was pointing a gun at her. Three, the doctor had a full syringe which he was preparing to stick in her upper arm, something that she would rather didn't occur. And four, her instructions from Melhuish had been clear: find out who was due to be assassinated, how and by whom, stop that happening, report back and please try not to kill anyone until all the above had been achieved. He had been at pains to emphasise this last point.

Still, she thought, situations change and she was pretty sure she could plead a convincing case. And she really, really didn't want that syringe stuck in her.

She heaved up with both arms, exerting as much strength as she could muster. As much strength as she could muster was a lot more than most people could muster and she'd already realised that the straps holding her to the bed were not, as they probably should have been, made from best-quality leather, Dyneema or Kevlar, but some form of polyester webbing. There could be only one winner.

Several things happened rapidly at this point. She threw herself at the doctor first. Always skittish, the doctor twitched to one side, overcompensated and skewed back. For once in his life, Dr Norton MD fulfilled his Hippocratic oath and did no harm – to the patient. Instead, he found that he had inadvertently injected himself in the neck. Had the syringe contained Ritalin, this would have caused him the minor inconvenience of keeping him awake longer than normal. He had just time to murmur, 'Oh shit,' before he slid, unconscious, to the floor with a suddenly limited lifespan.

By this time, Guna had wrapped one arm lovingly around Ralf's throat as her other hand busily relieved him of his gun. She only had seconds to realise her ambition of killing Ralf first before the doctor's demise beat her to the punch and using the gun would obviously be the quicker choice. But strangling was more fun.

As it turned out, Norton's and Ralf's deaths were virtually simultaneous. Which Guna could live with.

As Ralf hit the floor next to the doctor, the now ex-cook saw that during this brief kerfuffle, Stella Fish had vacated the doorway. It seemed to Guna that capturing her and finding Sapphire was the least she could do to get herself back in the CIA's good books after blowing her cover and killing Ralf and Norton.

She sprinted into the corridor. It was empty but it only took her a few more seconds to discover her prey holed up in a room at the other end of the passageway with a groggy Sapphire sitting on the edge of a bed rubbing her eyes. Guna noted that this bed lacked anything resembling polyester strapping or padlocks. Stella was backed up against a window holding a small automatic which was pointed straight at Guna as she slid into the room. Guna had Ralf's gun but realised that she'd made the embarrassingly rookie mistake of sticking it in a pocket before setting off down the corridor in pursuit of Stella.

She became the second person in only a minute to mutter, 'Oh shit,' as Stella's bullet hit home.

_\_\_ In which Sofija tapes a man to
     a chair, and Dawson asks some
     questions

When Dawson came round on the grubby, carpet-tiled floor, it was because Sofija was pouring water over his head from a large, dirty jug which she'd found behind the bar.

'Are you all right?' She sounded genuinely anxious.

'Apart from whatever bacterial infection I might get from that jug, yes, thanks,' he spluttered, wiping his face with a hand sticky from contact with the surface of the bar counter. The water at least removed most of the stickiness. It also helped the general waking up process so he started to push himself slowly to his feet, an operation that speeded up considerably when Sofija took a hand. Feeling woozy, he moved to a chair and sat. There was a pain centre situated just behind his left ear and when he reached up, his hand he felt a significant swelling. He studied his fingers. No blood. A good sign, he decided.

A muffled grunting caught his attention. He glanced up and saw the huge man who had crashed into him sitting on another chair not ten feet away. The man's arms and legs were securely taped to the chair and more tape encircled the lower part of his face, hence the muffled grunting. Although the man's nose was not taped he appeared to be having some trouble breathing; Dawson hadn't had time before he'd been flattened to check his attacker's nasal configuration but he had a feeling that its current misshapen appearance might be new.

'Did you do that?' he asked Sofija.

'Who you think do it? There no one else here. He squash you so I hit him.' Dawson nodded appreciatively. 'Then I find duck tape and tie him up. We question him together. He may know where is Lucy.'

'Good idea,' said Dawson. 'Perhaps he'll quack.'

'I take tape off face now,' said Sofija to the man whose eyes betrayed a trace of fear at the prospect. Having been on the receiving end of Sofija's fist, he was doubtless concerned about the amount of flesh he might lose during the removal of the gag. Dawson couldn't imagine Sofija being gentle about this and the man seemed to concur. Maybe the thought of even more pain would prompt him to spout information like a geyser.

This turned out to be a correct assessment on all counts. Sofija whisked the duct tape off his mouth in half a second flat, an operation that involved some skin losing its grip on the man's face. In the circumstances the scream of pain, although heartfelt, was surprisingly short-lived. 'Fuck!' yelled the man and then, in attempting to rub his bleeding mouth on his shoulder, he succeeded in jarring his broken nose, which prompted a second 'fuck!'. Dawson, genuinely concerned, would have liked to give the man something to mop up the blood and help assuage his pain but there was nothing available in the bar that wouldn't likely add salmonella to his list of ailments.

After gulping a few mouthfuls of air the man looked up at Sofija. 'You are a madwoman,' he mumbled. 'This is a respectable bar. My bar. You cannot just break in here and assault me. I am calling the police.'

'No police,' said Sofija. 'This not their concern.' She glanced at Dawson, as if for approval. 'I hit this *paks pätt* again and then he tell us where Lucy is.' She took a step forward, fist raised. It was enough.

The bar owner turned his battered face away from the prospect of more punishment. 'I don't know anyone called Lucy but the other two were taken away an hour ago. There's no one here but me.'

'Which other two?' demanded Dawson.

'Look, mister,' he said quickly. 'If you keep this madwoman

away from me, I will tell you everything I can. This is nothing to do with me. I'm paid to keep my mouth shut and not ask questions.' He repeated, 'This is a respectable bar.'

'Your idea of respectability doesn't agree with mine,' said Dawson, who nevertheless put a restraining hand on Sofija's arm. She glowered up at him but dropped the threatening pose and sat in the chair Dawson had just vacated. 'Carry on then. But make it quick. First off, what's your name?'

The man licked his chafed lips and nodded. 'Arthur Samson. I own this place. It's not much but it keeps me going. Only just though. Journalists and out-of-work dockers don't spend much.' He spat on the dirty floor, either to express his opinion about the munificence of his clientele or to get rid of some bloody phlegm. 'If people want to pay me to keep quiet about stuff, then I can't afford to object. And some of these people are very dangerous. It's not just money I have to worry about.' By now the floodgates had opened. 'Until today, it was only meetings. I kept my head down and let them get on with it. No harm done. I'm not interested in politics.' He spat again.

This was interesting. 'Politics?' echoed Dawson. 'Be more specific.'

Samson looked at them. 'You're not South African,' he said. 'What concern are our politics to you?'

There was a trump card waiting to be played so Dawson threw it on the metaphorical table. Not a real table; a card would have stuck to one of those. 'You've heard of MI6, I presume,' he said. 'The British Secret Service. That's who I work for and we have a very urgent concern.'

Arthur Samson looked as if he was about to burst into laughter, despite the blood still oozing from his mouth and nose. But then he looked at Sofija's still scowling face and thought better of it. He just shrugged. 'If you say so. Do you know of a man called Phukuntsi?'

'I do,' said Dawson. He remembered Rebecca Erasmus telling them about Phukuntsi that morning. He'd laughed when he'd heard the name, thinking it could knock Canaan Banana off top spot in the league table of World Leaders With Ridiculous Names. He wasn't laughing now. 'Go on.'

'Phukuntsi used to be a regular customer. Then he got elected to the National Assembly and suddenly this place wasn't good enough for him. But in the last few months he's been holding meetings here. In my back room.'

'Who's he been meeting?'

'It varied. But it was an Indian man in charge. Look, can you take the tape off my arms and legs? I'm helping you, aren't I?'

'Maybe. This Indian bloke. Does he have a name?'

'I was never told it. That's the truth.' Dawson believed him. 'I do have one more name though. A woman. She arranges the meetings and pays me. Her name is Asha. She's a dangerous bitch.' He glanced at Sofija. 'Like your friend here.'

Dawson came to a decision. 'Untie him, Sof,' he said. 'He's not the enemy.' Somewhat to his surprise, Sofija didn't object. She got up and went to the counter where she collected a knife and, with four easy movements, sliced cleanly through the bindings. She kept the knife.

'You said two people were taken away,' said Dawson. 'Do you know who they were and, most importantly, where they've been taken?'

Samson was rubbing his wrists. 'One of them,' he said without looking up. 'A police detective named Yeboah. He asks too many questions. I don't know the woman with him. She's older. White. Asha and her men had them in my back room overnight but took them away this morning. I was warned to keep quiet. Asha has a gun and wouldn't worry about using it. Perhaps you can deal with her, yes?' He looked at Sofija when he said this.

Captain Yeboah and an older white woman. Major General Brenda de Kock maybe, thought Dawson? 'And do you know where they were taken?'

'No,' said Samson, 'but I can guess. Phukuntsi has a house

backing on to the mountain at Bakoven. This place is usually full of journalists. Journalists talk. Drunk journalists talk more. I stand behind my bar and listen and I hear there is more to his house than meets the eye.' He pulled himself slowly to his feet and shambled to the bar where he found a pencil and a scrap of paper. 'This is the address.' Dawson turned towards the door but Samson placed a large paw on his shoulder.

'One thing more,' he said. 'We didn't get rid of apartheid all those years ago just to see Mandela's legacy shat down the pan by corrupt bastards like Phukuntsi, who are only interested in screwing our country for their own profit. If what you are doing helps to bring him down – and all the other fuckers like him – then I say, go get him.'

*When I woke up I was airborne. I was actually quite sur-
prised that I **had** woken up. It seemed high time that
Songsung Rong did away with me once and for all. At
first I had little idea how long I'd been in the helicopter
but a glance outside told me it could only have been a
matter of minutes. I could see the city laid out behind me
and we were flying low over what must be the far end of
Table Mountain, no more than three or four miles south
of the city. Geography is not a speciality of mine – I leave
that to Saul, who's a sort of human gazetteer – but Table
Mountain is a landmark even I couldn't miss.*

*We were low to the ground and getting lower. My
head hurt, as did my bullet-grazed shoulder. That was
twice Rong had hit me now and I was getting fed up with
it. Some people might say she'd evened things out as I'd
shot her in both feet back in Estonia, but I'm not some
people. My wrists were tightly bound and while my ankles
were free, I could see no obvious way of unlocking the
cross-strap seatbelt pinning me to the seat. Nor could I fly
a helicopter and were I to successfully disable the woman
next to me, we'd probably crash. Definitely crash. Low to
the ground or not, that didn't seem like the best plan. I'd
bide my time.*

*Rong glanced dispassionately across. 'You're awake,'
she said.*

*'Nothing gets past you, does it?' Speaking made my
head hurt even more and the rocking of the whirlybird
and the thwump-thwump of the rotor blades wasn't helping either. 'So, what's the plan then, Lanky?' I continued
conversationally. A chinwag might help me forget the
pain in my head. I was wrong. Or Rong, ha-bloody-ha. I
shook my head. I was getting befuddled. Being hit with a*

*blackjack can do that to a girl. It'd be good to know why I was still alive, preferably before I wasn't any more. 'You killed Charles Gulliver,' I stated. 'Was that deliberate or were you after me?'*

*'Hah. One year in this business and already milady has the inflated sense of self-importance. My instructions were to dispose of Andrew Gulliver's brother. I was unhappy about this. I should not have been taken away from South Africa at this important time. Somebody else could have done the job; it was a trifling matter.'*

*I kept my anger in check, bound as I was.*

*'But then I thought that if I could kill what you English call two birds with the single stone, then that would be satisfactory. My feet still give me pain, especially at night. I have spent months lying awake in my bed thinking of ways to make you suffer. And here you are, serendipitously.' Let's do right by Rong: her English was remarkably good. I don't think I'd ever used the word serendipitously in my life.*

*'So why am I not dead yet?'*

*'Killing you now would not satisfy me. I do not have time to make you suffer as my feet have suffered. The doctors say I may soon be in a wheelchair. So, suffer you must. But first, I have other duties to perform. Less pleasurable duties but the short additional wait is of no consequence. You will die tomorrow and you will not enjoy the experience, believe me.' I believed her. 'This is only what you would expect, Miss Smith, no?' she continued, peering through the plexiglass bubble, searching for something, a landing spot maybe. 'It is the game we play. We are alike, you and me, so in many ways it is a shame. You have been a worthy adversary.'*

*"Have been": so she was writing me off already. Also, I wasn't too sure about the "we are alike" part of that monologue, easily the longest speech I'd ever heard her*

make. She, after all, was a six-foot three-inch Chinese with cropped black hair, swimmer's shoulders and a strangely aquiline nose; I was nearly a foot shorter, blonde and pale and, though I say it myself, possessing a rather dinky little schnozzle I was quite proud of. Even so, I sort of caught her gist.

For now, I was still alive and the longer I could remain that way, the longer I had to free myself or for help to come along. Maybe from Saul's direction. I hoped he'd spotted the car into which the late lamented Cope and Best had bundled me and would be tootling along in, if not hot, then at least warm pursuit.

And then we landed, so softly it hardly registered. Rong certainly knew how to fly a helicopter, sore feet or no sore feet. Perhaps I could get her to teach me once I was back in charge of proceedings. We were in a small hollow on the mountain. Rong reached forward, flicked a couple of switches and turned a small key on the right side of the console. As she pocketed the key, the thwumping of the rotors slowed and stopped. I tried to memorise what she was doing for future reference. I was fully aware though that I'd have to learn how to (a) start the machine, (b) keep it in the air and, most importantly, (c) land it without killing myself and anyone with me. And before all that, I'd need to get the key off her, so all in all noting what she'd done wasn't really all that helpful.

She got out of the helicopter, disappearing from my sight before reappearing on my side of the contraption, cosh raised in her left hand. I thought for a moment she was about to biff me on the bonce again. Instead she flicked open the clasp of my seatbelt before stepping back. 'Out.' It seemed rude not to comply and there was also the cosh to consider.

But where the hell was she taking me?

__ In which some journalists try to
   look menacing, and Dawson gives
   van der Grieke 50 Rand

Dawson and Sofija were indeed in warm pursuit. Dawson
was mildly surprised to find their car still sitting where they'd
left it, right outside the Dockview Bar. However it was not sitting by itself; leaning on it were three men, seedy-looking,
down-at-heel. Two of them, both in their twenties and wearing
the sort of surly expressions that good mothers would have
told them to wash off with soap and water, straightened up
as Sofija and he reached the top of the steps leading up from
the bar's broken door. The third man carried on leaning on
the car. It looked as if he might fall down without its support.
He was old, almost emaciated, and Dawson could hear him
wheezing.

'What's been happening here?' asked one of the younger
men, moving closer. 'Why's the door broken? Who are you?
Where's Arthur?'

Dawson smiled. He didn't feel particularly worried by the
menacing air the men were doing their best to project. Partly this was because they hadn't really nailed the menace but
mostly it was because he had Sofija standing next to him.
And Sofija had just acquired a nifty little knife. Not that she'd
need it to do damage to these two should that become neces-
sary. He felt her stir beside him as the men approached and
put a hand gently on her arm. He thought he knew who these
blokes were, if only from the number of questions they'd asked.

'I believe you may be journalists,' he said. 'Yes, there's been
a small fracas in the bar but Arthur's fully open and will be
pleased to answer any questions you may have while he's pouring your lagers.'

Defused by Dawson's smile, his assertion that the bar was
now open and also, it must be said, by something indefinable

about the woman with him, the man who had spoken first said, 'OK, but again, who are you?' all the while keeping a wary eye on Sofija. His companion had taken a cautious step back.

'His name is Dawson,' came a thin voice from behind the two men. Their elderly companion was pushing himself upright and walking carefully across the pavement. 'He is British Secret Service and his companion, if I am not mistaken...' – by now he had reached the group at the top of the steps – 'is either Guna or Sofija Sesks. I apologise, my dear, my eyes are not as good as they were and it is nearly dark, *ja*?'

Over the course of the year, Dawson had been astonished on more occasions than he cared to remember but the old man's accurate assertion of who he was and, more remarkably, who Sofija was, jumped straight to number one in his personal astonishment hit parade.

The two younger journos were either entirely uninterested in the fact that a British spy was standing in front of them or were much more interested in the fact that the bar was now open and lager awaited them. They were already halfway down the steps to the broken door as the old man stopped speaking. Sofija took a pace towards him, scowling, and Dawson again laid a restraining hand on her arm, much good though it would do if she'd decided that damaging the old bloke would be a useful thing to occur.

There seemed little point denying who they were. 'You have us at a disadvantage, *meneer*,' he said, feeling quite proud that he'd brought to mind a word of Afrikaans. 'Who am I addressing?' Beside him, Sofija emitted a small growl. She didn't really do polite. Also, they were in a hurry.

But Dawson wasn't to be hurried. 'My name is van der Grieke,' said the old man. He looked about ready to fall down so Dawson opened a rear door of the car and showed him inside where he could sit. He'd thought about taking the bloke into the bar to have a chat in the limited comfort the Dockview could provide but doubted if Arthur Samson would be doing cartwheels – an unlikely prospect anyway, given his size – should Sofija in particular return.

'So, who are you, old geezer?' said Sofija, jumping into the front seat of the vehicle and turning to face van der Grieke as he made himself comfortable. Dawson slid in alongside him, wondering where Sofija had picked up the word geezer.

'Calm down, young lady,' said van der Grieke. 'You have no argument with me. I work for Die Burger.'

'What is that? Like McDonalds, yes? You too old to flip the burgers. You should retire.'

Dawson laughed. 'No, Sof, Die Burger's a local newspaper. So, Mr van der Grieke, you're a newspaperman who knows all about us. This is Sofija Sesks by the way, not Guna.' Sofija grunted from the driver's seat. 'I won't ask how you know. Your colleagues seem more interested in getting a drink.'

'*Ja*. They write what they are told to write. But everyone knows The Greek and I know everything.'

'And, knowing everything, you've come here to tell us something, is that it?'

The Greek laughed, which turned into a wheeze and then a cough. 'If he has something to tell us, he need to do it before he die,' observed Sofija. 'We are in hurry, remember?'

Van der Grieke waved a bony hand dismissively. '*Nee, nee*, I have nothing to tell you. This is a coincidence. I knew that you and your friend, Lucy Smith, the spy who is an English countess, were in Cape Town but I was not expecting to meet you here.' He paused. 'Perhaps, though, it is not surprising. I am simply here for a drink. I come here most nights. It is not a lovely bar but it is full of surprises. Tonight, the surprise is you, Mr Dawson.'

The old reporter really did know everything, reflected Dawson, although Lucy wasn't actually a countess, not until her father popped his clogs anyway. He had a thought and handed van der Grieke the scrap of paper with the address that Arthur Samson had written down. 'Before you get some lager inside you, what can you tell us about this place?'

'Lager, pah,' said The Greek. 'Watered down piss, especially here. *Nee*, I am a whisky man.' He looked at the address. 'Phukuntsi's house.' He made as if to spit dismissively, whether at the lager on offer in the Dockview or at the name Phukuntsi, Dawson wasn't immediately sure. Van der Grieke's next words clarified things. 'Yes, that is the place to go and the time to go is now. Phukuntsi is a pawn but even pawns can deliver checkmate and when the stakes are the natural resources of South Africa and the exploitation of its people, then pawns can become kings – and kings must be toppled. You hear what I say?'

Dawson had a dawning realisation that he was being asked to play a major role in trying to stop something very big and very bad.

'Do you have a gun?' said van der Grieke.

'Will we need one?'

'Maybe. My sources tell me that two police officers have disappeared.'

'Captain Yeboah and Major General Brenda de Kock,' Dawson said.

'Ah, you may be cleverer than they say, Mr Dawson.'

Dawson was used to comments like that by now. 'You mentioned my partner, Lucy Smith. You don't happen to know where she might be, do you?'

'Alas, no. I thought you would be with her.' He turned his near-skeletal head towards Sofija. 'She is prettier than this one, *ya*?' and he laughed again.

Dawson looked warningly at Sofija in case any thoughts of knifework were re-entering her head but she merely shrugged. 'What?' she said. 'Is true. We both know this.'

'Have you heard of a man named Patel, Mr Dawson?' said The Greek. Dawson nodded. 'Then you will know that you really should be going to this house armed.' The old man looked at Sofija. 'And not just with that knife you have under your jacket, Miss Sesks.'

Dawson climbed out of the Mondeo, reached into a back pocket and extracted a 50 Rand note. 'Get yourself that whisky,' he said, passing it to The Greek, who produced a business card in exchange.

'Call me when you have done what needs doing, Mr Dawson. Captain Yeboah is a friend of mine.' He paused at the top of the steps. Dawson thought about assisting the old man down them but imagined that, frail as van der Grieke was, he had already descended them successfully on countless occasions. 'But I think maybe I will see you at the rally tonight.' He laughed again before disappearing inside the Dockview.

_ In which Hansie Coetzee opens a drawer,
and hides behind some bushes

Hansie Coetzee had sent Lucy and Dawson off to the Dockview Bar on what he believed to be a fool's errand. He still harboured doubts about the two MI6 agents, especially the man, despite Rebecca's confidence in them. Having ensured they had seen him striding away down Wale Street, he returned to the SSA office via a back-double and made his way to the desk of the Assistant Deputy Director of Domestic Intelligence. He had always mistrusted Gilbert: the man was away from his desk without obvious reason far too often. Today's wholly unwarranted blocking of Asha Mbaso's personnel file had exacerbated that mistrust. And as he'd seen Gilbert drive away following the unsatisfactory conversation with Dawson and Smith, a sixth sense had suggested to Coetzee that now might be a good time to undertake a little investigative work.

At first, this investigative work did not produce any useful results other than the mild revelation that the Assistant Deputy Director's tipple of choice was Jack Daniel's, which he found in the only locked drawer in Gilbert's desk. Unlocking the drawer had taken him seconds and it took only a few seconds more to discover the other three drawers were mostly empty. Coetzee sat back on his ham-like haunches to reconsider. At which point it struck him that there was something odd about the bottom two drawers. He opened them both again. He was right. Although the two compartments were identical on the outside, the inside was a different matter. The one containing the JD was a little deeper than its counterpart, which contained nothing more than a stapler and a few pens.

The drawer had a false bottom.

Coetzee had no time to look for whatever mechanism opened the concealed compartment and the false bottom put up limited resistance when he smashed his gun butt into it to reveal a notebook, inside which was a hastily scribbled address. More accurately, part of an address but it was enough. 'Very careless,' he grunted in satisfaction. He believed he had time enough to find the place before he needed to return to Middelste Vallei. Rebecca would be angry but her anger would not last for long if his sixth sense proved correct. And it usually did.

As if on cue, his phone vibrated in his pocket. He needed no sixth sense to know that it was Rebecca calling to find out why he wasn't back at the winery to add his protective bulk and assist in escorting Jacob Dlamini to the rally later. He stared at it for no more than two seconds before switching it off. Collecting his car from the office car park, he drove out of the city, heading for Hout Bay on the southern side of Table Mountain.

It took the lieutenant rather longer to find the house he was looking for than he'd expected. The scribbled address was incomplete, and Hout Bay, especially on the Table Mountain side, comprised a considerable number of winding roads with widely scattered houses. He eventually tracked the property down along the upper reaches of the Hootbaairivier, some way north of the town. Leaving his car out of the way of prying eyes a little distance away, Coetzee trekked sweatily as close as he could to the house: white, two storey, colonial style, not large but with a long lawn leading to a stand of trees beyond which the lower slopes of the mountain reared.

He hid himself behind some bushes fifty metres away. What or who he was waiting for he had no idea but for the moment, he decided against going up to the house and knocking on the door. Whoever was inside, they were unlikely to be friendly and he had no idea how many unfriendlies he might face. He'd hardly begun his vigil when he heard the unmistakeable sound of a gunshot.

Deciding that the gunshot was too interesting a development not to be investigated, he hauled himself upright, pulled his own pistol out of its underarm holster and sprinted towards the house, gravel flying as he skidded to a halt with his back pressed hard to the white stuccoed wall next to the oak front door. He had heard no further gunshots during his mad dash across the front lawn and gravelled driveway.

Hansie paused to regain his breath, gun held in both hands, pointing at the ground. As silence still reigned, he edged sideways to the door and tried the handle. It gave under his touch and the door opened a few centimetres. With a violent rush, he hurled himself through the door and flung himself down on the highly polished oak floor, banging a knee painfully on a side table as he did so and sliding a couple of metres forward, his body twisting uncontrollably through ninety degrees on the slippery wood flooring. He was getting too old for this.

He listened but heard nothing, so pushed himself to his feet and started searching. The first two rooms, a dining room and adjacent kitchen, were empty, but the kitchen smelt like something dead had been kept unrefrigerated for longer than it ought to have been. The third room contained a dishevelled bed and a small table. Also, two bodies, both male. Gun to the fore, Hansie kicked both the corpses hard in order to confirm their deadness.

One of them had made it to late middle-age before he'd expired and it didn't take Coetzee long to suspect that the cause of death was whatever had been in the empty syringe sticking out of the man's neck. The second man was younger, bigger and had no syringe sticking out of him. Hansie rolled him over. No obvious bullet holes, so he wasn't the subject of the shot he'd heard from the bushes. He was still dead though. Hansie looked more closely. The man's neck was beginning to show heavy, dark bruising. Strangulation then but whoever had done the strangling had brought an enormous amount of force to the task; the victim wasn't puny. Coetzee tightened his grip on his gun and left the room.

*Songsung Rong and I were somewhere on Table Mountain in a small, flattened dip in the terrain. We were surrounded by rocky slopes with clumps of unidentifiable trees hiding us from any casual observers. I doubted that many casual observers strayed this far south on the mountain in any case. Thin swirls of mist curled around, nowhere near as thick as the last time I'd been on the mountain but even so, it had taken some skill to land the chopper here. The nearest branches of the trees were little more than a dozen feet from the rotor blades.*

*'Follow the path,' said Rong and pushed me in front of her. I'd almost forgotten the gunshot graze in my shoulder, so sore was my head but she pushed me right on the wound. A wave of nausea overcame me and I nearly fell.*

*'Fuck sake,' I shouted. Maybe a passing hiker would hear me but it was early evening with the light fading, the cable car was closed for the day and any hikers long since gone home for their supper. I took a few deep breaths and started walking, Rong and her cosh keeping their distance a few paces behind. I was quite honoured that, with my wrists trussed, my head pounding and my shoulder the recipient of a passing bullet, she was still so cautious. That was undoubtedly how she'd stayed alive for so long in this game, as she called it, and why my own future participation looked limited.*

*We didn't have to walk far. 'Stop,' she said after no more than thirty steps. I stopped.*

*'Look down.' I looked down. I could play this game for ever. I spotted a round metal cover set into the ground, maybe three feet in diameter. It had been virtually unnoticeable, what with the oncoming dusk and the swirls of mist.*

'Turn to me,' Rong continued. I did as she said and saw the cosh had been replaced by a vicious-looking knife and a small automatic had appeared in her left hand. A quick slice with the knife removed the rope from my wrists, quite impressive as her eyes never left my face. She stepped a pace back again, the gun in her left hand unwavering. For a moment, I considered the chances of her not being ambidextrous and if so, whether I could make a grab for the gun. But she was five feet away and the weapon was capable of rapid fire which would do away with any requirement for accuracy. I reconsidered.

'Open it,' Rong said. I couldn't quite see how at first but then spotted a handle set flush with the cover. I bent down, carefully in case of any returning nauseous interludes, and flexed my fingers to try to remove the numbness caused by the ropes. I got hold of the handle, which responded to my pull, at first easily and then, as the weight of the cover came into play, with more resistance. The cover reached a vertical position and I looked down to see a series of rungs set into the side of a concrete shaft leading straight down into the mountain. It was unlit. I couldn't see how deep the shaft ran but the darkness didn't seem to be a consideration for my Chinese friend, who prodded me in the back with the gun and said, 'Down.'

Down the vertical ladder I went into the dark. A few seconds later Rong joined me and as she pulled the cover back into position over our heads, some low wattage lighting came on automatically. Hardly thinking about what I was doing, I stopped my descent abruptly and made a grab for Rong's foot which had crept to within two feet of my head. I should have known better. She was expecting it and kicked hard.

I fell.

About a second later I landed on the ground. It wasn't

a deep shaft at all, something I should have checked before attempting to plunge my captor to her doom. Only my pride – not for the first time – was hurt. I started to push myself to my feet but as I did so, I noticed a small brass object on the ground, half-obscured by the bottom rung of the ladder.

A key. It must have fallen out of Rong's pocket as she kicked me. I furtively closed my hand over it as if I was dragging my palm along the ground for support, and stood.

By this time Rong was standing beside me. The fact that she towered over me was even more apparent in the relatively tight confines of the gently downward-sloping, poorly-illuminated tunnel that stretched before us.

'Kneel,' she said. 'Hands behind your back.'

'I don't think so,' I replied. It seemed unlikely she'd brought me all this way to shoot me in this passageway under Table Mountain; apart from anything else the floor was pale stone and my blood would stain it. She'd also seemed enthusiastic about the pain she was planning to inflict tomorrow.

'Do as I say.' To add emphasis to her words she kicked me behind my right knee which had the desired effect. I found myself back on the dusty floor of the tunnel. Before I could move she'd somehow produced some tape and wrapped it half a dozen times round my wrists. They were behind my back but that didn't bother me too much and it actually helped the pain in my shoulder. It was a very minor triumph, admittedly, my second minor triumph after finding the key.

'Walk,' Rong said and, as she still had the gun, I got to my feet and walked.

The tunnel was a lot longer than the shaft had been deep and it took us a few minutes to reach a solid steel door barring the passageway. There was a keypad beside the door. Rong punched the numbers 0086 into the keypad. 86, I recalled from somewhere, was the international dialling code for China. Why do villains have such exceptional lack of imagination? She was obviously unconcerned by my seeing the code but then she'd already said I was due to be eliminated with much suffering.

There was another short stretch of corridor, this one carpeted and altogether more salubrious, and then Rong pushed me through a second door into a comfortable room containing a desk with a computer monitor sitting on it, showing the passage we'd just walked along. There was a swivel chair in front of the desk and next to it a softly humming fridge. A well-upholstered, brown sofa was set against a side wall. Rising from the sofa as we entered was a young woman with dead, brown eyes. Her expression told me she wasn't particularly happy to see us, especially Songsung Rong. Now that was interesting.

'Where are the other prisoners?' demanded Rong.

After a long pause the dead eyes flickered towards one of two steel doors in the back wall of the room. Rong held out her hand imperiously and, after a brief pause, the young woman took a set of keys out of her jeans pocket and handed them over. A triple-locked, steel door; no one was taking any chances. Rong took three long strides across the room and opened the door. She glanced in, gun raised, then turned to me.

'In,' she said. I obeyed with alacrity. I didn't want to give her the time to realise that she'd left me fully capable of removing the tape from my wrists. Physically I might be something of a wreck but I pride myself on my flexibility and I still had a fully working set of teeth.

As the door shut behind me and I heard the click of the lock, I saw I wasn't alone. Two pairs of eyes looked at me from metal chairs bolted to the floor up against the far wall.

'Hail, hail, the gang's all here,' I greeted them. My parents had forced me to watch far too much Gilbert and Sullivan as a child.

___ In which Dawson knocks on a door,
and Sofija meets some hatless men


A narrow drive wound uphill between clumps of trees for perhaps seventy metres to a large, well-lit modern house – the
address given to them by Arthur Samson. Dawson drove slowly past it and turned into another driveway further along the
road. He switched off the engine. This property was in darkness, which hopefully meant no one was at home.

'What we do now?' asked Sofija. It was a novel experience
for Dawson to have her consult him. 'We have no gun. We not
know how many *kuradid* are in house and knife only good to
kill one unless get lucky.'

'Granted all that, Sof, but gun or no gun, we do need to see
what's going on in that house. It may be a wild goose chase
but I'm betting it's not. I think we'll find some of our mates are
in there, good and bad.'

'I not know what you talk about,' said Sofija. 'Who are these
wild geese and how can mates be bad?' She slipped out of
the passenger seat and by the time Dawson joined her, she
already had the knife in her hand.

'Right, this is the plan,' said Dawson. He had no plan so
was just talking and hoping that something sensible came out
of his mouth. 'I'm going to march up to the front door and
knock on it. That'll cause a distraction while you scoot around
to the back and find another way in.'

'It madness,' said Sofija. 'You will distract them by being
killed. And where is scooter?'

'Got a better idea?' Sofija did not have a better idea. By
now they had traversed two front gardens and were approaching Phukuntsi's well-lit house. Maybe China paid his electric-
ity bill for him.

Sofija looked down at the knife in her hand and, reluctantly, held it out to Dawson. 'You take this,' she whispered.

'I manage without it.'

'You mean, you'd manage a lot better than I can,' Dawson said equally quietly. 'You're right, but if I show up armed, I'm more likely to be shot without question. And you may be able to dispose of a few black-hats with it.'

'They not wear hats. It not cold enough. But maybe you right. You probably just stab yourself anyway. Do not knock on door until you hear me give signal. I will hoot like owl.' Dawson wasn't sure if owls were necessarily native to this part of the world but nodded and Sofija drifted off into the darkness. He waited.

Five minutes passed and then he heard a muffled 'Toow-it-toowoo,' from somewhere around the back of the house. It didn't sound like any owl he'd ever heard. He couldn't help chuckling to himself as he strode up to the door and knocked loudly three times.

———

The laundry room window had opened easily with a quick twist of the knife. No alarms sounded. 'Amateurs,' Sofija whispered to herself. The room was in semi-darkness but an arch led into a large kitchen where a light had been left on over a copper cooker-hood. 'This kitchen bigger than my flat,' she growled. A quick look revealed no more effective weapon than the knife she already had so she moved silently on into a wide, white-carpeted hallway.

She hadn't gone far when a door to her left opened and a man came out. He was followed by a second man. Sofija had been right: neither was wearing a hat. They weren't noticeably armed either, which meant they were either the amateurs she'd suggested or they just weren't expecting to find a stocky Estonian woman holding a knife walking towards them. Sofija carried on walking towards them. After all, she had the knife and there were only two of them. A couple of seconds later there was only one of them and, deciding he'd rather like to stay in one piece, he scarpered, leaving his colleague on the white carpet, which was rapidly becoming less white.

Sofija looked inside the man's jacket and found what she was looking for. She wiped the knife blade clean on the dead man's jacket and stuck it in her belt before checking her newly-acquired pistol for bullets and continuing up the corridor.

___ In which Coetzee spots some
Doc Martens, and Stella Fish
runs into a wood

A breath of air in the passageway told Hansie Coetzee that there was at least one person still alive in the Hout Bay house. Through an open door at the far end he could see part of a sofa, which suggested it was a lounge of some kind. He moved cautiously towards it. Halfway along the corridor another door was ajar. He peered in. The room contained a further bed and little else. The house was oddly configured, Hanzie Coetzee thought. If all the bedrooms were downstairs, what the hell happened on the upper floor?

Hansie was about to carry on to the lounge when he spotted something at ground level, poking out from behind the door. It was a foot wearing a black Doc Marten boot. He pushed the door wider open and a second, identically shod, foot came into view and then the rest of the person to whom the feet were attached. It was a woman, youngish, solid-looking with a bandage wrapped tightly around her head, short, tousled fair hair poking out of it. She was lying on her back and at first glance she too appeared to be dead.

The deep red stain blotting her not inconsiderable chest suggested as much but, edging carefully around the door and bending, Hansie could see and hear the slightest of breaths. He had no idea who she was but it looked like she was the unfortunate recipient of the bullet he'd heard fired a few minutes ago. He decided reluctantly that the woman was not his primary concern. He needed to know who'd fired the shot. He'd come back later and call the emergency services if she was still alive. But he doubted she would be.

So he continued to the lounge, took another deep breath and kicked the door open. It crashed against something and rebounded. But by that time he was fully through and spinning through 180°, pistol at the ready. The room was empty but in front of him a French window was open; it was this that had caused the ripple of air he'd felt from down the corridor. He looked out on to a wide lawn reaching down to some trees a hundred metres away.

Halfway down the lawn, heading for the treeline, were two women. They were making haphazard progress. The older of the two, smartly dressed, slim with shortish, greying hair was attempting to chivvy the second woman along but was having some difficulty. The latter, younger, taller and with a shock of bright red hair, seemed to be resisting, none too steady on her feet.

Hansie didn't bother raising his gun. Landing a fifty metres shot in the failing light was an unlikely prospect. Sighing, he broke into another run.

He'd made up half the ground when the grey-haired woman turned her head and spotted the boulder-sized man moving with alarming velocity. She clearly didn't have the same reluctance about shooting as Hansie had and he heard the crack of the shot at the same time as a bullet grazed his right ear. He flung himself to the grass.

From his prone position he saw the younger woman break free from the older one's grasp and start stumbling across the lawn at an angle. There was now a gap between the two women. He steadied himself and fired at the one with the gun. He missed but it prompted her to forget about the redhead and, crouching and weaving, sprint remarkably quickly for the trees. Hansie tried a second shot but that too failed to find its target and by then the woman had disappeared from view.

He wasn't going to catch her, that was certain, and in the darkness of the woods he'd more than likely take a bullet for his troubles should he try. He turned and saw the younger, redheaded woman trip and stumble over some indentation in the lawn and end up on her knees. She appeared to have expended all her available energy; she rolled over and lay flat on her back. Still holding the gun, Hansie walked across and peered down at her.

Back at the house, Hansie laid the woman carefully on one of the sofas in the lounge and considered his options. His rescuee remained groggy and hadn't uttered a word as he'd carried her up the lawn. He was left with four people in the house: two males incontrovertibly deceased and two females, one of whom might be dead by now and another insensible.

He closed the French windows to the dusk and, noticing a key, locked the windows and pocketed the key. There were no other exits from the lounge apart from the door to the corridor and he decided that he needed to see to the stocky young woman with the gunshot wound. He was short on time. He took a chance and left the redhead lying on the sofa.

To his surprise, the woman in the other room was awake but in a pretty bad way. She tried to get up and speak when she saw him but failed on both counts. 'Lie still,' he instructed, and called for an ambulance. He had to mention the gunshot wound so knew the police would tag along. He had about ten minutes before they showed up, he reckoned. He ripped a sheet off the bed, tore off a strip and stuffed it into the bullet hole to try to stem the bleeding. Carefully raising her a few inches to check her back, he could see there was no exit wound, which complicated things. A hand grasped his wrist, surprisingly firmly given what a dire state the victim was in. 'Sofija,' the woman murmured. 'Sister. Call...' before lapsing back into unconsciousness. Hansie saw the unmistakeable bulge of a phone in a trouser pocket and gently pulled it out. A quick scroll revealed only three saved numbers, all identified by a single letter. One was S: S for Sofija possibly.

This Sofija would have to wait. The paramedics would look after whoever her sister was and he had no intention of still being in the house when they and, more pertinently, the police pitched up. And there was someone else he still needed to talk to.

He returned to the lounge where the red-haired woman was lying where he'd left her, scooped her unceremoniously up in his arms and headed for the front door. He'd just reached his earlier vantage point in the bushes when he heard the sirens approaching. He adjusted his burden, straightened his shoulders and trudged off to find his car.

The front door was opened by a man holding a gun, which suggested he wasn't expecting an Amazon delivery. 'Hi,' Dawson said with a smile. 'My name's Dawson. I'm here to see Mr Phukuntsi.'

The man didn't reply but gestured with his gun and, arms raised because that's the way things are done in these situations, Dawson entered a plush lounge, the muzzle of the pistol pushing hard into the small of his back. Another man sat in a large armchair with his back to him, facing a picture window showing myriad twinkling lights in the distance.

He didn't rise to greet his guest, which Dawson thought quite rude until he was pushed in front of the man and realised what a feat it would be for him to rise, certainly with any alacrity. He was huge and almost completely round, with a small head that merged into the gigantic body without the benefit of any noticeable neck to assist. Dawson stared and he stared back through disconcertingly deep-set eyes. Dawson decided he was getting the worst of the staring match; his eyes were starting to water. It wasn't so much the mountain's roundness as the fact that he was wearing the sort of multi-coloured Hawaiian shirt that must have taken a dozen seamstresses, working flat out, a week to complete. If there was a known colour on the spectrum not included in the shirt's design – although design was perhaps an ill-fitting description for the ill-fitting garment – Dawson failed to spot it.

Eventually, feeling that the silence was becoming a little oppressive – even though it was a good indication that Sofija was still alive and kicking – Dawson said, 'Mr Phukuntsi, I presume.'

The man nodded, something of an achievement given the lack of a neck. He spoke in a high, thin voice as though he'd sprung a leak. 'And you are Mr Dawson.' A thrill ran through Dawson. It was quite exciting that so many people knew who he was. 'Somebody else giving me trouble. You can join the others.' The thrill disappeared as quickly as it had arrived. Were Sofija and he too late? Phukuntsi looked at the man who still had his gun trained on Dawson. 'Is Patel in the house, Skittle?'

Skittle? The bloke didn't look particularly sweet to Dawson.

'No, boss,' said Skittle. 'But Gao Chang's here. Downstairs.' Phukuntsi started to say something else but immediately broke down into a paroxysm of coughing and spluttering. The corpulent body shook as though an earthquake had hit. Dawson took a step back but the prod of the gun barrel prevented him going too far. If this bloke hoped to be president, he'd better make it soon; he didn't look like he'd last much longer. Was this man really the Chinese government's choice to become president of the republic? There was no way the international community could take this buffoon seriously. But then he thought back to the UK's own recent history and realised that buffoons did sometimes, goodness knows how, make it to the top.

Gao Chang was in the house. In other words, Songsung Rong. Dawson didn't know if Phukuntsi knew that Dawson knew who she was but the willingness to toss names around meant that they didn't expect Dawson to be in any fit state to make use of the information. The mention of a downstairs was interesting though. As the room they were in was on the ground floor that could only mean there was a cellar or basement, and if Major General de Kock and Captain Yeboah were alive there was a fair bet that's where they'd be. Maybe Lucy as well. He wiped the thought that they might not still be alive from his mind and considered his odds. He really just had Skittle to worry about; Phukuntsi would only be a threat if he fell on top of him. Even so, Dawson didn't rate his chances highly. Skittle looked efficient and he had a gun.

Then the already poor odds worsened. A door in the far corner of the lounge opened and Songsung Rong stooped elegantly into the room.

'Lugay, my dear,' she said, striding across and bending like a reed into the earthquake, seemingly unafraid that she might be swallowed up by the tremors emanating from the armchair. 'You must calm down.' She stood sharply to her full six foot three inches and looked at Skittle. 'Do not stand there like an incontinent panda,' she said. 'Get the president's pills.'

'But I gotta look after this one. He could be dangerous.'

'Dangerous?' Rong said. 'This man is the least dangerous specimen in South Africa. I can handle him. Now do as I say and get Mr Phukuntsi's pills or you will not be leaving this house upright. My men would be delighted to take your job and anything else they like while they are about it.' Skittle skedaddled, scowling. A small cosh appeared in Rong's hand. Rong with a cosh was more of a threat than Skittle with a gun.

The brief exchange between Rong and Skittle meant two things. Firstly, unless she was bluffing, any number of Rong's men were close by, which meant that Sofija might have hit trouble. Secondly, there was clearly little love lost between the South African and Chinese partners in this operation.

Rong moved closer to Dawson and was about to say something when two gunshots rang out from somewhere beyond the door, each followed by screeches of pain. Both were male screeches, so not Sofija. Rong glanced towards the door and Dawson threw himself at the momentarily distracted Chinese woman.

This manoeuvre achieved only partial success. Slim she may be, but Rong possessed a core of steel that failed to buckle. For a comical second or two Dawson found his twelve and a half stone clinging to her, his feet several inches from the ground, before she eventually started to topple backwards. She lost her grip on the cosh as she tried to break her fall and Dawson managed to grab it. He made a mental note to inform

Lucy that he was now two-nil up in the game of grabbing-weapons-out-of-thin-air contest that he'd just devised. Dawson slid off the falling skyscraper just as she landed on top of Phukuntsi, who was immovable in his armchair. Whether or not the prospective president's deep-set eyes had managed to fully take in what was happening, Dawson was unsure, but he didn't look capable of the sort of rapid motion that would have allowed him to avoid Rong's descent into his lap.

Dawson was surprised only that she failed to bounce off. Instead, the mass gave way with a loud release of air, from which orifice he preferred not to speculate. With her fall nicely cushioned, Rong remained highly dangerous. Dawson stepped forward, cosh raised.

Then the door behind him opened.

'Step back, idiot,' said Sofija laughing. 'This work for professional. And woman.' Sensibly, he stepped back. Sofija had somehow acquired a gun and was pointing it between Rong's eyes.

Three minutes later, Dawson, utilising a curtain cord, had bound Songsung Rong and Phukuntsi together. It wasn't a completely expert job but seemed effective enough. Rong wasn't going to move fast lugging thirty stone of politician behind her.

'Good, now we find the police people,' Sofija said.

'Is there any more opposition in the house?'

'I not know but three less than there was.' Dawson guessed that Skittle was one of three she'd knocked over.

'Apparently there's a cellar,' he said.

'Good. We start there then.'

They moved cautiously out into the corridor. Seeing the prone figure of Skittle lying there, Dawson bent and relieved him of his pistol. He now had a gun and a cosh but the continued presence of Sofija was even more reassuring. 'By the way,' he said as they moved off down the hallway, 'you do know that owls don't actually say toowit-toowoo, don't you?'

'Yes they do. I read this in books.'

Dawson couldn't quite bring an image to mind of Sofija reading; she didn't seem the type. 'Don't they have owls in Estonia?'

'Maybe. I not orthodontist though.'

_ In which Asha Mbaso has an itchy
finger, and Sofija faints


When Gao Chang left, she'd added Lucy Smith to the growing list of prisoners. Then she'd handed the key ring to Asha Mbaso. 'Do not open this door,' she'd instructed.

'Where are you going?' Asha had asked.

'That is not your concern. Stay here. Do nothing.'

Asha had not replied. Whatever she decided to do, it wouldn't be nothing but for the time being, she returned to her sofa. Her gun lay on the desk next to her. She looked at it. Her trigger finger was getting itchy.

An hour later, she decided it was time to scratch the itch. Rong and Phukuntsi would have long since left to get to the football stadium. Patel would also be there; Asha was sure he was no longer in the house. She reached into her pocket for the keys, checked her gun and prepared to face her chosen victims: the two police pigs plus the blonde English spy, Dawson's friend. A bonus. She thought about explaining to them first why they had to die but decided against it; Asha wasn't much of a talker. She calmly opened the three locks, click, click, click.

Two things happened at that point. As the last lock clicked, the door was pulled open forcibly from the other side and Asha stumbled forward into the prison cell and received a punch to the jaw which sent her spinning back into the room she'd just left. She glimpsed a brief flash of fair hair.

Then the door to the corridor opened and none other than her first choice of victim, Dawson, entered. He had a woman with him. Both of them held guns. Then Asha was kicked hard in the back of the leg, she presumed by the blonde bitch who'd hit her. She fell to one knee and saw the stocky woman with Dawson point her pistol at her.

'No, Sof,' said Dawson urgently, pushing down hard on her arm. 'Not this one. We need her to tell us what's going on.' Sofia started to lower the gun.

'About bloody time you turned up,' said Lucy.

It was all the distraction Asha Mbaso required. Rolling over twice, she brought her own automatic to bear and aimed it at Dawson, who still had his hand pushing down on Sofija's arm. Sofija shoulder-charged Dawson and he crashed into the wall. In so doing, she placed herself in the line of fire and a bullet went through her right forearm. Doughty as she was, even Sofija couldn't resist the pain and sudden numbness. She dropped her weapon.

Asha aimed a second time at Dawson but found her gun kicked out of her hand. It skittered across the floor.

'Stay there,' snarled Lucy. She saw that Dawson now had his gun trained on Asha and called back to the doorway of the prison-room where the two police officers were standing watching. 'Temba, old chap,' she continued, walking across and picking up Asha's pistol, 'perhaps you'd like to make yourself useful with that rope I've just untied you from.'

Yeboah stepped forward with the rope in question. He set about tying Asha up. He wasn't gentle.

'You know,' said Dawson thoughtfully to Lucy, 'you're going to have to stop running away from me once we're married. You seem to get into so much trouble without me. And look what you've managed to do to your hoody.' He could see the blood-stain around the rip in the garment and another dried red smudge on her hairline but knew that if his redoubtable fiancée wasn't mentioning it then she'd hate him to show sympathy.

Brenda de Kock was by now busy bandaging Sofija's arm with a strip ripped from her own thin jacket. Sofija kept still but looked furious. 'Guna kill me,' she muttered. 'I will be laughing gas.'

'This is all very lovely,' said Lucy. 'We can have a catch up later and you can explain Sofija's presence over a nice cup of tea. But first, have you seen our old chum, Songsung Rong anywhere on your travels?'

Dawson, whilst thinking that not even a psychiatrist, let alone he, could adequately explain Sofija, nonetheless laughed and said, with just hint of complacency, 'Yes, as a matter of fact we have. We left her upstairs hugging Phukuntsi.'

—

Rong was no longer hugging Phukuntsi. The lounge was empty but there was a pile of curtain cord lying next to the armchair where they'd been.

'Fuck,' said Dawson.

'Never mind,' said Lucy. 'I'm guessing someone's untied them and since he's currently unaccounted for, I'm also guessing that someone was Patel. I'm only surprised Sofija didn't just kill them.'

'I've been stopping her killing people all evening,' said Dawson. 'That's why there are only three bodies.'

'I wonder where they've disappeared to?' said Lucy.

And then it hit Dawson. 'What's the time?' he said, urgently.

'Nearly half eight, why?'

'The rally. That's where they've gone. We've got to get there quick.

'What the hell are you talking about? What rally?'

'The presidential rally, Luce. Keep up. Where the Chinese are going to ordain their man.' Ordain might be the wrong word – there was nothing holy about what was likely to happen at the stadium – but it didn't matter; the point was made. 'And Rong will be there to kill Jacob Dlamini to ensure that ordainment happens. Trust me.'

'No, you wrong. Not Rong.' Sofija said confusingly. She had appeared behind them, right arm in a sling. 'Is Sapphire woman. She is killer robot. Stella Fish control her with Nemesis codeword.'

Lucy had just started to say, 'Sapphire? But that's ridiculous,' when Sofija collapsed in a dead faint.

'I told her not to move and to wait for the ambulance,' observed Brenda de Kock from the doorway, Temba Yeboah behind her. 'But she wouldn't listen.'

'She doesn't really do listening,' said Lucy.

'Who the hell is she anyway?' said Brenda.

'Long story. But in the meantime, what did she mean about Sapphire killing someone?' Lucy looked at Dawson.

'I'm not entirely sure,' he said. 'Stella Fish has her under some kind of mind control. And it's going to be at the presidential rally at the football stadium. That's why Rebecca and Dlamini have been lying low.'

Brenda grabbed his arm. 'Rebecca?' she said. 'You mean you know where my daughter is?'

'Yes, Ms de Kock.' Dawson smiled. 'She's safe. She's been hiding out with Jacob Dlamini at a winery at Stellenbosch. Now they'll be at the rally and Rong's on her way there with murder in her heart. If Sofija's to be believed, then Sapphire might be a problem too, although I don't get that bit. I left a car up the road but there's no way we'll get to Green Point by nine: the traffic will be horrendous.'

'I'm not so sure about that,' said Lucy, grinning. 'Major General, can we leave you to sort out the mess here please?'

'Of course. I've already got ambulances and backup on the way.'

'In that case, follow me, boys,' and Lucy set off at a dead run.

\_\_ In which Coetzee and Sapphire go
   for a run, and Stella Fish
   wears a wig


Coetzee had left his phone in his car. It took him ten minutes of hard pounding to reach the vehicle. Powerful as he was, it had been slow progress. At first he'd carried the red-haired woman but after five minutes she'd demanded to be put down. He was grateful to comply.

'Who the fuck are you?' the woman asked him. She sounded Irish. And angry.

'My name is Lieutenant Coetzee,' he replied. 'South African State Security. And what is your name?'

Sapphire had to think hard before replying slowly, 'Sapphire Waters. I think.'

Assuming she was who she thought she was, then Coetzee had found Smith and Dawson's missing MI6 colleague. 'Can you walk?' he grunted. Sapphire nodded. '*Goed*. If you can run, even better. We must get to my car as quickly as possible. Keep up.'

'But...'

'No buts. Your questions can wait. As can mine.' And he pounded off again. As Sapphire had no idea where she was and the light was fading fast, she followed. She was feeling a little better and found she could keep up with the lumbering lieutenant quite comfortably.

Hansie reached his car and switched on his phone, which lit up like a Christmas tree. Twelve missed calls, all of them from Rebecca Erasmus. The time shone brightly from the screen: it was approaching eight o'clock. The rally was due to start at nine.

He dialled Rebecca's number, climbing into the driver's seat as he did so and beckoning Sapphire round to the passenger side. Whether or not this man was indeed with the security services, she really had little choice but to go with him. She had spent the previous five minutes whilst running through the woods, trying to make sense of what had been happening to her but had largely failed; there were a lot of gaps in her memory. Coetzee got the car moving as his phone squawked into angry life. 'Be quiet, Rebecca, *asseblief*. I will have to meet you at the stadium. *Ja, ja*, I am all right. Jacob? *Goed*. Listen. I have someone with me. A girl. Irish. Miss Sapphire Waters. *Ja*, her. I do not know. I will ask her while we drive. We will be there in half an hour.'

He switched the phone off and slid it into a pocket. The hardly noticeable track they had been following became a paved road and houses began to appear.

'Now, young lady,' growled Coetzee. 'What was that place, who was the woman with you and who in god's name did all that killing?'

'Killing?' Sapphire said, astonished. She knew nothing about any killing.

———

It took Coetzee longer than the half hour promised to reach Green Point. The roads around the stadium were packed and the concourses teeming. The stadium was already close to its 55,000 capacity. Despite the relative lateness of the hour, people had come out in their thousands to hear the candidates. Especially Jacob Dlamini. There was an overwhelming desire to see the uncorrupted elected.

But not by everybody, Hansie thought, as he flashed his security ID and squeezed into a VIP parking space. It was 8:45. Having listened to what Sapphire had been able to tell him during the drive, he now remembered where he'd previously seen the older woman who'd escaped into the trees. Stella Fish, Sapphire had called her. About two years ago, he and Rebecca had attended some do or other at the American Consulate.

He'd had to wear best dress uniform. He didn't like wearing any uniform, let alone best dress. It hadn't fitted him properly since before his thirtieth birthday. The Fish woman had been at the event, he was sure of it. He had the memory of an elephant. Jokes had been made about this in the past, although not for long. So she was American. CIA then. Jacob Dlamini had been confident the Americans weren't taking an active interest in the election but clearly he was wrong. This was not good news.

The football pitch was covered with temporary flooring and a large stage had been erected in front of the main stand. Colourful bunting abounded; this was the Rainbow Nation. The stage was still empty but the swelling music suggested it wouldn't be long before the five candidates appeared. A couple of hundred armed soldiers were in clear evidence around the stadium. Hansie would have expected nothing less but their presence failed to convince him that Jacob Dlamini was safe.

As they reached the suite reserved for Dlamini, he handed Sapphire over to a familiar security officer he believed to be reliable. 'Watch this one,' he said to the man and to Sapphire, 'We will speak again after the rally. Do not try to get away.' He disappeared into the suite.

—

Sapphire watched him go. The music was growing louder, full of the thump-thump-thump of African beats. Not knowing why she was there, she felt overwhelmed and slightly dizzy. The security guard, concerned, smiled at her and brought her a chair. 'Sit there, miss,' he said. 'Would you like a glass of water?' Sapphire nodded. The guard, deciding the woman looked harmless enough and actually not very well, went to get water from an adjacent kitchen. This was expressly not what Lieutenant Coetzee had instructed.

—

In an identical executive suite next door, a sweating Lugay Phukuntsi was receiving his final instructions from Mahatma Patel, who'd permitted the presidential stooge a glass of whisky to calm his nerves.

Patel regretted allowing himself to be mixed up in this Chinese charade but, whichever way it turned out, he had planned himself an exit route. He glanced around at the six other people in the box. Patel knew none by name. They were Gao Chang's men, three of Chinese appearance, the other three, local thugs. It seemed inconceivable that the Chinese government could be so candid about the whole business but it didn't seem to bother them.

—

Having delivered Phukuntsi to his suite, Songsung Rong had melted into the crowds in as much as any six-foot-three-inch Chinese woman could melt into a crowd of Africans. She was on the lookout for someone.

That someone was Stella Fish. While Rong was looking forward to doing away with the irritating, blonde Smith woman who had put bullet holes in her feet in Estonia, Fish's death was commanded by her superiors. Why, Rong didn't know. Fish would be here somewhere in this hot, overcrowded stadium and she was an old woman. It would be straightforward to finish her off, unnoticed in the throng.

—

Stella Fish had made straight for the stadium from the woods at Hout Bay. With Norton, Claxton and Ralf no longer available to her, only two of her men remained, the ones she'd sent off in pursuit of the appalling cook's accomplice, the person who had driven away from the house in the Kia. Stella cursed herself for not realising earlier that there were in fact two women but at least she'd left the cook dying. A mercy killing. Epicures everywhere would be cheering. Stella Fish's men had arrived within fifteen minutes of her call. They found her, a little bedraggled but still determined on her course of action, by the side of the M63. She'd slipped off her shiny, black court shoes as she ran so her feet were cut but that was of little concern. Once in the car and on the way to Green Point, she put her shoes back on and did her best to make herself look respectable. She donned a black wig from a bag on the back seat of the car.

Stella had several different identities available to her but her men did not, so on arrival at the stadium she was forced to leave them outside. They were of no use to her now anyway. Despite the concourses being packed and the music loud, she gained entry with no difficulty. She left her gun in the car. She wouldn't need it. All she needed was Sapphire Waters – Nemesis.

She had recognised the big Afrikaner who had showed up unexpectedly at the house, forced her flight and relieved her of Sapphire. He was Lieutenant Hansie Coetzee, State Security. Coetzee worked with Rebecca Erasmus. They were Jacob Dlamini's protection. Coetzee could therefore do one of two things, Stella concluded. He could take Sapphire to Wale Street but, given that Erasmus and Dlamini would be expecting him at the rally, he would not have time to get to the State Security offices first. Given that Coetzee had no idea how dangerous Sapphire was, he would take her with him to the stadium.

If so, then things were back on track. Hoping the wig would be disguise enough, she headed for the presidential hopefuls' executive boxes. Almost miraculously, there was Sapphire, sitting completely unattended in a corridor outside Dlamini's suite.

___ In which Temba Yeboah ducks,
     and some goats get
     a shock


'Where are we going?' The passageway led uphill and seemed to go on for ever. Dawson was puffing but was in a better state than Lucy, who had been shot in the shoulder and hit on the head. She was relying on sheer willpower. She unobtrusively flexed and unflexed her left hand a few times; it seemed to be working relatively well. It would have to do.

Behind them, Temba Yeboah stayed silent. He didn't know why he was there; no doubt he should have stayed with his superior officer back up in the lounge and furthermore, they were heading in entirely the opposite direction to central Cape Town and the football stadium. When Lucy Smith had said 'Follow me, boys,' and set off for the basement, it had seemed the most natural thing to do as she said. Access to the passage had been via a steel door just past the room where he and the major general had been locked up. Lucy had opened it using a four-figure code. How she'd obtained the code, Temba didn't know.

At the pace Lucy was setting, it took them only a couple of minutes to reach the foot of the shaft which led up to the secluded part of Table Mountain where Songsung Rong had left the helicopter.

'A helicopter? A purple helicopter. You're fucking kidding me,' said Dawson, poking his head into the night air. 'And who exactly is going to fly this thing?' Dawson peered at the maker's name to the rear of the door. 'This Robinson R22.' The only Robinsons he knew were a Crusoe and a Mrs. 'And how are we all going to fit inside? It's only got two seats.' This was true and, with a flat bulkhead hard up behind the seats, trying to get three people inside was going to be a squeeze, even if Lucy sat on someone's lap.

Temba joined them. Lucy turned to him. 'You're a policeman, Captain,' she said. 'Please tell me you're trained to fly a chopper.'

The look on his face wasn't promising. 'I'm a South African policeman, Miss Smith. I'm hardly trained to drive a car. I've never even been in a helicopter.'

'OK, then,' she said, smiling. Her watch told her it was now 8:40, too late to get back to the house. 'Dawson? Kev the Key ever give you any tips about piloting whirlybirds?'

Dawson was looking closely at the instrument panel and other controls. 'Not as such but it looks like we need a key to start the thing so let's take a shufty underneath.' Sitting in the pilot's seat, he bent down and peered under the console but couldn't see any obvious way of accessing the wiring. Lucy tapped him on the shoulder. She was holding the small brass key she'd picked up earlier at the foot of the shaft.

'This key, d'you think?' Dawson, without consciously considering the absurd thing he was doing, grabbed the key, inserted it into the keyhole and turned it clockwise. A light started flashing. 'Well volunteered, lover,' said Lucy, sliding into the right-hand seat. 'Good start,' she added. 'Try something else.' Dawson looked at her, lips pursed, and hand hovering over the mass of knobs and dials on the instrument panel.

'I thought you were going to drive,' he said.

'You're a much better driver than I am,' she said., 'and this looks like man's work to me. All the chopper pilots I've heard of are men. Princes mainly. You know, Andrew, William, people like that.'

'The only thing that's likely to happen if I manage to get this thing airborne is that it's going to fall like purple rain,' muttered Dawson.

'You can do it, big guy,' she said. She never called him big guy, not even in bed when he'd most like her to. 'But I'm happy to help.' She pointed to a switch, trying to remember what she'd seen Songsung Rong do and then thinking backwards.

'Try that one.' Dawson clicked it downwards. 'Now this one.' She reached over and clicked the second switch herself. The blades over their heads started moving, thwump-thwump-thwump. 'See? I'm helping. How hard can this be? I watched Long Tall Sally land it so we just have to do the opposite to that.'

Dawson shook his head. If he was a Catholic, he'd be crossing himself. Despite his lifelong atheism, he crossed himself anyway, hoping he'd been theologically wrong all his life.

Temba Yeboah, still standing close to the helicopter, ducked as the rotor blades started moving. 'What about the good captain?' said Dawson. 'Where's he going to sit?'

'Excellent point,' she said. 'Fancy hanging on underneath, Captain?' she shouted across Dawson over the noise of the rotors, which were now turning ever more quickly, although the chopper remained glued to the ground. Yeboah was already edging backwards in a crouch, miming a telephone call. 'I guess not,' she concluded.

'Better get back to the house, Temba,' Dawson yelled. 'See you at the stadium.' He paused. 'I hope.'

'Oh ye of little faith,' said Lucy but the increasing noise of the rotors drowned out her words. She pulled her door shut and Dawson followed suit. Remembering Rong's ear-defenders, Lucy unhooked them and placed them on Dawson's head. 'Pilot's privileges.'

The little machine was now vibrating so much that unless it took off pretty damn quick it would likely shake itself to pieces.

Lucy seemed relatively unconcerned. She pointed to a pedal. 'Press on that, mate,' she said. 'It's not there for ornament.' Dawson pressed down experimentally on the pedal and behind them the tail rotor burst into life, the shaking increasing as it tried to spin them sideways.

'OK,' Dawson murmured. He was beginning to enjoy himself. 'That does that. Now this looks like a hand brake.' He gripped it and, with a deep breath, released the handle. The helicopter shot upwards like a jack-in-the-box and spun dramatically through 540°. Lucy, still looking for some ear protection, lurched sideways and crashed into the door, which burst open. She found herself falling head-first out of the cockpit but managed to reach for and grab the skid before she fell the thirty feet or so back to the ground. Luckily she grabbed it with her fully operational right hand. With Dawson entirely unaware of how he achieved the feat, he somehow made the machine tilt to the left and Lucy, after a first failed attempt, managed to hook a leg over the skid and haul herself slowly upright. She climbed back into the cockpit and sat down, breathing heavily.

'If you didn't want me to come, you should have said before we took off,' she laughed.

'We've both come up with alternative careers now: me, chopper jockey and you, circus acrobat. Could come in useful when MI6 sack us again.'

Lucy had spotted the second pair of ear-defenders under the seat as she'd clambered back inside, so fished them out and put them on. Belatedly, she clicked the cross-belt firmly in place across her chest.

They only experienced a couple of near misses before Dawson, experimenting with the two pedals under his feet and what he thought of as the rudder and handbrake in front of him (actually, he later learnt, the cyclic and collective), brought the chopper under some measure of control. For half a minute they found they were carrying a sizeable bush with them that Dawson had inadvertently scooped up with the left skid as they'd traversed the top of the mountain. Two Himalayan Tahrs, who had been taking refuge behind the bush, narrowly avoided the same fate. 'I didn't know there were goats on Table Mountain,' said Dawson, conversationally, as he swerved to avoid a flock of Knysna Warblers, disturbed from their slumber by the rotors slicing off a few branches of the tree in which they'd been blissfully sleeping.

They were making erratic progress across the northern slopes of the mountain. Cape Town was stretched before them. Lucy touched Dawson on the shoulder and pointed to their left. 'There,' she said, having found the switch on the ear defenders that allowed them to converse. A couple of miles ahead was the floodlit doughnut of the football stadium. 'We'll be there in a minute. Better try and slow down and start to bring us lower. Have you thought about where you're going to land?' She'd nearly said crash but didn't want to ruin his confidence.

'I'd thought about inside the stadium,' Dawson said as it grew steadily larger through the windscreen. 'It's a football pitch, isn't it? Should be plenty of room and it'll avoid all that tiresome business getting through security.'

'That sounds like a good plan, dearest, but just in case you'd forgotten, there's a presidential rally about to start. There'll be lots of soldiers with guns who could decide it's a fun idea to shoot us out of the sky and ask questions later. Mind you, that would solve the landing problem.'

She wasn't wrong. By now the stadium was virtually beneath them, close under their skids, and they heard the double-crack of two bullets too close for comfort. 'Just warning shots,' said Lucy but as the pitch came into view they saw that landing on it wasn't an option anyway. It was covered with a throng of people, tens of thousands more filling the stands and all of them staring up at them. Three more bullets flew past and a fourth cracked the plexiglass windscreen. They were followed by a veritable hail of others.

The fusillade of bullets had the advantageous effect of scattering the crowd on the pitch. 'OK, that works,' said Dawson, and thrust the stick forward. They hurtled, nose down towards the stadium. The helicopter's unpredictable progress wasn't doing the soldiers' aim any good.

Dawson was wrestling with the sticks and pedals, sweat breaking out on his brow, as the firing intensified. Lucy, mouth clamped shut and holding grimly on to the sides of her seat, had a brief glimpse of Rebecca Erasmus and Hansie Coetzee standing on a balcony a few metres in front of them before, finally, a bullet hit something intrinsic to the helicopter's ability to stay airborne, and Rebecca and Coetzee disappeared, to be replaced by another balcony and a plate glass window.

They weren't going to make the pitch, Lucy realised.

She covered her eyes. Beside her, Dawson muttered, 'Oh fuck,' and did likewise.

___ In which a woman hides behind
a drinks trolley, and a plate
glass window breaks


The security officer emerged from the kitchen with a glass of water just as Stella Fish said 'Nemesis' in a clear, calm voice from the top of the stairs a few metres away. The word meant nothing to him but he saw the red-haired woman snap to attention, all signs of illness gone, and look around with narrowed eyes. Whether Sapphire's programming was fully operational – or not, as the late Dr Norton had suggested – Stella could do no more and melted away down the stairwell.

'Are you OK, miss?' he said, moving closer. 'Here's your water.' Sapphire stared at the man, then turned and headed towards the door into Dlamini's suite. A second guard stood outside.

Sapphire approached him. The flap of his gun holster was tucked back, affording rapid access should it be required. Apart from a slightly strange look in her eyes, the woman appeared harmless and he'd seen her arrive earlier with Lieutenant Coetzee and saw no reason for concern. He smiled and took a step across to block the door. 'I'm afraid I can't let you in, miss,' he said, 'But I'm happy to pass a message to Lieutenant Co...'

He got no further. His colleague, still holding the glass of water, saw the redhead come to a halt and then, in the blink of an eye, she had a gun in her hand and his fellow officer was falling to the ground clutching his midriff. The woman helped him on his way with a shove and calmly opened the door. Dropping the water, the first guard fumbled for his own gun and fired off a shot which crashed into the door as the woman shut it behind her.

Sapphire looked calmly around the suite. There were only four people in it.

None was the person she was looking for.

Seeing the gun in Sapphire Waters' hand, Hansie Coetzee realised he'd made a grievous error in bringing her to the stadium. He ran towards her, groping for his own weapon in its under-arm holster. Before he could free it, Sapphire side-stepped and hit him over the head with the butt of the gun she'd taken off the security guard. He fell to the floor, fully conscious but with a cut opening above one eye. Rebecca Erasmus flung herself at Jacob Dlamini and pushed him to the ground. The young, female stadium employee, tasked with es-corting the presidential candidate to the stage, screamed and dived behind a drinks trolley.

It was quickly apparent that Sapphire, after a quick scan of the room, had no interest in any of them. There was a sliding door out to a balcony overlooking the pitch. She walked calm-ly to it, slid it open, and left the suite. 'Stay down, sir,' Rebecca hissed at Dlamini as she and Hansie sprang to their feet. They saw Sapphire halt and take a rapid look in both directions be-fore disappearing towards the next suite. The suite occupied by Lugay Phukuntsi and his entourage.

Rebecca beat Coetzee to the balcony by a couple of sec-onds but she was brought to a halt by a crescendo of sound. A small, purple helicopter appeared to her left, breasting the roof of the stadium by a matter of inches, the pulsing noise of its rotors fighting for supremacy over the music blaring from the loudspeakers. The crack of multiple rifle shots also filled the air as the mass of soldiers securing the rally took hurried aim.

They had little initial success as the chopper, flying errati-cally, either by design or accident, headed downwards in a jag-ged, zig-zaggy series of jumps and twists. These uncoordinat-ed manoeuvres, together with the gunfire caused a stampede of people away from the pitch below, where it seemed the chopper would crash-land. Or just crash. Screams and shouts from the dispersing crowd added to the cacophony.

But the helicopter's nose rose again as its pilot wrestled with the controls and Rebecca, realising it was now heading straight for her and Coetzee, leaped to the side, attempting with only limited success to pull Hansie's bulk with her. She suddenly, shockingly, realised that the pilot was Dawson with Lucy Smith beside him, as they were briefly illuminated through the plexiglass windscreen by the stadium floodlights. At the last second, as the machine seemed certain to crash into her and the lieutenant, one of the hundreds of bullets fired wildly by the army found its target on an integral part of the helicopter. The tail rotor came to a sudden stop as its assembly mechanism was hit and the chopper veered to its left and crashed through the plate glass window of the adjacent box.

Lugay Phukuntsi's box, into which Sapphire Waters had just disappeared.

There was a horrendous crash and a screeching of metal as the helicopter came to rest wedged in the doorway, rotors mangled and tail poking out over the arena. The army stopped firing and, apart from a few remaining screams, the crowd, their rush away from the pitch halted by the spectacle, fell quiet.

'Out!' I screamed in Saul's ear, leaned across, unclipped his belt and pushed him towards the other door. He needed no second invitation and we both scrambled out on to a sea of broken glass.

The scene was slightly clearer outside the helicopter. The bullet-scarred windscreen had evidently been doing as much to restrict our vision as the dust and smoke, which were slowly beginning to clear. The noise of people moving about and starting to talk became louder, and indistinct shapes appeared ahead of us. I didn't immediately recognise any of the shapes but best to be prepared. I pulled out the pistol I'd taken from Asha Mbaso back at Phukuntsi's house. As it was, the first person to loom discernibly up in front of us was the fat politician himself and it was a fair bet that nobody with him would be particularly friendly. Especially as we'd destroyed the suite, covered them in dust and brought the rally to a premature halt.

I heard Saul say, 'Keep back,' forcefully from the other side of the whirlybird's nose cone but, looking around, no one was listening. Or they were choosing to ignore him. Some were Chinese and all had sprouted guns although they seemed confused about who to shoot. I wondered if Songsung Rong was in the room somewhere but if she was, I couldn't see her and, as there was now clear air above the smoke and dust, she wouldn't be hard to spot if she was standing up. Maybe we'd run her over with the chopper. We could hope.

Then there was a gunshot and Phukuntsi, who had been stumbling around in the gloom, dropped out of sight with a cry. I saw who had pulled the trigger. Astonishingly, it was Sapphire. She came into view from behind a group of Chinese men and moved closer to the fallen Phukuntsi, primed for a second shot, which suggested the first had only winged him. Well, it had several inches of blubber to penetrate before hitting any important internal organs, so that made sense.

Sapphire's presence made no kind of sense. I glanced at Saul who said, 'Sapphire, drop the gun.' Something in his voice told me he was less surprised than me to discover Sapphire Waters, slightly-wet-behind-the-ears MI6 desk-jockey, kidnapped in London three days ago, in an executive box at the Green Point Stadium trying to pop off a South African presidential candidate. Given Phukuntsi's loathsomeness and total unsuitability for the job, more power to her elbow. Nevertheless, I guessed we should try to stop her.

But she was ignoring Saul. I stuck my gun in my belt, took two steps and dived on top of her.

She seemed to be totally preoccupied with the task of killing Phukuntsi and didn't see me coming. We crashed onto the floor but, strangely, I ended up underneath. How had that happened? I'd seen Sapphire's service record and she hadn't been trained to pull a stunt like that. So there I was flat on my back with Sapphire's green eyes – no black-rimmed specs now, I noticed – staring at me and her gun raised in my direction.

I say staring **at** me but she was actually looking straight through me. As if she didn't know me. This wasn't how I expected to go. I made a desperate grab for her arm but she must have borrowed some steel sinews from Sofija and it didn't budge. Was that a flicker of something behind the eyes? I wasn't sure.

Then she fell sideways to the floor, unconscious. Saul stood over her. He'd thumped her hard behind the ear with what looked suspiciously like Rong's little cosh. 'Quite effective thing, this,' he said, admiring the weapon. He reached out his hand. I grasped it and he pulled me to my feet. I gave him a big hug. I didn't care if half a dozen goons were looking on. Looking on, I now saw, with their hands in the air.

'How are you making them do that?' I asked Saul, mystified, before realising that the room had become more crowded while I was being pinned to the ground by Sapphire. A dozen or so soldiers had streamed in and, faced with the heavy armoury they carried, the Chinese, together with a few more local-looking minions, had surrendered en masse. I unhooked myself with some difficulty from Saul as one of the soldiers, with captain's pips on his shoulders, came up to me. He had a handcuffed Patel with him.

'Sorry about the mess,' I said, spotting Major General Brenda de Kock and Temba Yeboah behind him. I was surprised they'd got to the stadium so quickly; it made the whole stealing-the-helicopter thing rather pointless. Fun though. Six goons were led out of the suite behind Patel by more than enough soldiers to do the job efficiently. Four paramedics arrived to tend to Phukuntsi himself, although they'd need a lot more than that to carry the stretcher. One of them bent down over Sapphire.

'Careful, mate,' said Saul, stepping forward. 'She's more dangerous than she looks.' He turned to Temba Yeboah. 'Could you arrange to have her restrained, please, Captain?' Temba nodded. We'd been joined by a few police officers and, at Temba's command, one of them approached with handcuffs for the still unconscious Sapphire.

I looked at Saul. 'Was there something you'd forgotten to tell me?'

He couldn't have looked more innocent. 'What's that, darling?'

'Sapphire?' I prompted. 'Care to explain why she was about to kill me? You appear to have some sort of inside knowledge.'

'Oh, she wouldn't have done that,' he said. He looked doubtful though. 'She wasn't programmed to kill **you**.'

'Programmed? What the hell **are** you talking about?'

'Sofija and Guna... You know about Guna, do you?' I nodded. He carried on. 'They found out that Stella Fish had turned Sapphire into what Sofija described as some sort of robot. There's a code word.' He glanced down at Sapphire who remained out cold and was also now securely cuffed. 'Nemesis,' he whispered.

'Nemesis? Code words? Robots?' I shook my head 'If not me, then who was she programmed to assassinate? And why?'

'They didn't know. Just one of the presidential candidates but there were five to choose from. I'll be honest, I wasn't expecting it to be Phukuntsi. I assumed Dlamini.'

We were interrupted by a commotion from inside the stadium. Down on the pitch, Jacob Dlamini was moving among the few remaining people, helping them, calming them, the only presidential candidate to stick around. But that wasn't the cause of the commotion. Up on the temporary stage, a fight had broken out.

Stella Fish and Songsung Rong were going at it hammer and tongs.

—

None of us knew how or why they'd come to blows. What was clear though was that the ex-CIA woman was losing the fight. Songsung Rong had the advantage of nine inches and twenty years. The one-sided battle was going to be over pretty damn quick, and certainly before anyone in uniform could reach the stage. The army captain was speaking urgently into a radio but so far neither soldiers nor police had appeared on the football pitch.

Shooting either of the combatants with a handgun

*would have been difficult from that distance, with no guarantee of hitting anyone, let alone the right woman. And who **was** the right woman? Not Rong. She was officially a member of the Chinese Consulate staff and had diplomatic immunity. Her murder would cause all sorts of ructions. And not Stella either; there would be a lot of people keen to keep her alive for questioning. The CIA for example.*

*But then two shots **did** ring out. Not from the balcony and not from any of the soldiers who were now starting to appear at tunnel entrances around the stands. Instead, a young woman emerged from behind the stage, took up a stance and, aiming carefully, shot Songsung Rong in the thigh.*

*It was Kaya Rabada.*

*Rong, her hands clamped round Stella's throat, squealed like a stuck pig, attempted to rise and face her new assailant but then collapsed back on top of her older adversary.*

*'That's exactly the noise she made when I shot her in the foot last summer,' I said.*

*Kaya herself looked in poor shape. She had a bloody bandage wrapped around her head and, even as we watched, she too collapsed in a heap and, like Rong and Stella was soon surrounded by men and women in uniform.*

'This seems to be the place,' said Dawson two days later as he and Lucy entered the small ward. 'The wing for unsuccessful international espionage agents.' There were only six beds lined up against the left-hand wall. The first four were occupied, possibly in order of Seriousness of Injury. The two furthest beds were empty.

At the end of the ward, a good-looking male nurse giving off a strong air of capability – not necessarily confined exclusively to nursing – sat behind a desk. He smiled as they entered, displaying two rows of perfect teeth. The teeth looked American and Dawson suspected the smile was directed more at Lucy than himself. Opposite the beds was a pair of French doors, open to allow fresh air into the room. Through the window, Dawson could see a garden with views across Table Bay towards Bloubergstrand where Andrew Gulliver's headless body had washed ashore four days earlier. Dawson briefly wondered if the police had ever tracked down the cabin cruiser that had deposited the body into the water but it was irrelevant now. It had doubtlessly been piloted by some of the Chinese thugs arrested by the army at the stadium on Monday night.

Somebody had paid for all this, the CIA probably, and it was their agent, Kaya Rabada, who occupied the first bed. She had a number of tubes linked to drips sticking out of her and her head was tightly bandaged. The doctor Lucy and Dawson had encountered on their way in had said she was mending well and would be fine.

She'd been left for dead by Songsung Rong's men at the CIA's temporary building. Rong hadn't killed her outright but neither had she been sparing in the use of her wicked little cosh; and her men had thought it fun to pile in with their heavy-duty footwear when Rong herself had departed to capture Lucy on the roof. It was a wonder that Kaya had still managed to make it to the stadium to take her revenge on the Chinese agent before collapsing.

Next to Kaya was a wide-awake Guna. She glowered briefly at Lucy and Dawson then broke into a smile. 'I didn't expect to see this,' said Dawson cheerfully. 'The indomitable Guna Sesks laid low by a single bullet.'

'Stella could not shoot fish in a barrel,' said Guna. 'How she missed my heart from three metres I do not know.'

'That easily explained,' said Sofija from the next bed. 'You have no heart.' Apart from the sleeping Kaya, everyone laughed, even Anthony Melhuish, lying in the fourth bed. He looked fully recovered from inhaling the gas two days earlier but was being kept in for observation, like Sofija, for whom a bullet through the forearm appeared to be a minor inconvenience. Seeing Dawson's questioning face, she said, 'I just here to keep eye on incontinent sister.' Her far-from-incompetent sister grunted.

'Who are the other two beds for?' asked Dawson. Lucy tried not to think of Best and Cope, who had been less fortunate.

'You two, but you have luck of Devon,' said Sofija. Devon, where Charles Gulliver had met his untimely end at the hands of Songsung Rong, seemed a long time ago and not at all lucky. If it was the luck of the devil she meant, then maybe she was right. Dawson had come through everything completely uninjured although Lucy hadn't got away entirely scot-free. She pulled her t-shirt off her left shoulder revealing the gauze padding over the bullet wound.

'I think I must just be tougher than you, Sofija,' she said, blue eyes wide. 'So who's running the local CIA now you and Kaya are laid up, Mr Melhuish?'

'That would be me, Ms Smith.' The sort of deep, mellifluous voice that would give Morgan Freeman a run for his money came from behind them. The male nurse had walked silently across from his desk. He was still smiling. Dawson began counting the ultra-white teeth but stopped when he reached forty.

'Meet my successor,' said Melhuish. 'Benjamin Hammond. As soon as Kaya is fit enough to fly, she and I will be heading back to Langley for debriefing. Guna too. I doubt it'll be pleasant; the CIA hates to be upstaged by the Brits.'

'Also by girls on holiday,' added Sofija.

—

'Would you be so good as to step this way,' said Hammond, extending an arm towards the doors into the garden. He allowed Dawson and Lucy to precede him and shut the doors behind him. There was a shaded table at the far end of the lawn, with chairs. They sat.

'Is this **our** debrief then, Mr Hammond?' asked Lucy.

'Of course not, Ms Smith.' There were those teeth again. 'You don't work for us. I just thought you might like a few gaps filling in, at least as far as I'm able to do so.'

'Thanks,' said Lucy. 'The main thing that's puzzling us is who Stella Fish was really working for.'

'As I believe Anthony told you, she's ex-CIA who went rogue, taking the information about poor Ms Waters with her. Who was she actually working for?' Hammond paused and smiled again. He clearly liked smiling but then with teeth like that, why wouldn't he? 'It seems she too was working for the Chinese.'

'What?' said Dawson. 'How so? Stella Fish set Sapphire up to kill Phukuntsi and, unless I'm missing something, Phukuntsi was the Chinese government's pick for president.'

'Exactly so, Mr Dawson. The Chinese government's choice. Unlike Songsung Rong, Stella wasn't working for the Chinese government but a different Chinese power base. This was why

Rong was beating the hell of out her before Kaya came to the rescue.

'Thing is, guys, China's a totalitarian state but not everyone's happy about that. Big business particularly. Totalitarianism is restrictive and expensive; it's hard to make money unless an awful lot of official palms get greased and there can be sudden reversals of political fortune. There are a lot of insanely rich and powerful people who'd prefer China becoming a democracy, if only because they think it'll be better for business and as a result, they'll make even more money. That's a long way off so for the time being they're just chipping away at the edges, weakening the government. This next part is top secret, OK? There's a, er, let's call it a secret organisation – and I know this is something of a Bondian cliché but it's no less true for all that – a cabal of big business and opposition politicians and supporters, working hard behind the scenes to bring about change at the top.'

'What's the CIA's involvement?' said Lucy.

'Hey, we didn't want anyone killed. Live and let live. If South Africa wants to elect a dodgy president, then let 'em. Preferably not one working for the Chinese government of course, but we ran checks on Lugay Phukuntsi and he's so stupid we were pretty sure his election would backfire in a year or less, and Xi Jinping would end up with egg on his face. Not enough egg to unseat him but it might earn him a few minus points. Obviously, we'd prefer Dlamini. A more honest government is good for trade with America. Dlamini's probably not the purest of the pure himself but who is? He's certainly better than anyone else.'

'And Kaya?' asked Dawson

'Kaya's a recent recruit, like your interesting friend, Guna Sesks. Stella didn't know her and as we weren't sure what Stella was up to and needed eyes on her, we inserted Kaya as her driver. When Kaya told us about Sapphire Waters, there was some rapid dot-joining so we added Guna to the crew.

Dr Norton advertised for an agency cook, very amateur, that. Basically he signed his own death warrant.'

'And Guna decided to get Sofija in to help.'

'That was nothing to do with us and we sure as hell aren't paying her.'

'Hiring Guna was dangerous if you didn't want anyone killed,' said Lucy.

'Calculated risk. No harm done, eh?'

'Not sure that Norton and the other bloke she did away with would agree,' said Dawson. Or Cope and Best, Lucy thought.

'The official line is they killed each other. Same with the third guy, Claxton, the one that Ms Waters unknowingly shot.'

'Why are you replacing Melhuish?' asked Dawson.

'The South Africans are expelling him. They didn't take kindly to discovering he was moonlighting within their own security service. And someone has to take the rap for damaging the football stadium. The future president of the republic doesn't think it should be you, so...'

Lucy interrupted. 'I presume that's the last we'll see of Songsung-bloody-Rong.'

'I expect so. She's disappeared into the bowels of the Chinese embassy in Pretoria. I imagine she'll be on a plane to Beijing before too long.'

'Where she might well disappear rather more permanently.' Dawson and Lucy grinned at each other.

'Thanks, Mr Hammond.' Lucy rose to her feet. Dawson followed suit. 'We'll say goodbye. We've got to collect Sapphire from the other end of the hospital and then we have a plane to catch.'

'Yes. We're happy to let MI6 take charge of fixing Ms Waters, although strictly speaking at least part of her is the CIA's property.'

Lucy flared up. 'What, her brain, you mean? She's not a piece of meat.'

'Forgive me. I hope your guys in London can sort her out. Genuinely. I was never involved in the Nemesis programme myself and, in light of events, Langley's view now is that it never actually happened.' He held out a hand. Dawson shook it and, after a pause, Lucy did too. 'One more thing,' Hammond said, his dark eyes looking directly at Lucy. 'If you ever fancy a job, give me a call.' He held out a card. She took it. 'We're going all international now in the Agency. Witness Guna Sesks.'

Lucy put her good arm around Dawson's waist. 'We come as a pair.'

'And unless Underwood's sacked us again, we've still got jobs with MI6,' added Dawson. 'I think they're expecting us to start tracking down Gaddafi's lost loot.'

Hammond laughed. 'They'll be disappointed, I'm afraid. We've already got most of that.'

___ In which Dawson wields a letter
    opener, and Lucy goes for
    a shower

New Year had come and gone. Lucy's shoulder was in full working order and outside the snow was falling. Again. England was having a dreadful winter. Dawson had quite enjoyed his own winter but was already talking about another holiday, the first one not having gone quite as planned.

Jason Underwood, while not actually sacking them this time, had gone out of his way to avoid giving them any meaningful work since they'd returned from Cape Town. 'I told you we should never have gone back,' said Lucy, who was keen to pick up the phone to Benjamin Hammond and discuss the job offer from the CIA. Dawson was less sure about that, especially as they'd seen fit to dispense with Guna's services, which he thought showed a lack of appreciation.

Lucy agreed. 'They'll come to regret that,' she said. 'Mark my words.'

'I certainly wouldn't want to be stuck between Guna and the CIA if it comes to blows. I think Sofija's trying to get her to join her in Estonian Security.'

The doorbell rang. Dawson came back with a large crisp envelope and waved it in the air as if to emphasise its stiffness and thus its likely importance. Lucy glimpsed some sort of embossed badge on the flap.

'Post's very early,' she said. This was twenty-first century, home counties England so mail rarely arrived before eleven o'clock.

'Special Delivery,' Dawson intoned. 'Youngster with a posh uniform. Shall I?' He waved the envelope around again.

Lucy smiled sweetly. 'Only if we want to know what's in it.'

Dawson produced the brass letter-opener he'd received as a Christmas present from an aunt twenty years earlier and which he had used precisely twice since. 'Don't want to tear the paper,' he said. 'It looks expensive.'

'Get on with it, lover,' she said. 'I'd like to get in the shower before lunchtime.'

Dawson carefully slit open the envelope and pulled out a card. Lucy took it from him.

'Manners,' he said, smiling.

Lucy read from the card. 'The Government of the Republic of South Africa cordially requests the presence of Lady Joanna Leigh Delamere and Mr Saul Dawson to the Inauguration of His Excellency Jacob Dlamini as President of the Republic on Monday 29th January. RSVP.'

'Reply Soon Very Prompt,' said Dawson. 'Shall we? I reckon we're due another holiday.'

'I agree,' Lucy said. She handed back the card, rose to her feet and started to loosen the cord from her robe. 'But I've seen enough of South Africa for one lifetime, thanks all the same. Besides, it's addressed to Lady Somebody and a bloke called Saul. I don't know who either of those people are.'

'Absolutely,' said Dawson, tearing the invitation in half. 'Anyway, we don't want to be ruining Jacob's big day. I should think Rebecca and Hansie will have enough on their plates keeping him safe without worrying about people trying to bump us off as well.'

Lucy had nearly reached the door by now and let the robe drop to the floor as she disappeared towards the bathroom.

'Now, about that shower...' he continued, jumping to his feet and neatly hurdling the robe as he followed her.

___ The End

## About Steve Sheppard

Steve was born in Guildford and grew up in a house with a river at the bottom of the garden. This makes him sound quite posh but it wasn't a very big house and it wasn't a very big river. Nine years at boarding school taught him absolutely nothing about how to be an adult and actually becoming an adult also failed in this respect. One thing he did eventually learn, however, was that he should have tried writing a book much earlier than he did although he also now realises that he ought to have tried to become a celebrity first, as this would have made selling it much easier. Steve now lives in Hampshire, having moved there after the success of *A Very Important Teapot* and *Bored to Death in the Baltics* in an attempt to avoid the paparazzi. This worked a treat, thus leaving him undisturbed to write *Poor Table Manners*. He is also working on a standalone thriller that does not include Dawson and Lucy.

**www.stevesheppardauthor.com**

GREAT STORYTELLING
DOESN'T JUST ENTERTAIN,
IT ENERGISES

Claret Press' mission is simple: we publish engrossing books which engage with the issues of the day. So we publish across a range of genres, both fiction and nonfiction. From award-winning page-turners to eye-opening travelogues, from captivating historical fiction to insightful memoirs, there's a Claret Press book for you.

To keep up to date about the going-ons at Claret Press, including book launches, zoom talks and other events, sign up to our newsletter through our website at:

**www.claretpress.com**

You can also find us through Instagram **@claretpress** Twitter **@ClaretPress** and TikTok **@claret.press**